MONEY CAN KILL

Wonny Lea

Money Can Kill

Copyright © Wonny Lea 2012

This edition published by Accent Press 2014

ISBN 9781783754564

The Author asserts the moral right to be identified as the author of this work.

All rights reserved.

Disclaimer: This book is a work of fiction. It has been written for entertainment purposes only. All references to characters and countries should be seen in this light. All the characters in this book are fictitious, and any resemblance to actual persons, living or dead, is purely coincidental.

Chapter One

It was twenty-five past nine and the teachers on the second of three coaches did a final head count of the children and the adults accompanying them.

'We're still missing two,' shouted Claire Masters as she looked through the list on her clipboard.

'Course you are,' called back Angela Roberts, one of the parents. 'No sign of Jason and his mother yet, is there? She'll be arriving in her taxi and she'll expect the bus to be waiting even if she's ten minutes late.'

Miss Masters refrained from making any comment but she could see that Mrs Roberts was right, as Jason Barnes and his mother Christine, better known as Tina, were the only names not yet crossed off her list. The general conversation that ensued in the bus ranged from mildly abusive to positively vitriolic as most of the adults and even children as young as six had something to say about the two missing people.

'I bet it's quite a struggle, having to decide which of their designer labels to thrill us all with today,' suggested a grossly overweight woman who occupied the best part of two seats, spilling into the aisle and squashing her young son's head against the window. She had nothing more to say on the subject and turned her attention towards the boy, who was taking too long to open a large pack of bacon sandwiches.

Claire squeezed past their seat and the smell of bacon caught her attention. 'Mrs Hall, as you know, we have been asked not to eat on the coach. It'll only take us about half an hour to get to our destination and there are plenty of picnic areas there.'

Mrs Hall couldn't reply, as her mouth was now stuffed full of what would be the first of many bacon butties, and shrugged her shoulders as Miss Masters moved towards the front of the coach. She sat down next to her colleague and voiced her frustration. 'We've brought black bags for the rubbish and vomit bags for those who are sick from travel or over-indulgence, but we've been told that if any of the coaches are left in a mess today this will be yet another travel company that blacklists our school.'

Holly Road Primary was a typical inner-city school, with nearly five hundred pupils aged between four and eleven and from every conceivable ethnic and religious background. Claire Masters had only been teaching at Holly Road since September and was already thinking back fondly to the small school with just two hundred pupils in Llantrisant, where she had taught until the end of the last school year. She had left because she was ambitious and knew that in order to be eligible for some of the more prestigious teaching posts in Wales she would have to be able to demonstrate experience in a variety of educational settings. She would have to be able to show that she understood the meaning of diversity and was capable of developing strategies that would enable every child to get the best from the system.

According to the latest thinking, a big part of educating the children holistically was to get them and their families away from the school environment and introduce them to opportunities for learning within the local community. Today's excursion was the first of four arranged for the school year and Claire prayed that they would be less challenging than the accounts of last year's outings, related by her colleagues in the staff room. These ranged from the usual teasing and spats between the kids to very public verbal abuse and even full-blown fights amongst some of the parents. A trip to a local working farm had resulted in the death of two chickens and a seven-year-old girl being tied to the wheels of a tractor.

The school changed its policy after that visit and now each child had to be accompanied by a named responsible adult, but looking around the bus Claire doubted the efficacy of that arrangement. One of the so-called responsible adults was already on her third bacon sandwich and a young dad appeared to be singing songs more suitable for a rugby trip – and the coach hadn't even left the school!

Today's excursion was to take Years Two and Three to the Museum of National History at St Fagans, and in particular to get the children to look at the tools used by farmers throughout the ages. The youngsters had been looking at how their food got to the table and the majority had been quite amazed to discover that it had not all just come from the shelves of the local supermarket.

Claire was offering a silent prayer that all the equipment would be nailed down when the anticipated taxi pulled up alongside the coach and Jason Barnes and his mother got on board.

There was an uncanny silence as they made their way down the central aisle looking for a double seat, and although no one looked Christine Barnes – Tina – in the eyes, most of the adults took in every detail of her appearance. Bling was the order of the day for a number of the women and some of the men on the coach, but everyone knew that Tina's bling was the real thing. She had no concept of the idea that 'less is more', and although she wore designer jeans and a leather jacket, nothing was coordinated, and the overall effect, topped by her black and blue streaked hair, was tarty.

Pushing Jason into the only remaining pair of seats Tina recalled how different it had been on the school trips last year, when she had been one of the girls and would have been seen laughing and joking with everyone on the bus. Her clothes and chunky jewellery would have come from the market and Jason's clothes would, at best, have been some cheap copies handed down from her neighbour's son.

It had been just after the Easter holidays when Tina had come up trumps on the Euromillions lottery, winning tens of millions of pounds and having only Jason to share it with.

She initially gave generous hand-outs to friends, but instead of showing some gratitude they had just become greedy and wanted more. Some of those friends were on the coach today, but she had been crossed off their Christmas card lists and they were now the leaders when it came to slagging her off. Part of her wished that she could wind the clock back; wished she had never won the money; wished she was still part of their world.

It didn't help that Jason was showing off his new black Kickers boots to a boy whose trainers were falling apart and the boy's mother was openly voicing her opinion of people who thought they were better than anyone else. There is a general misconception that money will solve problems whereas in reality it can bring more than it takes away. In Tina's case it had taken her out of her social comfort zone and left her completely isolated. Although she had tried to adapt to her fortune, she simply didn't have the ability to do so. She was thirty years old and for most of her life she had been a hard worker, often holding down a full-time job and then doing part-time bar work in the evenings. Tina was not bright and had left school with no qualifications; she had still been living at home with her father when she became pregnant at twenty-three. Her father hadn't worked in years and had been more than happy to live off Tina's money, and when he found out his daughter was pregnant he tried to persuade her to have an abortion.

It was one of the few times in her life when Tina did exactly what she wanted to do, and from the moment that Jason was born he became the very centre of her existence. She left home and for the first six and a half years of her son's life she struggled, with the help of state benefits, to make ends meet. They had been housed in a two-bedroomed maisonette in Llanedeyrn, surrounded by families in similar situations, and for the most part they were very happy there.

When Jason started school Tina had taken on several jobs as a cleaner, and when she looked back now it was with a longing to be still in that little house and not rattling around in the five-bedroomed property she had been persuaded to buy.

The coaches had left the school and were driving in convoy along Eastern Avenue and just as the ten o'clock news announced the death of Dame Joan Sutherland, the driver slammed on his brakes and swerved to avoid going into the back of the coach in front. There was uproar as women screamed, men swore, one little boy was propelled down the centre of the bus, and two girls were sick.

The driver spoke into his microphone. 'Sorry about that,' he said. 'I had no choice as some idiot in front of our coaches suddenly changed lanes. Still, it'll teach some of you to wear your seat belts and let me remind you that County Coaches will not be responsible for any injuries if you don't follow the rules.'

Miss Masters felt she had no alternative than to break the rules as she got up and returned Tomos, the human cannonball, to his seat and belatedly handed out sick-bags and generous amounts of wipes. The atmosphere was already getting heavy as the smell of vomit mingled with what was now a variety of sandwich fillings and definitely cheese and onion crisps.

Claire returned to her seat and on the way heard the hiss of a can opening and got a definite smell of cider. She would have preferred not to have witnessed the occurrence but having done so she couldn't ignore it. 'Mr Ponting,' she said. 'You don't need me to tell you that the school does not allow alcohol on school trips.'

'Sorry, Miss, but I wasn't thinking of giving it to the kids. Not much I can do about it now, so I'll just down it quickly.' The words were spoken by a skinny man in his twenties with a sculpted hair style that was copied by his two young sons. One the boys spoke in defence of his father.

'Don't have a go at my dad, Miss. He doesn't like fruit and so he's got to drink cider to get his five-a-day. It's only apple juice, don't you know?'

Claire made no comment as she watched father and son make a high five in recognition of their perceived victory over the teacher. When she re-joined her colleague, Mrs Locke, they mentally left the school trip and spent a few minutes discussing the recent death of Dame Joan Sutherland.

'I'm not an opera buff but I have to agree with Luciano Pavarotti when he said her voice was like heaven. It sends shivers down my spine,' said Emma Locke. 'What a wonderful gift. It puts what I have to offer in a very poor light.'

'Oh, that's rubbish,' insisted Claire. 'I think that anyone who works with the mix of kids we get at Holly Road year after year deserves a medal.'

Their next words were drowned out as the driver turned up the volume of the radio controls and some of the responsible adults joined in the chorus of 'Love Me Do' and a medley of hits from The Fab Four. So, accompanied by The Beatles, and with the majority of the people on coach number two murdering 'Eleanor Rigby', the last ten minutes of the journey passed without incident. Soon the coach turned the corner and stopped alongside a number of other similar vehicles.

The National History Museum of Wales was among the best of Europe's open air museums and allowed visitors to experience what life was like in Wales in the days before widescreen TV, iPads, and fast food. For the past ten years entry to the museum had been free of charge and consequently it was an obvious venue for schools and large family outings.

Although there was a plan in relation to the perceived educational output of today's visit, the teachers knew that many of the carefully prepared handouts given to each child would never be read. Individual groups had already decided how they were going to spend their time at St Fagans and a few would not be going further than the children's play area.

Claire used the driver's microphone to ensure that everyone knew the arrangements for the day and encouraged the use of the worksheets. She reminded the children that the blacksmith was going to give them a special demonstration at eleven o'clock and told them to make sure they didn't miss out.

'The most important time for you all to remember is two thirty. That is when we leave here and we must be on time because the coaches will be needed for the normal school runs after we get back. Anyone who is not on the bus by two thirty will be left behind and will have to make their own arrangements for getting home.'

Claire looked at some of the glazed-over expressions and had serious doubts about how much of what she was saying was being absorbed, and so she concluded. 'Have a great day. There are six members of the teaching staff here today so if there are any problems one of us should be able to help.'

Several people had already left the coach before she had even finished speaking and the ones that hung on to her every word were the ones that didn't really need to listen. They were the adults whose children had already proudly written their names on the front of the booklets, and had pens and pencils poised to make sure that there would be a tick in every box before they returned to the coach. Claire recognised gratefully that they were the majority and they took up less than ten per cent of her time. She sometimes felt a bit guilty that she couldn't give them more because the demands of the thankless few were overwhelming, but her job was to ensure that as many horses drank water as she could persuade.

Jason and his mother were the last to leave the coach and Claire noticed that they stood apart from the various groups, and the first thing Tina did was to light up a cigarette. She was a very heavy smoker, as the nicotine stains between the index and middle fingers of her right hand indicated, and she was one of the few people left who refused to smoke filter-tipped cigarettes. She had previously rolled her own, but since she no longer needed to worry about the cost she had a constant supply of Pall Mall soft packs.

The driver had looked down the aisle of the coach and huffed and puffed, before telling Claire that it would be in the best interest of Holly Road School for her to have a quick clean up before he took the bus back to the company depot. It only took five minutes for Claire to half-fill a black bag with empty packages and a few cans and to clean up the sick patches, getting the driver's nod of approval.

As she stepped off the coach she noticed that two of her teacher colleagues had been doing a similar clean-up in the other two coaches. She joined them with her black bag and the three of them looked for a large rubbish bin.

The plan was for the six teachers to have a cup of coffee and then wander around in pairs, giving advice and assistance as required and rounding the pupils up for the two planned sessions. One was the blacksmith's demonstration and the other was a short talk on the tools used by farmers during the past couple of centuries.

Claire told her colleagues that she would join them at the coffee shop and made her way to the toilets to wash her hands free of the smell of stale vomit.

Jason was kicking around the wrapping from an ice-cream cone just outside the ladies' toilets and he saw her coming towards him.

'It wasn't me, Miss, I didn't chuck the paper on the floor, it was there already.'

'Hello, Jason,' said Claire. 'I wasn't going to suggest that you had caused the litter but if you want to be a really big boy you could pick it up and put it in the bin.'

'Somebody else chucked it down so somebody else should pick it up. My mother says we aren't servants to nobody, Miss.'

Claire bent down, picked up the cardboard cone, and placed it in one of the many rubbish bins, hoping that her example would register. She looked back at Jason. 'What are you doing here on your own anyway?'

'I'm not on my own, Miss, my mother needed a pee so I'm just waiting for her to come out of the toilet – here she is.'

As Jason spoke his mother appeared and chastised her son for making a nuisance of himself before yanking his arm and dragging him in the direction of the children's play area. Claire stared after them, wondering why she was feeling sorry for someone who had more money than she was ever likely to see in her lifetime, but she did feel very sorry for Christine Barnes.

Joining her colleagues for coffee she was not surprised to learn that Emma Locke had already entertained the group with the happenings from their coach, and she sat and listened to the stories from the other two coaches. The avoidance of a traffic accident had caused a nosebleed in the first coach and Peggy Lloyd told them that one of the dads was going to sue the coach company for the trauma his six-year-old princess had endured.

'I'll change coaches with anyone,' said the youngest teacher,

8

Kerri Powell. 'Mandy Perkins' mother has brought her two youngest girls with her and they have screamed non-stop, but that's the least of my worries. Mandy's mother, who is *very* pregnant, is looking decidedly uncomfortable and I don't fancy playing the midwife on the return journey.'

This caused a great deal of laughter but no one volunteered to change coaches; all the plea did was to make the group of teachers realise that today was likely to be a long day and a round of assorted cakes was needed to gird up the loins.

Dragging Jason behind her, Tina walked up the path towards the children's park but decided against going into the area when she saw some of the women standing around and staring in her direction. Jason let out a howl as he was spun around and left in no doubt that he would not be swinging from the climbing frame any time soon.

'I want to go to the park,' he shouted. 'I want to play with my friends, I don't want to see the animals, I want to play with my friends.'

'Shut up, Jason, just shut up. You can play with your friends in school. I'm not going to the park and that's that. Just stop shouting before I give you something to shout about.'

Tina was tall and thin to the point of looking gaunt and for every one of her strides Jason was forced to take five or six running steps and he pleaded to her to slow down.

'You're going too bloody fast,' he told his mother.

'Don't you dare say bloody unless you want a smack across the face,' replied Tina. 'It's a good job Miss Masters didn't hear you swearing or you would really be for the high jump.'

Tina suddenly stopped and gave Jason a big hug. 'Look, Jase,' she said. 'It's just you and me since we won the lottery, or at least until I find you a new dad. That lot back there are just jealous and it's for the best that we don't bother with them.'

Jason looked horrified. 'But I don't want a new dad. Have I even got a dad? I didn't know I had one. Have I got a dad?'

Realising she had opened a can of worms Tina ignored her young son as she didn't really want to be reminded of Jason's biological father. As far as she knew he was totally unaware that Jason existed. She had registered her son's birth using her own surname and told the registrar that she could give no information about his father. The registrar had assumed that this meant there were so many possibilities that Tina couldn't decide who to name, but the reality was very different.

Tina was not, and never had been, promiscuous. She knew exactly who had fathered Jason, and she still caught sight of him from time to time. There had been one occasion in the schoolyard when he had spoken to Jason and for a moment Tina had imagined that the light of recognition had flashed across his face, but it was unlikely he even remembered their brief sexual encounter.

Jason had not stopped firing his questions. 'Why haven't I got a real dad? I want a dad like my friends. Molly-Anne has got two dads. One of them lives with her mother and one of them lives with another girl's mother. They all go to the cinema together, I know 'cos Molly-Anne told me.'

'What are you going on about?' asked Tina.

'She did tell me, I'm not telling fibs, she did tell me.' Jason suddenly changed tactics and told his mother that he was starving and wanted to go to McDonalds.

'Don't be stupid, Jason, there is no such thing as McDonalds here, and anyway we've brought sandwiches.'

'I don't like sandwiches. I want a burger and fries, not sandwiches.' Jason sulked and plonked himself down on the path.

'Get up,' his mother shouted but he refused to budge and she walked on, thinking that he would soon get bored with sitting on his own and catch up with her. 'If you sit there too long the pig man will come and get you – and good riddance is what I would say.' She called the words back over her shoulder. After a few minutes she stopped walking and waited to hear his footsteps running towards her but a few other children passed with their families and no sign of Jason.

The families that were walking past were not from her son's school and were all speaking Welsh so she did not feel able to ask them if they had passed Jason. She made her way back to the spot where he had been sitting but he was not there. She wasn't worried as hide and seek was one of his favourite games and she began looking behind trees and over the walls of the circular dry-stone pigsty. 'Jason,' she shouted. 'Jason, that's enough now. I give in, I can't find you, so you've won and if you like we can get some ice-cream.'

Usually the very mention of ice-cream would see Jason running towards her but still nothing and now there were children from Jason's school walking towards her so she confronted them.

'Have you seen Jason? He was sitting on the path and must have decided to play hide and seek but he's too good for me and I can't find him.'

'Mam, am I allowed to talk to Jason's mam?' asked the son of one of the women Tina had at one time considered to be her friend.

'Best not or she'll only think you're after her money, like she thought your mother was.' Smirking at another woman who was walking alongside her, Pam Woodland answered her son's question, but now Tina was getting worried and so she ignored the intended insult.

'Look, Pam,' she said. 'Forget about me and just answer the question. Have you seen Jason? He was sitting in this exact spot but now he's nowhere to be seen and I'm getting concerned.'

'Your concerns are no concerns of mine. I've got three boys to look after and I've managed not to lose one of them,' Pam retorted. 'We passed two of the teachers near the red farmhouse so I suggest you ask them.'

Claire Masters and Emma Locke were listening to the history of the Kennixton farmhouse, and how the owners had lived in the red-painted house and farmed the land in the Gower over the centuries. Like all the other historic buildings it had been relocated to the museum and was a terrific example of a particular way of life. Their interesting history lesson was interrupted as Tina ducked her head to enter the low doorway.

'Have you seen Jason?' she asked breathlessly. 'I can't find him anywhere.'

A missing child was top of the list of incidents that must not happen on a school trip, only topped by the loss of more than one child, but it was never a permanent loss. Usually the missing children were being naughty and one of the other children could be persuaded to reveal their whereabouts. But it was always a worrying time for the parents and teachers alike and Claire responded to the situation, treating the matter as serious from the outset.

'OK, try to stay calm,' she suggested. 'I doubt he's gone far; he's probably gone to look for one of his friends. Mrs Locke, will you find the other four teachers and check if they've seen him, and I'll go back with Jason's mother to where she last saw Jason. We're due to see the blacksmith in fifteen minutes, so I guess lots of the school will be on their way there and Jason's possibly tagging along.

'I also suggest you speak to the staff of the museum as this is probably not a rare occurrence and they may be able to suggest special hiding places that are used by children.'

Even as Claire made the suggestion she was remembering what she had learned about St Fagans prior to the trip and especially the bit about it being set in a hundred acres of parkland. The boy could be anywhere, but she reined in her imagination, as she remembered that there were a hundred and sixty-two adults and children from Holly Road walking around, so someone would have seen him.

His mother had lit up another Pall Mall, and her cheeks caved in as she sucked heavily on the cigarette as if her life depended upon it. As they returned to the spot where Tina had last seen her son they passed several of his classmates. The majority had come from the playground and were en route to watch the blacksmith bending some seriously hot iron, and no one had seen Jason.

'He hasn't come in this direction,' said one of the dads. 'I think young Carla here has a soft spot for him and she would have spotted him, wouldn't you sweetheart?' He grinned down at his daughter and she dealt him a swift kick on the shins accompanied by a load of cheek, but this seemed to amuse him all the more.

Claire shook her head and wondered what her own father's reaction would have been if, when at the age of six, she had kicked him and suggested that he was sick in the head. She was hardly in her dotage but she did believe that society as a whole had changed dramatically since her childhood.

The two women walked around the area from where Jason had gone missing and, with renewed vigour, looked around every hedge, fence, tree, and wall. There was no sign of the boy and Claire was starting to get really worried. She was puzzled by the fact that there was a definite pathway along which Jason would have had to go, either forwards towards his mother or back in the direction of his classmates. It appeared that he hadn't gone in either direction, so he must still be hiding somewhere – there was no other explanation.

Both women made a beeline for the pigsty. There were no pigs in the enclosure, just an area enclosed by stone walls, with a gate that allowed access to a small area that was paved in stone and had a stone feeding trough. Claire had no idea if pigs were ever kept there, but today it all looked clean and there was nowhere here for anyone to hide. However there was the sty itself. There was a small opening into the actual circular sty, but it was dark inside and the area looked undisturbed. Although it was just possible that a small boy could have crawled inside, Tina said that Jason was terrified of the dark and didn't like being stuck in small spaces, so there was no way he would hide in there.

A number of others had now joined in the search for Jason and one of the dads jumped over the wall of the pigsty, and getting down on his hands and knees stuck his head into the low square opening at the bottom of the bee-hive shaped stone building.

'It's black as hell in there,' he said 'I can't actually see a bloody thing, we would need a torch to be sure, but I can't see a kid staying in there and I can't hear a sound either.'

No one had a torch but Tina handed him her cigarette lighter and he knelt back down to get a better look. After just a few seconds he confirmed that there was no one inside, and he scrambled back over the wall.

At that moment they were joined by Mrs Locke and two of the museum staff, who were closely followed by the other four teachers. Claire smiled at the museum staff who introduced themselves as Andy Marsh and Clive Kane, and she asked if they had any ideas on how they should go about finding Jason.

Clive said that he was the head groundsman and knew every nook and cranny, and he tried to reassure Jason's mother. 'At least once a week we get a call to look for a missing child but it usually takes no more than ten minutes of our time, so don't worry, we will soon find your son. Show me exactly where you left him and I'll tell you all the possible places he could have made for from that point.'

Tina gave the man a half-hearted smile and lit another cigarette. 'He was exactly here,' she pointed to the spot. 'He was miffed because he didn't want the sandwiches I brought, he was insisting on a McDonald's happy meal, and so I just left him to sulk.' Recalling her last words to Jason she started to cry and smudged her blue-black mascara across her cheeks. 'I told him the pig man would come to get him … but I didn't mean it … I was only teasing.'

Claire offered her a tissue from the seemingly endless supply that was available to primary school teachers, but Tina was now sobbing pitifully and thinking that the situation was getting out of hand. Clive Kane took control.

'OK, let's get the "find Jason" show on the road, and I suggest we look in groups, with each group headed by a teacher or one of the museum staff, so that will give us seven groups and we can each head off in a different direction. I want Miss Masters to stay here with Jason's mother and I bet by the time we all get back Jason will be here with them.' He gave each group an idea of the direction he wanted them to take and suggested that they just walk and look for ten minutes and then retrace their steps so that he could re-assess the situation.

He turned to Tina. 'Apart from Andy and me everyone

knows what Jason looks like and will spot him a mile off, but if you describe him we will also know who to look out for.'

'I can do better than that,' sobbed Tina. 'I took a picture of him on my phone this morning. We were standing in the drive waiting for the taxi to take us to the coach, and I made him stand next to the pool for me to take a photo.'

Clive was surprised when he looked at the image on Tina's phone not to find the kid's paddling pool he had expected, but a beautifully designed patio area surrounding a state-of-the-art swimming pool.

He focused on the boy standing awkwardly at the side of the pool and used the phone's touch technology to enlarge the image of the boy and showed it to his colleague. 'Is he still wearing these clothes?' he asked Tina.

She nodded and Clive took a fresh look at her. Because he had thought she looked a bit common, he had assumed that her clothes and jewellery were imitation but now he could see that his first impressions had been wrong. Although she completely lacked any style, there was no doubt that her designer labels and gold chains were the genuine article. He recalled the setting in which the child's photograph had been taken and some uncomfortable thoughts registered in his mind.

There appeared to be some serious money attached to this woman and so maybe her son's disappearance was more sinister than a childhood prank. Maybe he had been snatched.

Clive told himself to get a grip. This was Cardiff, not London or New York, and when kids went missing in St Fagans they were always found safe and well. Jason would be no different … would he?

Chapter Two

DCI Martin Phelps stared up at the Victorian design of bunches of grapes and bold flowers etched into the ceiling of his office in Goleudy. It was good to be back. The past couple of months had taken him to some very dark places and caused him at times to doubt the very foundations of his profession, but the outcome had been worth the trauma.

He had only been working outside his substantive role for three weeks, but it felt much longer than that and he was keen to get back to normal. Matt Pryor, his detective sergeant, had been acting as a DI in Martin's absence and just lately he had wondered how Matt would feel about reverting back to being a DS.

Rather than just let it happen Martin decided that a bit of social time together would ease the transition, and he knew that Matt was desperate to know the details of the Vincent Bowen case that Martin had been charged with re-investigating.

Sacrificing a weekend at his cottage with his girlfriend Shelley was not something he had really wanted to do, but at least nowadays Shelley was spending more time with Martin in Llantwit Major than she was at the home she shared with her father, thanks to her dad's new-found courage.

For years Shelley's father had been an insulin-dependent diabetic, but in spite of masses of encouragement from Shelley and the community nurses he had never been able to give his own insulin injections. It had always been Shelley's responsibility to check his early morning blood sugar levels and adjust his insulin requirements according to the results. She had never minded doing this for her dad, as there had only been the two of them since Shelley's mother had died of a malignant brain tumour almost twenty years ago. Her father Pete had been mother and father to Shelley, enlisting the help of his sister Fran for the 'girlie bits' of his daughter's growing up.

Shelley had only been a young teenager when her father's diabetes became really unstable and needed to be kept under control by rigorous blood sugar tests, careful control of food intake, and appropriate adjustments to his insulin levels. Over the years the community nurses had been brilliant and were always available to give Shelley some time off but she knew that her father preferred her to give him his injections.

Pete had watched his daughter grow into a beautiful young woman who looked so much like her mother, and who had also inherited her mother's gentle but determined nature. She did well at school, got a 2:1 at Cardiff University, and then stayed on to get an MSc in Occupational Health. Throughout her university days she had lived at home, working every weekend and a couple of evenings a week to ensure a more comfortable financial state for herself and her father.

In spite of his precarious health, Pete had held down a middle-management position as a finance officer in the NHS and had then taken early retirement with a reasonable pension. His position now was one where he could stand alone financially but he could barely remember a time without his daughter and didn't really want to. Although Shelley hadn't been short of boyfriends there had never been anyone special until she had taken the job as head of training and development at the South Wales Police Headquarters, Goleudy, based in Cardiff Bay.

The redbrick Victorian building had been purposely adapted to bring together all the elements needed for twenty-first-century police work. Until she had started working there she, like most members of the public, just thought it was a large police station, but had been amazed to discover just how many different facets of police work it facilitated.

She had expected to see cells and interview rooms but not things like the state-of-the-art laboratories, post-mortem rooms, identification suites, specialist IT facilities, and above all she had been impressed by the way the various departments worked together.

Her own domain was based on the second floor and comprised of one very large seminar room, several smaller discussion rooms, a couple of offices, and a good-sized cloakroom area. Since Shelley had been appointed the training programme had expanded and news of her own particular expertise in all matters relating to health and safety in occupational settings had spread to the rest of Wales and beyond. A participant on one of Shelley's courses had commented in his written feedback that he wouldn't have believed that it was possible to get so excited about H&S law and suggested that the course-leader's enthusiasm should come with a government health warning.

Although Shelley used IT effectively she neither knew nor wanted to know about the technical side of it and was delighted when she was introduced to Charlie Walsh, who headed up the IT department that was based on the same floor as Training. The two women soon became good friends and when Charlie had changed her surname to Griffiths, Shelley had been at the wedding.

It had only been her second week of working there when she was introduced to DCI Martin Phelps and her whole world had changed. Her father claimed to remember the day when his daughter came home from work wearing the look of a woman in love, and had been surprised not to be visited by the object of her affection for over a year! It wasn't that Martin hadn't noticed Shelley, but they had met at a point in his life when he was not looking for a special relationship and certainly not with someone who worked in the same place that he did.

Consequently they were afforded the time to become good friends before moving on, for Martin to realise that Shelley was the love of his life, and for her father to decide that administering his own injections was a small price to pay for his daughter's happiness.

Martin knew that he had reached a crossroads in his life and that his career and his personal circumstances were in the process of a big shake-up. Just over a month ago Chief Superintendent Colin Atkinson had been transferred to Cardiff from the Greater Manchester Police, and was proving to be a no-nonsense man and someone whom Martin could both work with and respect.

The two men had met at the conclusion of a case where a serial killer had been caught by Martin's team virtually at the point of stabbing to death what would have been his fourth victim. The identity of the killer had been a shock for the public, but even more so for the police force, as the murderer was a former DCI, Norman Austin, someone with whom Martin had worked.

Each of Austin's killings had been heralded by a bizarre poem giving clues to the identity of his victim. From the beginning it had been obvious that Martin was one of the killer's intended victims, but absolutely no one had suspected his old boss. As soon as the killer's identity had been realised it had unleashed a flood of memories from Sergeant John Evans and others, regarding cases that the former DCI Austin had managed.

In particular Evans had remembered his concerns regarding the conviction of Vincent Bowen for the murder of young prostitutes in Cardiff. The cruel ritualistic killing of these women had happened over a period of time, with the first one being six months before another three separated by just a few weeks.

The murders had caused a public and political storm and DCI Austin had been under enormous pressure to bring an end to what the press called 'the terror of the ladies of the night'.

At the time Martin had only recently been appointed as a detective sergeant, and although he had been partly involved with the investigations surrounding the second and third killings, he now realised that he had been deliberately left out of the fourth murder and its subsequent investigation that had led to the arrest of Vincent Bowen.

All four murdered prostitutes were considered to have been killed by the same man, but only three had been proven to be the work of Bowen. It had been one of those euphoric moments when, with the arrest of the serial killer, the whole country had applauded the efforts of DCI Austin and his team. The discovery of a knife stained with the third victim's blood in the suspect's home provided the copper-bottom evidence of guilt and Vincent Bowen was convicted of the murders.

Just twenty-three years old at the time, Bowen was known to have moderately serious mental health problems but had never been considered a risk to himself or others. His psychiatric workers were lambasted in the press for not recognising his evil potential but his main caseworker had always held her belief that Bowen was not capable of carrying out these killings and had joined his mother's campaign for her son's release.

Sgt Evans· had always considered that the finding of the knife in Vincent Bowen's flat was loaded with doubt, as he had been part of an original search of the property when no knife had been discovered. He had voiced his concerns at the time, but the then recently appointed Superintendent Bryant was basking in the glory of his new team solving such a high-profile case and agreed with DCI Austin's convenient view that Evans was as blind as a bat.

The recent murders, and the revelation that Norman Austin was the killer, had given Sgt Evans new-found courage to take his previous concerns above the head of Superintendent Bryant. This time the concerns he revealed to Chief Superintendent Atkinson were taken seriously, and were part of the reason that DCI Phelps had spent the past three weeks looking at the circumstances surrounding the conviction of Vincent Bowen.

Atkinson had appointed Martin to head up the new enquiry and had raised the issue of a possibly unsafe conviction, due to police corruption, with the chief constable and Home-Office officials. Consequently the manpower and facilities needed for a thorough review were thrown in Martin's direction, and an area of the sacred top floor of Goleudy turned into a major investigation unit.

Teams worked around the clock checking and re-checking every detail of the case and finding a number of anomalies.

Witness statements were re-examined and members of the original investigation team, some still members of the force, were interviewed.

One of the first people that Martin had spoken to was Vincent Bowen's mother. His initial contact had been a telephone call and he had followed it up with a meeting at Mrs Bowen's home, where he had not been surprised to see Emily Wiseman waiting with her.

In fact it had been Emily who had let him in after he had spoken into the intercom system that linked the main entrance of the building in Fairwater to the individual flats. As soon as she had realised who he was, Emily had released the locking mechanism, something buzzed loudly, and the door literally burst open.

'Third floor, flat number nine,' she told him as he stepped inside and the heavy external door snapped back into place behind him.

The building was built in the mid-seventies and was fit for purpose but not a pretty structure. The front faced the main road, separated by just a footpath, and the area to both sides and at the back was concreted over and used for parking. In spite of the uninspiring appearance it looked well cared for, with a number of strategically placed litter bins actually being used for the correct purpose, and the area had recently been swept clean. It looked neat and tidy but without soul.

Martin had the same feeling about the inside of the building as he looked at a number of bikes and pushchairs chained to a central bar just inside the door. Everything was well ordered and the place had a vague smell of pine-scented disinfectant. The lift looked as if it was in good working order but Martin decided to take the stairs. On the first floor was a good-sized square landing and four doors numbered 1-4. Here was the first sign that individual tenants were making an effort to put some personal stamp on their surroundings. Different coloured doors had been decorated with a variety of bells, handles, and door-knockers and outside two of the flats were tubs of plants that looked to be thriving.

It was a similar picture on the second floor and when Martin reached his destination Emily was waiting for him.

'I wondered why I hadn't heard the lift,' she remarked. 'Not many people use the stairs – come through, Cora is anxious to meet you.'

Outside Cora's front door Martin caught sight of a six-foot-high rubber plant with shining leaves standing in a gleaming copper container, and Emily saw that he had noticed it.

'It's an amazing specimen, isn't it? Vincent bought that for his mother for her birthday about six weeks before he was arrested for the murder of those women. It didn't look like that then – it was just a small plant in a plastic pot, but in the absence of her son Cora has cared for his last gift to her. She calls it her "plant of hope" but from what I can see the more it grows and flourishes the more her hope diminishes. My own hope now is that you're not going to give her any more cause for despair.'

Martin followed Emily down a short passage into a light and airy lounge where Cora Bowen sat in an armchair that was positioned so that its occupier could look out over the nearby tree-tops. She didn't get up but turned her head as Martin approached her and made his usual official introductions. She shook his hand with a faint smile and confirmed that Emily had previously been her son Vincent's primary caseworker.

'I don't know how I would have got through the years of Vincent's incarceration without Emily,' said Cora. 'Apart from me she has been the only one who has always believed in his innocence and has never faltered in her support.'

'That's not difficult when you know that what you believe in is the truth,' said Emily. 'Have you met Vincent?' she asked Martin. 'He got into a whole heap of trouble when he was in school, and sniffing solvents over quite a long period led to changes in his behaviour, and indeed his whole personality. There were issues at the time that led to him being referred to the community mental health teams and that's how I first met him.'

She looked at Cora as she continued. 'Despite his problems

23

Vincent never showed any tendency towards violence, and even when he had left home to share a flat with a friend he still spent a lot of his time back here with his mother.'

Martin accepted the offer of a coffee and Emily left Cora to talk to the DCI in more depth about the time of Vincent's arrest.

'It happened when I was beginning to see some signs of the return of the Vincent that he had been as a young boy. He had always been fun loving, always up for a laugh, and too adventurous for his own good. Look at that photograph over there, Chief Inspector, it was taken when Vincent was eleven and was in the days when he woke up every morning with a smile on his face, and was so much alive I could barely keep up with him.

'I haven't seen my son smile in years, and the man that I visit once a week has had every ounce of life sucked out of him. I have never doubted his innocence but a few years ago even I tried to persuade him to confess to the killings and express profound contrition. The only reason I suggested it was so that there would be a chance of his release sometime in the future. It would appear that the first step towards that has to come from Vincent owning up to the crimes and demonstrating how sorry he is for his actions.'

Cora stood up and looked through the window, and then with eyes brimming with tears she turned back towards Martin. 'The thought of even his own mother apparently believing he was guilty of such horrendous acts of depravity were too much for Vincent to bear, and he attempted to kill himself. He had no weapons or pills at his disposal and so he simply kept banging his head against his cell door until he lost consciousness.'

Emily put three mugs down on a central glass-topped coffee table and put her arm around Cora's shoulder. 'I don't think Vincent really intended to kill himself, and like Cora I have never believed he could be guilty of killing those women.'

Emily looked directly at Martin as she handed him his coffee. 'Like everyone else we've been following the events surrounding the recent murders in the area, and we were shocked more than everyone else to find that the killer turned out to be Norman Austin. He was the DCI leading the investigation into the murder of those women, but then of course you will know that.

'What you may not know is the number of times in the early years following Vincent's conviction that we tried to get him to take a fresh look at the evidence, and we even asked his superior officer, Superintendent Bryant. Our case was not helped by the fact that there were no further killings and the police and the public were convinced that the killer had been caught and justly punished.'

'Cora rang me this morning after getting your call and we are both anxious to know why you are here, and Cora had even suggested that maybe Austin killed those prostitutes and framed her son.'

Martin took a mouthful of coffee and the three of them settled down for what Martin suspected was going to be a long session. Cora's last comments had rung alarm bells with Martin but mainly because they mirrored some of his own thoughts. Once he would never have come close to suspecting his former DCI of slitting the throats of those prostitutes, but the past few weeks had shown Austin to be a psychopath with an incredibly unbalanced mind; unbalanced but clever. Who knew what would come out of the re-investigation of this case?

For the moment Martin was more concerned with investigating the evidence that had led to Vincent's arrest, and although he still had material to check and witnesses to interview it was becoming more and more obvious that Vincent's conviction was unsafe.

He didn't want to raise the hopes of Vincent's mother and her devout friend too much but he did explain to them that certain things had come to light following the arrest of Norman Austin and that a number of his old cases were being re-examined.

'I have been specifically charged with undertaking a comprehensive review into the murders of the prostitutes. We realise that a miscarriage of justice may have occurred and want it remedied as quickly as possible, and that is why an unprecedented level of manpower and support services have been put at my disposal.'

Although Martin had specifically warned Cora about not getting her hopes raised too high the level of excitement in the room was palpable. When Martin had entered her home he had seen a worn-out woman who looked to be in her mid-sixties and whose eyes were almost bereft of life. Now, looking at her, he realised that she was probably ten years younger than he had first thought and it was the new light in her eyes that had caused the transformation.

'Please try and contain your expectations,' he begged. 'My only purpose here today is to tell you that the case is to be re-opened and not to give you any indication that my findings will be any different to those of the original investigation.'

'That's all we have ever wanted,' Emily said. 'We both believe in Vincent and we both believe that your investigation will get to the truth; we can't ask for any more. What will happen now?'

Before he left Martin explained that his next job was to review all the witness statements and examine all the evidence that had been documented. He added that the team expected to be able to make a decision within days.

'If we conclude that Vincent's conviction appears to be unsafe we will apply to the courts to have it overturned. There is interest in this case at the highest level: hence the speed at which it is being moved.'

'If you find the conviction unsafe and the courts agree, what will happen then?' asked Cora, barely able to contemplate the answer.

'Vincent will be released and your fight for compensation regarding his wrongful arrest and years of imprisonment will begin,' Martin told them. 'I have arranged a session with your son tomorrow morning and it's possible that even as soon as that I may be able to give him some news.'

As he left Martin handed a card with his direct phone number to Cora with a special plea that she keep things to herself for the moment and in particular avoid any contact with the press.

Thinking back now Martin remembered how, when he had left those two women and driven his Alfa Romeo back to Goleudy, none of them could have envisaged what the next three weeks would bring.

He had visited Vincent in Cardiff Prison the morning after meeting his mother and had been introduced to a man in his early thirties with dark hair that emphasised the pallor of his gaunt face. He could once have been good-looking, but he was far too thin and had a totally blank expression. Martin introduced himself and received no indication of whether or not Vincent even knew he was there.

It took less than half an hour for Martin to tell Vincent what he had previously told his mother, but the news did not appear to have the same effect. Throughout the meeting Vincent remained motionless and didn't say a word, but he'd managed a simple nod of the head when at the end Martin asked him if he had understood what had been said.

On the way out Martin had spoken to one of the prison officers who told him that Vincent rarely spoke and was such a gentle person that she and her fellow officers often quizzed over how he could have committed such appalling murders.

By the end of that week Martin and his seconded team had shown numerous reasons why Vincent's conviction was unsafe and in fact left no doubt that he was totally innocent of all the charges that had been made against him. The court supported the findings and Vincent was released amidst a fever of media activity.

Hours after his release and in line with the arrangements organised by Martin the reunion of Vincent with his mother took place miles away from the glare of the media. The only other person who knew that they were staying at a cottage in Dorset was Emily and she joined them after a couple of days.

The press, as expected, had camped outside Cora's flat in Fairwater for almost a week following Vincent's release but had to be content with the sightings of Vincent leaving the prison, as after that he had seemingly disappeared.

Martin guessed that what lay ahead of Vincent and his mother would be years of struggle as they attempted to return to some sort of normality. He was pleased to think that they had the support of Emily Wiseman and he knew that in the fullness of time there would be a mega payout to Vincent, ostensibly to compensate for his wrongful arrest and years of imprisonment.

No amount of money would ever be able to give him back his lost years, and if Vincent had been a damaged man at the time of his arrest it was likely that the harm had deepened during his time inside. It could only be hoped that the love and devotion his mother had shown would continue and would bring her son to a better place.

Martin felt really good about Vincent's release, but of course it had begged the question as to who was the real killer of those prostitutes. Although his brief had been to concentrate on the conviction of Vincent Bowen, it had been agreed that the team should take things further and their efforts took them to Bristol.

It had been a year or so after the murders in Cardiff when a fifty-year-old man had been arrested for the slaughter of two sex workers on a large housing estate fairly near Bristol city centre. Although these women had been killed by having their throats cut, in the same way as the prostitutes in Cardiff, there had been no reason to link the crimes. After all, the perpetrator of the Cardiff killings was behind bars and this was just another man who, in his own mind, had a reason for 'cleaning up the streets'. What had led Martin to Bristol was the fact that the review team had brought to his attention: that all the women killed in Cardiff had links with Bristol. He had learned from the local vice squad that it was not uncommon for sex workers from Cardiff to work for a period in Bristol and vice versa.

None of this had come to light at the time of the killings in Cardiff and as soon as Vincent had been arrested the then-DCI Austin had quickly closed down any other possible leads. The second week in the re-opened enquiry had taken Martin and some of the team to Bristol's Cambridge Road prison.

Mike Waverley was still the acting governor, and

remembered Martin from a previous visit when he and Matt had been there to see the father of a gay man who had been butchered in Cardiff. The two men had spent a few minutes reminiscing on the results of that case before turning their attention to Jeff Norris, the man Martin had come to interview.

Martin learned that Norris had confessed to cutting the throats of two women in Bristol and boasted that he was better at cleaning up the filth on the streets than the politicians. They only talked about it, but he did it. At the time of his arrest he had bragged about having killed many more before the Bristol two and indicated that Cardiff, Swindon, and Reading had been part of his mission to 'get the whores out of the city centres'.

His claims to crimes in other places had been checked out, but the only area where there had been similar killings in that time frame was Cardiff, and the perpetrator of those deeds had already been tried and convicted. Nothing more had been done at the time, but when Martin spoke to Norris the man was able to give details of the Cardiff murders that only the killer could know. All the details of the Norris investigation were transferred to the team in Goleudy and the comparisons between the cases that Norris and Bowen were convicted of left no doubt that all women were killed by the same hand.

The timing of the Bristol murders gave Vincent Bowen a cast-iron alibi, as he was already in prison and in any event Norris was more than willing to confess to what he considered to be a valuable service to decent people.

For Martin the worst part of the last few weeks had been meeting up again with his old boss, Norman Austin. An armed response team had been used to capture him and during the operation Austin had received a bullet wound that had almost been fatal. Thanks to the initial response of an excellent medical team and the subsequent work of surgeons Austin had survived to face the consequences of his deranged murderous intentions.

He had looked like a pathetic old man when Martin had visited him at the hospital, and just nodded his head when he had been asked if he understood his rights and the charges that were being made.

Although his wound had been life-threatening, it was only a few days after surgery when he was back on his feet and the team were able to question him about his bizarre killing spree. He had shown no contrition or remorse and as his health improved and he returned to his normal self he became ludicrously proud of his crimes.

A week ago Martin had interviewed Austin regarding his actions around the time that Vincent Bowen had been arrested. Discharged from hospital, Austin was on remand and would remain so until after his trial. Now he looked and sounded more like the boss that Martin remembered. Gone was the frail look of a man who had just recovered from near-death, and back was the arrogant bully and obsessive controller.

It had taken several attempts to get Austin to realise that Martin was not there to talk about his own killings but to go over the events surrounding the arrest of Vincent Bowen. Eventually he laughed in Martin's face and not only admitted had he arranged for the knife to be planted in Bowen's flat but also implicated the other officers who had helped with getting it coated with blood from the second murdered woman.

He had gone on to tell Martin how he had rubbished Sgt Evans when the sergeant had taken his concerns to the newly appointed Superintendent Bryant. As if on a roll Austin had continued to boast about his success in solving crimes and admitted to using any methods he could lay his hands on to get the results he wanted. Names of fellow officers and their part in sorting out appropriate evidence poured out of his mouth and into the memory of the tape recorder.

Martin could not remember a more demoralising moment in his career and felt physically sick with the knowledge that at least three other possibly innocent people had been convicted as a result of Austin's methods. It was also possible that if dubious evidence had been used to convict even the guilty, then their lawyers could now get them released. Two of the officers named by Austin were still serving and would now have to be suspended and investigated. Walking away from that interview Martin had reflected on the bloody mess that one man had made and the hit that the police force would take in terms of public respect and confidence. He was a firm believer in the old adage that 'behaviour breeds behaviour' and could see how the practices encouraged by Austin would have influenced some of his fellow officers and subordinates.

Martin had spent the past two hours giving a report to Chief Superintendent Atkinson and the Chief's positive response had been reassuring. Everything would be done to respond to the mistakes of the past and he had told Martin about some anti-corruption plans that were going to be implemented. He turned his attention from the detail of his office ceiling that seemed to focus his memories and looked through the window. Matt had a day's leave booked but they would catch up tomorrow – and yes, it was good to be back.

Chapter Three

'We've been looking for coming up to an hour now,' whispered Claire Masters to Clive Kane. 'I still think he must be hiding somewhere, but considering the number of people who've now got involved with the search it seems incredible that we haven't found him.'

Claire spoke quietly because Tina Barnes had freaked out the last time anyone mentioned how long her son had been missing.

Clive shook his head. 'You're forgetting the size of this place. The museum itself has lots of different exhibitions and then there's the restaurant, the café, the shop, and the park. Away from the central area we have the stand-alone sites and in all there are more than forty original buildings.'

'Then there's the Iron Age Celtic Village and St Fagans Castle with the gardens and fish ponds – they would attract me if I was a small boy who had managed to break loose from my mother.'

'I'm not forgetting the size of the place,' replied Claire. 'It's just thinking of the countless possibilities for hiding a small boy that worries me the most. What I don't understand is why nobody has seen him since his mother left him and she says she was only gone for a few minutes. I certainly believe her on that score, as the weird thing is that since she came into money her circle of friends has dwindled to virtually nothing and Jason is the centre of her life.'

Claire's phone rang and she recognised the number of her headmaster. 'Any news, Claire?' asked Paul Prosser. 'I've just come back from a meeting in Cardiff and Miss Holden has said you've been trying to reach me. These things are usually a storm in a teacup so I guess the little monkey has come out of hiding.'

'You guess wrong this time, Paul,' Claire snapped. 'The world and his wife have been looking for Jason for nearly an hour, and I think it's time we handed the search over to the police, but I wanted to check with you before I did anything like that.'

'Bloody hell, what do you think has happened to him?'

Claire listened in disbelief to her head's question and wanted to say that if she had the foggiest idea she would be acting on it and not wasting time talking to him. Instead she raised her concerns about the possibility of the boy being injured.

'It's the only thing that makes any sense. Jason has got quite a short attention span and if he had been hiding he would have been bored by now – and even in the process of finding a hiding place it's likely that someone would have seen him. I certainly don't see him leaving St Fagans, he's not that brave as he knows his teachers and his mother would be furious with him.'

Paul Prosser interrupted. 'The decision regarding the involvement of the police is down to Jason's mother as she is with you, but the school could do without any negative publicity.'

This time Claire didn't hold back with what she was thinking. 'Sod the negative publicity, all I'm concerned about is finding Jason, and I think you should take the responsibility of phoning the police now so that at least we will be seen as taking the issue seriously even if it turns out to be your *storm in a teacup*.'

'OK, Claire, calm down. I wasn't suggesting bad publicity was more important than Jason's safety, and I can hear from your tone that you're really worried so I'll get on to the police immediately and let you know what they suggest.'

Jason's mother had heard the part of the conversation where Claire had suggested sending for the police immediately and became uncontrollably hysterical. They had returned to the spot where she had last seen Jason and Tina threw herself onto the

34

ground and sobbed into the grass.

Claire knelt down beside her and tried to console her, even suggesting a cigarette would calm the nerves. She asked Clive to go to the entrance to the grounds and wait for the police and they would follow when Tina was a bit more stable.

Tina looked at her through eyes that were red and puffy and that reflected the terror she was feeling. 'I'm not going nowhere, Miss,' she spoke with a voice that wobbled and shoulders that shuddered. 'I'm staying put 'til my Jase gets back.'

She suddenly sat up and ran her fingers violently through her hair. 'I'll kill the little bugger when I get hold of him,' she said, and immediately regretting her words stared anxiously at Claire.

'I heard you telling Mr Prosser that my Jason could have had an accident, but if he has, why haven't we found him? That man Clive knows this place and says how big it is but he doesn't know my Jase. He's not keen on walking and that's the truth, and he was hungry so he wouldn't have gone far. I think something terrible has happened to him.' She had barely finished the words before a new deluge of tears arrived and she had once again buried her face in the ground.

As Claire bent to comfort Tina she was pushed aside by Pam Woodland, who no longer cared about her differences with her former friend, understanding what the loss of a child could bring to any woman. Her own three boys watched in total confusion as their mother cradled the woman who less than an hour ago had been on the receiving end of her cruel tongue.

'We'll find him, don't you worry, we'll find him. I've phoned my brother and he's sorting out some of the rugby boys to help us look. They'll find your Jason.' Pam sounded confident and her words appeared to be calming Tina.

Claire decided to enlist the help of Mrs Woodland further and asked her if she would remain with Tina while she went to see what was happening with the police. Pam nodded and then shouted at her boys to behave themselves as they were rummaging through her rucksack looking for sweets. 'Make yourselves bloody useful and look around for Jason, but for

God's sake stick together,' she told them.

One of the boys had discovered a packet of Haribo Supermix, and pocketing his find called to his brothers to help him find Jason and inevitably eat their way through the large packet of sweets.

Before Claire left the two women Tina was already sitting up and drawing heavily on a cigarette. If anyone could bring a touch of normality back to this tense situation it would be someone like Pam Woodland, thought Claire as she walked quickly back towards the car park. Although her stomach was now churning and she was deeply worried about Jason she knew that having no children of her own she would never be able to truly empathise with Jason's mother. She may have her own family sometime in the future but for now she could barely imagine what it would be like to give birth to a child, share his ups and downs, and then have him cruelly taken away. With some effort she controlled her over-fertile imagination and tried to reassure herself that in a little while this nightmare would be over and Jason would have bounced back.

Even before she reached the car park Claire could see the flashing blue lights of two police vehicles. When she had been taking a shower at seven o'clock that morning she had smiled at her mind imagining what pranks would be played during today's school outing. She wasn't smiling now. This was every teacher's worst nightmare and she was pleased to see that her colleague Emma Locke was already speaking to four officers.

Mrs Locke had years of experience under her belt and was dealing with the situation calmly and she waved to Claire. 'I take it Jason hasn't been found?' she questioned, but Claire shook her head. 'I've been telling the officers how he went missing and the efforts that have been made to find him, and we were just deciding what needs to be done next.'

Clive Kane indicated that there was a room set aside from which the officers could work and following formal introductions the group made their way through the main entrance. The lead officer was PC Alan Lewis and he asked his colleague PC Tucker to go straight to where the boy had last been seen and interview the mother. She indicated that she knew the exact spot that had been described and went off in that direction. Claire discovered that all the officers were local and that they were familiar with the layout of the grounds and buildings and had conducted a couple of successful searches in the past.

PC Lewis suggested a plan for thoroughly combing the area within a ten-minute walk in all directions from where Jason had disappeared. Clive explained that they had already completed a similar exercise but agreed that with additional manpower the search would be more rigorous. No one wanted to sit around and as they all started to walk in the direction PC Tucker had taken Clive came up with an idea.

'Ms Barnes, that's the boy's mother, took a photograph of her son this morning and it's on her phone. If you get her to email that to this address I'll get some copies printed and pass them around.'

As he spoke he wrote down the email address and handed it to PC Lewis. 'The staff here will help in any way they can – just let us know what you need.'

Walking away a sudden thought occurred to PC Lewis and he spoke to Claire. 'Miss Masters, has anyone checked the bus you came on? On one occasion a child we were looking for had returned to the bus and was found fast asleep on the back seat.'

'I'm pretty certain our coaches weren't hanging around. We're less than half an hour from the school and so they're able to fit other commitments into their day. They'll be coming back for us at two thirty as scheduled. Nevertheless I'll check the coaches and then catch up with you.'

Claire could see most of the coaches from where they had all been standing, but there were now quite a lot of them and she carefully looked for the blue and gold colours of County Coaches. She hadn't expected to see them and within a few minutes she was satisfied that they were not there and guessed that they would have been long gone before Jason went missing.

She decided that guessing was not the order of the day and

so she used the emergency number she had for the company and asked if there had been any problems when the coaches had returned to the depot. The manager told her that all the coaches had gone back out as they were ferrying women to some sort of special WI lunch at the Rhondda Heritage Park. 'I think they're pushing it somewhat to get back to pick you up by two thirty but the drivers seem to think it's doable. The only problem we had when the guys came back from you was a smell of sick in the second coach but a few blasts of the air conditioning soon sorted that. Why are you asking about problems?'

Claire explained the situation and the manager expressed his concern. 'I can assure you that there was no small stowaway when our drivers got back and I hope you find the young man soon. I've got three boys of my own and most of the time I feel like banging their heads together to stop the constant bickering, but if anything happened to any one of them I'd go to pieces. Look, I hope you find little Jason soon, and if we can do anything just let us know.'

As she ended the call Claire reflected on the love-hate relationship between children and their parents and wondered if she would ever be strong enough to survive the roller-coaster ride that seemed to be an inevitable part of bringing up a child. She hurried to where she had left Jason's mother and prayed with every step that she would find Jason sitting with her.

Her prayers were not answered, although at first it was difficult for her to know as Tina Barnes was surrounded by a mass of people including the four uniformed officers. Their very presence seemed to up the ante from being a worrying situation to a potentially horrendous nightmare. As she approached PC Lewis pulled her to one side.

'I've done as Mr Kane suggested and emailed him the photograph of Jason that was taken this morning. The picture was taken at their home and without wishing to sound too prejudiced I was surprised to see the background and I asked Ms Barnes about her circumstances.'

Claire interrupted him. 'It's no secret, Constable Lewis, that Tina had a big win on the lottery and although I couldn't tell you how much she got I know it was several million.'

PC Lewis nodded. 'I haven't said anything to Ms Barnes yet, but from my point of view her vast wealth puts a different perspective on her son's disappearance and we have to consider that he has been deliberately taken and may be held to ransom.'

In spite of herself Claire laughed spontaneously but quickly controlled herself as she had received some scathing looks from some of the parents.

'What?' she questioned, keeping her voice at the level of a whisper. 'Are you seriously suggesting that Jason has been kidnapped?'

'Under the circumstances we have to consider the possibility and now that I've entertained that thought I have a responsibility to inform my superior officers get the CID involved. With any situations involving children we would rather do too much than too little even if it proves to have been overkill.'

PC Lewis moved away from Claire and spoke into his phone, explaining the position to his local sergeant and looking relieved that he was able to pass this one up the line.

Both of them were startled by a sudden wail from the centre of the crowd surrounding Christine Barnes and Claire knew instantly that the almost inhuman sound had come from the woman herself. She pushed her way through the parents and children to find Tina holding a small Lego figure.

'It's Jason's Ron Weasley,' she screeched, and thrust it in the direction of the child who had discovered it. 'Where did you find it, Chelsea?'

The little girl cringed at being the centre of everyone's attention and her bottom lip quivered as tears welled up in her eyes. Claire knelt beside her. 'It's OK, Chelsea, you're not in any kind of trouble and you did really well to find Jason's toy. Do you think you could show me exactly where it was before you picked it up?'

Chelsea wiped away her tears with the back of her hand, leaving some dirty smudges across her cheeks. 'It was just by there, Miss. Jason's mother was nearly sitting on it – it was just by her bum, Miss.'

PC Lewis spoke to the other officers and suggested that people would be better used by continuing to search for Jason and they organised the small crowd into groups each led by an officer. Even before they had sorted themselves out Clive Kane had returned and handed out pictures of the missing boy to the officers. Word had spread of his disappearance and more and more people became involved with the search.

Individuals took a copy of the picture and whole outings forgot about the purpose of their visit and abandoned all thoughts of a day out in order to find a missing child. Claire was moved by the level of concern shown by compete strangers and prayed as she had never done before that their efforts would be rewarded.

With the majority of people off on a mission the only ones left were Tina, Pam, PC Lewis, and Claire. Tina was staring lovingly at the small plastic figure that she was holding as if it represented her son, and PC Lewis was asking her about it.

'It's definitely Jason's, it's the only figure he's put together out of the Diagon Alley set I bought him. It's got over two thousand pieces and it's meant for a much older child but Jason is Harry Potter mad and thinks he is Ron Weasley just because the two of them have ginger hair and freckles.'

A fresh torrent of tears accompanied her memories of her son and Pam coughed and spluttered as she attempted to light up a cigarette for Tina. 'God only knows how you can smoke those things,' she said, handing it over and watching Tina draw long and hard, inhaling the smoke with no difficulty.

It took all three of them to persuade Tina that they should walk back to the museum and wait for news of Jason. She seemed to think that moving from the spot where she had last seen her son was in some way betraying him, but she finally agreed that there was nothing to be gained from just sitting there.

Tea and coffee had been provided but Tina didn't stay in the room, but walked out of the fire doors to light up yet another cigarette. Pam followed her. She had left her own boys in the care of one of the other parents and was now firmly in the role of best friend and felt able to ask Tina some questions that others were loath to broach.

'Did you and Jason have an argument? I fight with my lot all the time and I've given them all a clip across the ear on more than one occasion. I know it's not the thing to do these days and the last time I smacked my Ben he threatened to report me. And last week Harry ran away. He didn't get far 'cos my cousin saw him at the end of our road and brought him home, but they know how to worry you, don't they?'

Tina nodded. 'Jason does sometimes say he's going to find his dad, but he just *says* it, and we had been talking about his dad but that wasn't the issue when I walked away from him. We were arguing about food. I wouldn't even call it arguing, it was just that he was having a strop because he couldn't go to McDonalds.

'What are we doing here anyway, just standing around and talking isn't going to find Jason, is it? We should be out there looking for him.'

Tina looked helpless and her head and shoulders dropped even further as she stared at nothing with eyes that were almost closed with the swelling of tears.

'There are literally hundreds of people looking for him,' said Pam quietly as she gripped hold of Tina's hands. 'Look, Tina, everyone still thinks Jason is hiding somewhere, and you know what kids are like – he could even have curled up and gone to sleep, but the police don't want to take any chances so they've called in the CID.'

Pam got the reaction she was expecting as Tina's howls were probably loud enough to have been heard by her son if he was anywhere on the hundred-acre site.

The call that had been made by PC Lewis' sergeant went through a number of offices and ended with a call from DC Helen Cook-Watts to DCI Phelps.

'Someone up there must know you're back, guv, we've just been notified about a missing child and the sergeant from St

Fagans seems to think he could have been snatched. He was on a school trip with his mother and has been missing for about an hour now, and it seems that panic has really set in.'

'Don't tell me any more now, Helen, you can fill me in with whatever else you know on the way. See you in the car park in five minutes.'

En route to St Fagans Helen briefed Martin on what little she knew and they discussed the possible reasons for a child being taken. In their view the worst-case scenario would be a paedophile on the lookout for easy pickings, and such perverts knew that children on school trips were likely targets. These monsters had kept up with the desires of youngsters and were less likely to tempt them with sweets as in the past. Some of the recent cases had seen kids seduced by the latest apps on expensive iPads and drawn into conversations on how best to complete the levels of some of the more popular games.

'There's so much help given these days to enable them to recognise things that are not quite right but I think we forget that at the end of the day they are just kids and God forbid that we have to teach them to regard every grown-up as a potential enemy.' Helen looked at the image of Jason that had been sent to her phone and as Martin was driving she described what she saw.

'He looks as if he was reluctant to pose for the photograph if the sulky expression is anything to go by,' she said. 'It's not possible to see from the picture but apparently he's of average height for his age and his arms and face are covered in freckles. With that mop of ginger hair he isn't a child who would fade into the background, and his clothes are very distinctive. None of your supermarket gear for this young man: it's all genuine designer labels and the background to this picture adds to the money-is-no-object impression. That's what prompted one of the local officers to think about the possibility that the kid has not just hidden himself away somewhere but may have been deliberately taken.'

Martin interrupted. 'Are there any issues surrounding the child's parents? I'm thinking maybe a father who has been denied access. The boy would have gone with his father if he had turned up, wouldn't he?'

'I don't know,' replied Helen. 'All the information I got was that the boy's mother recently had a big win on the lottery and it's now being considered that her son may have been snatched and could possibly be held to ransom. Have you ever dealt with a kidnapping before?' she asked Martin.

'Never,' he said shaking his head. 'I hate crimes that involve children, and let's keep our fingers crossed that this turns out to be a false alarm and that young Jason is already reunited with his mother.'

Helen nodded but thought it was unlikely to be the case, as she had been promised an immediate call if the boy was found and her phone was silent. She had only joined the CID a few months ago and already had under her belt the experience of investigating a serial killer and now a potential kidnapping. Part of her was excited by the prospect of being involved in such a case and she remembered that she had fought down a similar feeling of excitement when she had been called to the first murder of the serial killer. Helen wasn't proud of her feelings and tried to convince herself that she was not responsible for the crimes and the excitement stemmed from her anticipation of helping to capture the perpetrators.

She had worked with Matt Pryor while Martin had been seconded to the investigation into Vincent Bowen's conviction but they had only dealt with day-to-day crime – nothing major. Matt would want to be involved with this case if it turned out to be a kidnapping and she mentioned the fact to Martin.

'He's going to be meeting us in the St Fagans car park. I flipped a coin to decide whether or not to interrupt his day off but then gave him a call and left the choice to him.'

Martin laughed. 'It wouldn't have taken much for him to decide to take work over what he was doing, so with a missing child as an excuse he was off the hook.'

'What was he doing, gardening, decorating, or baby-sitting one of his numerous nieces?'

'Well, sort of the latter,' replied Martin. 'The thing with

Matt's nieces is that there are so many of them, and I think the youngest is only three but the oldest is starting her university course and she's the one who Matt's with today. Apparently there's a jobs fair at the Atrium on the uni campus and they've gone along to find a suitable part-time job for Lowri to fit in with her studies. Judging by the conversation between the two of them when Matt got my call, I would say it was a toss-up as to which of them was the most relieved.'

Helen smiled and used the relaxed atmosphere to make a comment and dig for some information. 'It will be good to be back working with the full team but rumour has it, sir, that there are big changes ahead and you're likely to be moving onwards and upwards.'

Martin turned his Alfa Romeo away from the Culverhouse Cross junction and seconds later was on Michaelston Road, no more than five minutes from their destination.

As she looked at the suddenly stern face of her boss Helen wondered if she had been a bit cheeky using the situation to fish around, but the jungle drums had been pounding hard over the past few weeks and everyone was keen to know what the future held for the team.

'At this moment in time I know as much or maybe as little as you do. Everyone's aware that there are going to be some major changes and the merging of some departments is almost inevitable, but when it comes to the position of individuals within the new set-up I haven't got a clue. All I can say is that Chief Superintendent Atkinson has pledged to speak personally to every officer affected by the changes and the various staff organisations are expected to be fully involved. With all that on the agenda, I suspect it'll be the beginning of next year before the new arrangements are in place. Some staff may choose to take voluntary redundancy, but there'll be no compulsory departures, and that genuinely is all I know for the moment.'

Martin had already spotted a black 4x4 and headed in the direction of the tall, tanned figure of DS Pryor, who had arrived just minutes ahead of him and was staring up at the black clouds that were circling above.

'You look well,' remarked Helen. 'I only saw you last Friday but you seem to have shed a good few pounds – and where did you get that tan?'

Matt grinned at Martin. 'Well, two days surfing in Llantwit Major should have seen me at least a stone lighter, but it was off-set by far too much excellent hospitality. But we got addicted over the weekend and Sarah and I have barely been on dry land for the past two days. She's back at work this morning and I got roped into going with my niece to some job fair. If you listen carefully you will probably hear Lowri and her friends cheering at my departure – I was certainly cramping her style!

'What's all this about?' he asked Martin. 'You mentioned a missing boy and the possibility of foul play but have we got anything else?'

The three of them made their way to the front entrance of the museum and were greeted by PC Lewis, who had been told to expect their arrival.

Helen had previously met Alan Lewis at a training session and so she facilitated the introductions.

'It's been well over an hour now since the boy was last seen and there must be hundreds of people who are now involved in the search. We all thought it was just a childish prank to begin with but my own suspicions were aroused when Jason's mother showed me the photograph she had taken this morning.'

PC Lewis went on to describe the setting of the picture and to pass on the information he had been given by Miss Masters regarding the mother's lottery win. 'That puts her in a position to be able to pay a sizeable ransom for the release of her son and apparently her win has never been a secret, so loads of people know.'

'What about other family members?' Martin asked. 'Is Jason's dad around?'

'I spoke to two of the teachers and they both agreed that they had never seen another member of Jason's family and when we asked Tina, that's what everyone calls his mother, she said it was just her and Jason.'

'Where is she now?' Martin questioned.

PC Lewis pointed in the direction of the room Tina had gone into and Martin turned to Matt.

'I suggest that PC Lewis takes you to the place where Jason was last seen and that Helen and I go and speak to the mother. It seems ludicrous to suggest taping off the area as it sounds as if the world and his wife have already trampled over it, but do whatever you think and get some advice from Alex Griffiths.'

Matt nodded and walked off with PC Lewis. Alex was the head of the local SOC team and could find a needle in a haystack, so Matt put through a call to him.

'Hi, mate,' was the immediate response. 'Don't tell me, the dynamic duo are back together and need my help – see you as soon as.'

Chapter Four

'Shut that bloody kid up or I will,' screamed Susan Evans. 'I mean it, his constant bawling is doing my head in. Can't you give him some more of my sleeping tablets? On second thoughts perhaps a smack across the head would be quicker. For the love of God, will you shut up, you stupid little freak?'

Susan accompanied her demands with a wine glass that she threw in Jason's direction, missing the boy but smashing to pieces just above his head.

The result was an even louder noise from Jason who screamed that he wanted his mother and seemed distraught to have been separated from Ron.

'Who the bloody hell is Ron?' shouted Susan directing her question towards the man who was eating a sandwich made from chunks of cheese and pickle barely contained within two pieces of white sliced bread. 'I thought you said the kid didn't have any brothers or sisters. Maybe his mother will be less concerned about him if there are more of them – maybe she won't want him back.'

Although he was sobbing loudly Jason heard the woman's words and the thought of his mother not wanting him was too much. He kicked at the leg of the table in front of him and the whole thing collapsed, causing the remains of a jar of pickle to collide with a bottle of gin as it joined a tub of butter and two mugs sliding almost in slow motion towards the floor.

Jason was terrified by the result of his actions and knowing that it would spell big trouble for him he tried to make himself disappear by covering his face with his hands and keeping totally still and quiet.

Still and quiet were not two words that could in any way be attached to Susan as she leapt from her seat and rescued her gin but not before at least a few measures of her favourite liquid had been swallowed by the thin brown carpet. 'Fucking hell, the boy's a bloody nutter,' she screamed. 'Get those bloody boots off him before he does any more damage.'

With her one hand clasped firmly around the neck of the dark green gin bottle she raised the other hand and was about to strike Jason when her shoulders were grasped from behind. Dan Painter was not a tall man, but he was strong and with very little effort he turned Susan away from the boy and forced her to face someone far less vulnerable.

'You know the rules, bitch,' he shouted into her face. 'The kid is our ticket to his mother's money but not if he's damaged goods. We may have to give her proof that her son is alive and pictures of him covered in bruises from your fists won't be much help.'

The very mention of money calmed the situation and Susan shrugged off the hands that were still holding her shoulders and returned to her seat. There was no table in front of her now and no glass for her gin and so she took a large swig from the bottle.

'For Christ's sake, lay off that stuff,' shouted Dan. 'You're supposed to be here to keep an eye on the kid when I go and do things like picking up the ransom money. If I hadn't put a stop to it you would have laid into him just now, so how can I trust you, especially if you get drunk. Maybe we should just forget about the whole thing and let Jason go and maybe I should never have let you talk me into it in the first place.'

'Maybe, maybe, maybe,' mocked Susan. 'Maybe was the only word you knew before you met me. It's me who's changed "may be" into "will be", if it was left to you nothing would ever have been done.'

Dan looked at Susan and at the chipped scarlet nails that still held the gin bottle and not for the first time regretted having told her that he was Jason's father. He was at least twenty years older than her but Jason's very existence was testament to the fact that Dan liked younger women.

Tina was the daughter of Mike, one of Dan's drinking pals, and it had not been unusual for the two men to finish a Saturday night session at Mike's house with Tina providing their preferred feast of beans on toast. Although Dan was the same age as Tina's father he was in much better shape and generally thought to be a good-looking man and he was aware that Tina was attracted to him. She puzzled him and he quite often asked Mike why she wasn't out enjoying herself on a Saturday night instead of hanging around the two of them. His mate's reply was always the same, suggesting that Tina was saving herself for Mr Right and had inherited her lack of interest in sex from her mother.

One Saturday night Tina was persuaded to join the men and he remembered how she had sat down at the kitchen table and opened a tin of tobacco. He had never seen a woman roll her own cigarettes and he was fascinated to see her slim fingers produce a perfect roll-up. Even then she was a heavy smoker and that night she matched him one for one with cans of cider and cigarettes.

It was obvious that she was getting drunk and sending out blatant signals that she was more than a little interested in her father's friend. For some reason her father had found the situation amusing and had taken himself off to bed.

The inevitable happened but it had been very different from anything that Dan had ever experienced before. He was not short of sexual experience but it soon became clear that Tina was a novice and as he kissed the top of her head and let himself out of his mate's house he realised that he had just robbed Mike's daughter of her virginity.

He hadn't known what to think about the situation and ranged from congratulating himself for achieving such a conquest at his age to wondering if he would be locked up if she decided to cry rape. Not that it had been rape but with his mind in such turmoil anything was easy to contemplate. It was hard to believe that at the beginning of the twenty-first century there were still twenty-three-year-old virgins around, and Dan wished he had been sober enough to have enjoyed the experience.

Dan's Saturday evenings at his friend's house came to an abrupt end, and Mike accused his daughter of scaring off his best mate by putting him in an impossible position and almost begging for it, though he never realised what had actually happened. In reality Tina and her father had always had a strained relationship and he would have turned his daughter out years before were it not for the income she provided. Tina had stepped into her mother's shoes when she had died two days before her daughter's seventeenth birthday, and as well as doing the cooking and cleaning she held down two jobs. It was little wonder that she hadn't experienced sex, as she rarely went anywhere other than to work, and it was not surprising that her contact with her father's friend had become the highlight of her week and she actually believed that she was in love with him. She became depressed when her father told her that they were bored with beans on toast and chose instead to visit the local curry house on Saturday nights.

Tina knew that the real reason for their change of plans was that Dan was scared to face her and may have been expecting repercussions. After all, he had a wife and family, and one of his daughters had been in school with Tina and was pregnant with her third child.

It was months after her first experience with a man that Tina told her father that she was pregnant. She knew what his reaction would be and it had been for that reason that she had kept her secret until the pregnancy was past the point of legal termination. In spite of that Mike had tried to persuade his daughter to get rid of the baby, but had been surprised by Tina's new-found strength and determination to do what she wanted to do.

They parted following a heated argument during which her father accused her of having sex with the man who lived next door and was mentally retarded. He said her baby would be thick as shit and that it would be better to put it down before it was born. Although she was sickened by his words Tina was grateful to realise that at no time had her father considered that his mate Dan could actually be the father of his grandchild.

For years Tina had no contact with her father and although she still lived in the area, before Jason started school, she only once saw Dan when she was buying tobacco at a local supermarket. She realised then that her son was the living image of his father and she would do everything possible to ensure they didn't meet. Dan's ginger hair was getting more and more streaked with grey and this was making a match less obvious; in time the possibility of people linking the man with the boy would not be an issue.

Tina's plans were confounded when for the first time ever when Jason was five. Dan brought Megan, one of his granddaughters, to school and she made a beeline towards Jason in the playground. Dan followed her and spoke to her little friend, just as Tina appeared to say goodbye to her son. No words were spoken but as Dan looked from Tina to her son his stomach turned over and he rushed off and was through the school gates within seconds.

That evening Dan had fished out some photographs of himself as a boy and was totally convinced that Jason was his. He couldn't believe it. They had only had sex once and he had been pretty drunk at the time – and why hadn't Tina told him, and at the very least made him pay maintenance?

Dan remembered how he had agonised over what he should do. He had always wanted a son but had three daughters and between them they had given him four granddaughters. Thinking of the pros and cons of confronting Tina he had decided to let sleeping dogs lie and pushed it all to the back of his mind.

For about two years Dan said or did nothing, and then he heard of Tina's lottery win. His marriage had broken up when the last of his three daughters had left home and he had moved in with Susan Evans, who was the same age as his eldest daughter and was proving to be something of a handful. Susan wanted much more than he could afford to give her and she drank far too much, but she offered sexual favours that were beyond his wildest imagination. He desperately wanted those to continue, but she had other offers and was about to take up one of them when he told her about Jason.

He regretted it almost immediately but she had been like a dog with a bone and pointed out to Dan that he was the father of a boy who had access to millions of pounds. She had fantasised about what they could do with that sort of money and with her own special means of persuasion she convinced him to hatch a plan for getting his hands on some of it.

Their first thoughts had been to confront Tina with the fact that they knew who had fathered her child and would make it public knowledge unless she agreed to parting with some of her winnings. There were obvious flaws to this plan, and it was Susan who said that if she was in Tina's position she would not pay up.

Dan remembered her exact words were 'The stupid cow would be chuffed to let the world know that you're Jason's dad. Rumour had it when she was pregnant that she'd been stuffed by the retard who lived next door and she's never denied it.

'If she tells us to go ahead and tell the world we're done for and she wouldn't give us a penny. True, you'd be recognised as the kid's father, and perhaps that's what you want, is it? Want to go and play happy families with Tina and Jason, do you?'

Susan had screamed the words at Dan and it had taken him some time to convince her that Jason's mother was the original Miss Frosty Knickers and there was no way he wanted anything from her other than her money.

It had been Susan who hit on the idea of kidnapping Jason and holding out for a big ransom.

'It's the one thing that the skinny bitch will pay up for.'

The planning over the next couple of weeks had been what had led them to their current position, but it was proving to be more traumatic than either of them had envisaged.

The caravan they had brought Jason to was *not* what Susan had anticipated, but she would put up with the conditions for a few days if it meant getting her hands on a fortune. For now the most important thing was that nobody knew about their hideout, as the building work for which it had been positioned had been abandoned almost four years ago. Dan had been involved in digging the foundations for what was going to be a luxurious single-storey dwelling with views overlooking a little-known part of the South Wales coastline. Difficulties with planning regulations, a serious matrimonial dispute, and a downturn in the economy had initially put the project on hold and then resulted in various parties pulling the plug on the whole thing. Dan had been back to the site a few times since the work had finished and had taken away anything that could be sold on, so he knew that the caravan was still on site and that the fenced-off area was deserted.

It had been easy for him to reconnect the water and electricity supplies and fix up some gas bottles for cooking. He had stocked up with food and drink, although the plan was to be there for just a few days and for the two of them to be flying from Heathrow to Mexico City on Thursday. Dan felt a pang of regret that he probably wouldn't see his family again, but he soon put it out of his mind as he thought of the money and the long, luxurious days in the sun with Susan at his side – and in his bed.

They already had their tickets and Dan had taken out a loan to book business class seats which had cost him over three thousand pounds. He told Susan that by the time they set foot on the plane they would be millionaires and so should have tickets that reflected their standing. Once they got to Mexico they would disappear with a cool million in their pockets. In order to avoid suspicion they had return flights booked, but would not be using part two of their tickets and would certainly not be repaying the loan.

At no time had either of them considered the possibility of Tina not paying the ransom and all they had to do now was put in place the plans they had agreed. Persuading Jason to hide in the recently purchased cricket bag had been easy, as Jason had recognised him as Megan's granddad and was up for a bit of fun. The school trip to St Fagans had been a golden opportunity, and Dan had bought the cricket gear as he thought he would blend in, because there was a cricket club very near to the museum. He watched the coaches pull into the car park as he adjusted the strap of his Slazenger Ultimate V180 Holdall and made pretend strokes with an unfamiliar cricket bat.

He thought it unlikely that Tina would pair up with any of the other parents and he was proven to be correct. All he had to do was to wait for an opportunity to get Jason on his own and it came much sooner than he had anticipated. Dressed in white trousers and a white V-neck sweater, and sporting a white floppy cotton hat and sunglasses, Dan believed that he was a perfect representation of the cricketer images they had Googled.

At first he had stood back and watched at a distance and saw a great opportunity when Jason seemed to be standing on his own outside the ladies toilets. He moved in quickly but had been forced to walk away as suddenly Jason was talking to a woman that Dan recognised as one of the teachers from the school.

Initially he had cursed the woman but then inwardly thanked her for preventing him from taking the risk of picking up Jason in an area where there were lots of passers-by. He prayed that Tina would not go into the play area and his prayers were answered as she seemed to change her mind at the last minute, dragging her son away. Keeping a safe distance Dan followed behind and was pleased to see that everyone else from the school had either gone to the park or had stopped at the red farmhouse.

Dan wondered how he was going to separate the mother and son and once again his prayers were answered as they appeared to be having an argument and Tina was walking off leaving her Jason on the grass verge.

He grasped his chance immediately, and taking off his sunglasses so that the boy would recognise him he sat down next to Jason. There was no time for preliminary banter and so Dan gave Jason his biggest smile and suggesting they play a trick on his mummy persuaded him to hop into the cricket bag and hide.

Jason caught on immediately and grinned from ear to ear as he snuggled down inside the bag and drank the very sweet apple juice that Dan had given him. It was effortless for Dan to pick up the bag and walk back in the direction he had come and with his head down and his sunglasses back on he passed several people he knew from the school without a glimmer of recognition from any one of them.

It was warm and dark inside the bag and even before they reached the car park Jason had started to wriggle about and Dan whispered to him to be quiet, telling him that his mother was coming and they would soon surprise her.

Dan zapped the remote of a silver-coloured Ford Focus and placed his cricket bag containing a now frightened little boy into the boot. The car didn't belong to Dan; with Susan's help he had borrowed it, without asking, from her sister. At that moment Diane, the real owner, was tucked up in bed having done a night shift stacking shelves at the Asda supermarket, and would never know to what evil use her car had been put whilst she slept.

Fear, the warmth, and the dark had overcome Jason and with the help of the sleeping tablets dissolved with lots of extra sugar in the apple juice he was now fast asleep.

Just a few miles away from the museum Dan had pulled into a lay-by and changed from his cricket gear back into the black jeans and sweater he had brought with him.

There was no sound from the boot and Dan was almost physically sick as he thought that maybe the boy was dead. He had persuaded Susan to crush up fewer tablets than she had originally intended but had they still exceeded the dose needed to kill such a young boy?

His fear caused him to be careless and he had pulled out from the lay-by almost into the path of a police vehicle. They were about to pull him over when some boy racers zoomed past and became the new object of their attention.

Even as he thought back over the incident Dan's blood ran cold and he visualised the police opening the boot of his car and possibly finding a dead body in his cricket bag. He shook his head. It hadn't happened and the rest of the plan had gone like clockwork, as Jason was transferred into Dan's car and he drove Susan and their captive to the caravan that was to be their base for a few days.

To Dan's relief Jason was not dead and he was amazed to realise that as he opened up the cricket bag and carried the boy into the caravan his relief was much more than he would have expected. Looking at the boy's face was just like looking at photographs of himself when he was Jason's age and he found himself wishing he had not agreed to Susan's suggestion of kidnapping.

It was too late now to turn back and as he started to lay Jason on the bed Susan had stopped him.

'I feel like celebrating,' she had said. 'Put the kid on the seat by the table and we can make good use of the bed.'

She poured them both a hefty measure of gin and drank hers even before he had put Jason down. Gin was not his tipple and he offered her the second glass and she finished it in two gulps.

Susan didn't need gin to relieve her of her inhibitions – she didn't have any in the first place, and for the next hour she reminded Dan of why he wanted to be with her and why his kid could have no place in their lives.

It was the sound of Jason trying to stand up that brought Dan back to reality and once again he surprised himself as he pulled on his jeans and threw a sheet over Susan's naked body to avoid the boy any embarrassment.

Jason looked dreadful, with eyes that were still puffy from previous tears and that were staring around in complete terror. Dan tried to reassure him and offered him a drink but Jason had memories of the last drink he had been given and shook his head violently. He started to cry and his wailing woke Susan – and instantly World War Three broke out between the two of them.

For hours Dan listened to Jason sobbing and the scantily clad Susan screaming at him, and the moment at which Jason kicked the leg of the fold-down table and upset her gin was a turning point. Although he had rescued the situation Dan was getting concerned about leaving Jason with Susan and he would have to be doing that the next morning if their plans were to have any chance of working.

Although he had asked her to stop drinking Susan defiantly lifted another glass of gin to her lips and seeing red Dan knocked it out of her hands. She lashed out at him and her red nails clawed at his face and he retaliated by striking her across the face with the back of his hand. Instead of stopping her, his actions prompted a vicious reaction of her own and she picked up the bottle of gin and smashed it on the side of his head.

He reeled backwards and then with a rage he didn't even know he was capable of he grabbed hold of her neck with both hands and shook her and shook her so that her movements resembled those of a rag doll.

Jason had been screaming and now he was quiet.

Susan had been swearing and now she was quiet.

As if the quiet had suddenly registered Dan released his hands and Susan dropped like a stone, landing in a crumpled heap at his feet.

He couldn't move, being paralysed with fear and knowing with absolute certainty that the woman at his feet was dead. He had strangled her and his first reaction was to lose control, and to add insult to injury he was sick all over her.

Jason had found his voice and started to call for his mother but one look from Dan soon silenced him. He hadn't liked Susan when she was shouting at him and he certainly didn't like the look of her now.

In a robotic fashion Dan picked Susan up and was in danger of triggering another bout of vomiting as his hands slipped on what had previously been the contents of his stomach. He swallowed hard and was surprised that Susan was so heavy as he awkwardly moved her from the floor onto the bed where she had just a few hours ago been extremely active.

Dan had only seen three dead people in his life, and all of them had been very old and had died peacefully of natural causes. Susan was not old and had certainly not died of natural causes. He had killed her – and the thing that was now uppermost in his mind was the fact that Jason had witnessed the whole thing.

He could not bring himself to look at the boy and slammed

the bedroom door before turning the cold-water tap on full and putting the whole of his head under the feeble stream that came from the pipes. The shock of the cold water was just what he needed and he rubbed it all over his short hair and massaged it into his face and scalp.

There was no sound from Jason but he was watching what looked like some sort of ritual and his little body was trembling as he wondered what was going to happen next. He had liked Megan's granddad and couldn't understand what was happening. Although he was only seven he had made some sense of the conversations between Dan and Susan and realised that they were planning on giving him back to his mother if she gave them some of her lottery winnings.

Jason wasn't worried on that score and he knew that his mother would gladly give them all her money, as she often told him he was more important to her than anything. He had never seen grown-ups fight before but had heard stories from some of his classmates and now he believed them. It had been the most terrifying experience of his life and as he thought about it tears ran down his cheeks and he wondered if he would be killed next. Jason knew nothing about death and dying but he was sure that Susan was dead and wouldn't pop back up again like some of the characters in the cartoons he liked to watch.

He shuffled in his seat and Dan raised his head from the sink and rubbed his face and head with a bright yellow towel.

Dan didn't know what he was going to do but was beginning to realise that time was on his side. Because of the very nature of their original plan neither he nor Susan had told anyone where they were going. Susan's sister wouldn't be worried if she didn't see Susan for weeks and there was no one else who was in the remotest bit interested in her welfare.

He would have to get rid of Susan's body but that wouldn't be too difficult as the disused building site would give him plenty of possibilities for burying it, and it might be years before it would be discovered.

No, it wasn't Susan that was his biggest problem, it was Jason, and Dan tried to focus his mind on the possibility of continuing with the original game plan regarding the ransom for Jason. In many respects it was more important than ever for him to get his hands on the money as he was now definitely going to have to disappear permanently.

He knew that tomorrow morning Tina would be receiving a letter setting out in no uncertain terms exactly what she had to do in order to get her son back. The letter had been computer-generated and handled with gloves to eliminate the possible pick up of fingerprints and Dan had driven to Swansea to post it, so avoiding a Cardiff postmark.

The plan had been to give Tina time tomorrow to get a million pounds from the bank. Susan had seemed to think Tina could easily do that because after all it was her money and they couldn't refuse to give it to her. Dan had expressed reservations about any bank having that sort of money readily available and that was why they had decided to give her a full day.

The letter would tell her that any contact with the police would blow her chances of ever seeing Jason alive and tell her where to leave the money that would ensure his safe release. All of that was already in place and Dan now had to consider if not having Susan around would make any difference.

Her only role was to have been to look after Jason when Dan went to pick up the money and of course she would have had a major role in spending it. Dan reckoned he could do without her input and would have to ensure Jason was locked in the caravan when he went to the agreed pick-up point. That would be no problem but there was now a very big issue with Jason and Dan had to come to terms with the fact that it would no longer be possible, even on receipt of the million, to let Tina know the whereabouts of her son. Jason had seen Dan strangle Susan and would be persuaded to tell the psychologists who would undoubtedly be called in to counsel him following his ordeal.

There was always going to be an issue regarding the fact that Jason would be able to identify at least one of his kidnappers, but by eight o'clock Friday Dan would have picked up the ransom money and he and Susan would be on the way to Heathrow airport. That was the original plan and they were going to wait until just before boarding the plane before Dan made the call to Tina telling her where she could find her son.

No one would know where he was at the time of the call and he would use one of the pre-paid phones he had picked up to make the call. Susan had said that would prevent the police tracing the whereabouts of the phone and as Dan knew absolutely nothing about cell-phone technology he had assumed she was right.

They knew that when Jason was found he would tell his mother that it was Megan's granddad who had taken him from St Fagans, but by then they would be halfway to Mexico. Dan had even considered the possibility that when he made that phone call to Tina he could persuade her to get the police to forget about the kidnapping. After all, he was the boy's father and was only catching up on the rights to know his son that she had denied him for the past seven years.

But now Jason would have another story to tell his rescuers and whereas he might have got away with kidnapping his own son, murder was a different ball game.

Jason was the only person who knew about Susan and how she had died and this meant that the phone call to Tina telling her where she could find her son alive and well was no longer an option.

Chapter Five

Martin introduced himself to Tina and was updated on the details of Jason's disappearance and the subsequent searches that had been made. It certainly seemed as if a great deal of effort had already gone into finding the boy and the DCI suggested that only he and DC Cook-Watts needed to speak to Tina, and that everyone else could continue looking for Jason.

Pam Woodland was reluctant to leave, as she was enjoying being at the centre of all this excitement, but Martin assured her that Helen Cook-Watts would take over her role and support Tina whilst he was questioning her. In her usual down-to-earth way Helen had already persuaded Tina to sit at one of the tables and had coaxed her into drinking a cup of coffee.

Now that he had more details about the timescale since the boy was last seen and the intensity of the search, Martin was convinced that he was dealing with a carefully crafted plan to relieve the boy's mother of some of her money in exchange for her child's return.

He remembered some of the workshops he had attended over the years when approaches to different categories of crime had been explored and best-practice protocols developed. The one thing that kept coming to the forefront of his memory was the issue of time. The words of one of the workshop facilitators crossed his mind.

'*Yes, there is a need for sensitivity, but better a crying mother than a dead child. Make the parents think thoughts they can't bear to think and do that at the very start of the investigation. There's no point in holding back difficult questions that could give vital clues about the reasons behind the kidnapping and the possible identity of the kidnapper.'*

It had been easy to nod in agreement in a warm and comfortable seminar room, and without the grief that Martin was now witnessing on the face staring down into an empty coffee cup.

He pulled up a chair and faced Tina directly. 'It's been well over an hour now since Jason went missing and hopefully he will soon be found. But he is unlikely to have been hiding all this time – do you agree?'

'Yes,' mumbled Tina. 'I gave up thinking he was playing hide and seek after about ten minutes. He'd already said he was hungry and I think he's either had an accident or someone's taken him.'

She was more composed than Martin had expected and he felt able to pursue the possibilities she had suggested.

'I think we can rule out an accident given the very short timescale between you noticing his disappearance and a search getting underway. He couldn't have gone far in that time and as I understand it every nook and cranny has been explored.'

'It's my job to get Jason back to you and with that in mind we need to explore the possibility that he has been abducted for some reason.'

Tina looked as if she was going to collapse and Helen held her hands tightly.

'You mean some pervert has got my little boy. Please God, not that. My Jase's still a baby … he's still my baby.'

Tears streamed down her face and Martin jumped in quickly to prevent her thinking any further along the lines of her little boy being the victim of a sex offender.

'I don't think that is what has happened,' he said loudly and clearly. 'I don't think Jason has been taken by anyone who wants to do him any harm. I really believe that at this time your son is alive and well but I do believe he has been kidnapped and that very soon the kidnapper will make contact with you and be asking for money.'

Tina stared at Martin with a look of utter confusion but the tears had stopped and she was clearly trying hard to focus on what was being said, so Martin continued. 'I have been told that you won a considerable amount of money on the National Lottery but no one seems to know exactly how much.'

'It was eleven and a half million pounds and it was on the Euromillions,' said Tina. 'I shared a pot of £46m with three other people. To be perfectly honest a win of a few hundred thousand would have been better for me. I'm sure there are lots of people who would know how to make good use of millions of pounds but I'm not one of them. I bought the house with the pool that you can see Jason standing next to, and gave money to some of the people who asked for it and a lot of good that did me. They just wanted more and with some of the people I thought were my friends things got very nasty.

'Jason is the most important thing in my life – nothing else matters and if it takes all the money I have to get him back then whoever has taken Jason can have it.

'Just find my boy, Inspector, if you don't find him I'll die.'

It was difficult for Martin to hear what Tina was saying as every word was accompanied by sobs and she suddenly got up and headed for the door.

'Give her five minutes,' suggested Helen. 'She smokes like a chimney and at the moment nicotine will be her version of a comfort blanket.'

Martin nodded and indicated that Helen should follow Tina and try to get her talking.

'I don't want to appear callous but time could be critical and if we can get some names from her we could start checking them out. My initial feeling is that the person we are looking for is known to her and to Jason.'

Martin rubbed the sides of his face and went on to explain his thinking. 'From what we have been told no one witnessed a struggle of any sort and I doubt the boy would have willingly gone off with a total stranger.'

Helen latched on to Martin's sense of urgency and after just a few minutes she had persuaded Tina to return and Martin questioned her about her family and friends.

'Tell me about Jason's father,' he began. 'Are you together

and what part does he play in Jason's life?'

'No and none,' answered Tina bluntly. 'Jason has never met his father, in fact I'm the only person who knows who he is and that's the way it is going to stay. I doubt Jason's father even knows of his son's existence so you can cross him off your list of suspects.'

Martin decided to let that go for the moment but knew it was something he would be coming back to if other lines of enquiry didn't produce results.

'What about your own family? I want you to think about your parents, grandparents, brothers or sisters, aunts or uncles, cousins, or anyone who knows about your circumstances and may want to cash in. Have you fallen out with any of them since you won the money? Is there anyone in particular who has a grudge against you and would know that the best way of hurting you would be through your son?'

There were no longer any signs of tears as Tina focused on the task in hand. Martin could almost see the cogs in her brain whirling as she mentally trawled through her family and friends.

'My mother died years ago but she did have a sister and when I was a child Auntie Betty was around quite a lot. She wasn't like my mother, she was much more in control of herself and she and my father were at daggers drawn. When my mother died she came to see me a few times but each time she argued with my father and then she stopped coming.

'I doubt she even knows I have a son or about my lottery win. She used to live in Bridgend but that was years ago and for all I know she could be dead. There was no one else on my mother's side that I can remember. Auntie Betty didn't have any children and I don't think she was even married – I certainly can't remember any uncle.'

Helen was making a few notes and asked Tina for her aunt's surname and for an address in Bridgend.

'She always was just Auntie Betty to me but if she never did get married her surname will be Goldsmith. It's one of the few things I remember about my mother, she always said that she'd never been any ordinary old Smith, she'd been a Goldsmith. It was one of her little jokes that my father hated.'

Martin was a bit worried that Tina would get upset again as she recalled memories of her mother but over the past ten minutes Tina had transformed from a frightened quivering wreck to a woman on a mission to find her son. A tigress and her cub sprung to Martin's mind and he didn't fancy the chances of anyone who got between Tina and her determination to find Jason.

'I couldn't give you an address for Betty but I did go to her house once with my mother and I remember that it only took us a few minutes to walk there from the bus station.'

'You mentioned your father,' said Martin. 'Do you and Jason see much of him?'

Tina scowled. 'If my father had had his way Jason would never have been born. I was six months pregnant before I even told him about it but even then he wanted me to have an abortion. I was his beer ticket. I worked around the clock and paid all the bills and put money in his pocket so that he could meet his mates for a pint most nights and unlimited pints on a Saturday.'

She suddenly stopped talking and it would have served Martin well if he had been able to read her mind, as it went back to one particular Saturday night when she had lost her virginity and gained a son.

'My father is still around, Chief Inspector, at least I think he is.' she told Martin. 'I moved out after we fought over my refusal to get rid of Jason and I haven't seen him from that day to this. I can give you his address if he still lives in the same place but if you are looking for someone who Jason knows then I can assure you he wouldn't know his grandfather from Adam.

'I was amazed when my father didn't turn up like a bad penny when I came into money but much as I have no love or respect for him I can't see him kidnapping his grandson, he simply wouldn't have the balls. It's possible that one of his mates would be up for it, but I don't know what company he's keeping these days.

'There is a couple who I used to be friendly with and who kicked off when I refused to give them money for some pretty dodgy business plans. I'm not the brightest, Inspector, but even I know that buying an ice-cream van doesn't require an investment of two hundred thousand. I would probably have given them that amount of money to settle their debts if they had come clean and said that they wanted to do that but I don't like being taken for an idiot.'

Martin's opinion of Tina was changing as she spoke. When they had first been introduced Martin had seen a woman distraught over the disappearance of her son and he had felt very sorry for her, but he certainly hadn't credited her with much intelligence. He was now seeing a woman who was showing amazing spirit and he was impressed by the logic of her thinking especially under the circumstances.

'Just give DC Cook-Watts any names and contact numbers and we will check them out if only to eliminate them from our enquiries,' said Martin.

'What happens now?' asked Tina with a voice that had started to shake and was showing signs that a new wave of worry was hovering and waiting to take over her mind and body.

Before Martin had a chance to answer he was interrupted by Matt. As soon as he entered the room Matt realised that the three people there would be expecting feedback from the site of Jason's disappearance and he quickly brought them up to date, but wished his news could be different.

'Sorry, but there is nothing I have to tell you other than that our SOC officers are combing the area for any clues to Jason's disappearance.'

Realising that Tina and Matt hadn't yet met, Martin made the required introductions and asked him to tell them exactly what had been happening. 'We have managed to identify the people from Holly Road School who were coming from the park and walking in the direction of the pigsty at the time when Jason would have been sitting on the grass verge.

'I have spoken to most of them but there are still one or two people who are apparently somewhere in the grounds looking for Jason that I haven't been able to interview yet. Not one of them saw Jason when they got to the pigsty and all of them are certain that Jason hadn't passed them whilst they were walking towards it. The women especially were adamant that if they had seen Jason walking past without his mother they would have stopped him.'

'It would appear that a number of people were walking in the opposite direction, that is to say going back towards the museum, but that's all I have been able to establish. No one is able to say if the people they passed were men or women, short or tall, black or white, families or just lone figures. The children proved to have been marginally more observant than the adults as they recalled a boy with a toffee apple and a girl who was whizzing along on roller blades but none of them had seen Jason either on his own or with anyone else.

'These people were all on the scene within minutes of Jason having been left there and I'm struggling to make any sense of it.' Matt looked towards Tina. 'There are only two ways Jason would have chosen to go unless he decided to get over a fence or a hedge and head for the fields.'

'He wouldn't have done that,' responded Tina. 'There are animals in those fields and although Jason likes to watch them from the path he would be terrified to go anywhere near them, especially on his own.'

'That's what I thought,' said Matt. 'At the risk of sounding ridiculous, are you sure that Jason didn't sneak past when you were waiting for him to catch up with you? I don't have any kids of my own but I spend a lot of time with a dozen nieces and I know how artful they can be and they often seem to pop up from nowhere when you think they're somewhere else.'

Matt's suggestion generated a wry, watery smile from Tina.

'That's not such a ridiculous suggestion,' she replied. 'I've thought about it myself but it didn't happen. I walked on for no more than a minute but I do take quite large strides and initially I had hurried off to make a point with Jason. Then I leant against a stone wall and lit a cigarette and there was only that path in front of me. Jason would have had to walk over my feet to pass me but he didn't and neither did anyone else. No one came past at that time – no one at all.'

'OK, then that rules out a few things,' continued Matt. 'Jason didn't go forward in your direction and I agree with you that it is highly unlikely he would have gone into the fields on his own, so that just leaves two possibilities. Either he had company and he braved the fields, or he managed to pass at least twenty people who know him without being spotted by one of them.

'A number of the people I've spoken to have been taking photographs with cameras and phones and one of the fathers owns a new iPad and has been photographing anything and everything. I spoke to Charlie, our IT expert, and she's on her way here and will gather together every photograph that has been taken.'

'How will that help us find Jason?' asked Tina, who had reverted to being the confused and despairing woman Martin had first met, and as he responded to her question he wondered how she was going to receive his next suggestion.

'The people DS Pryor has spoken to were all bound up with sorting out their own children, taking photographs, and generally looking around the area. In spite of what they say they could easily have missed your son, especially if he had decided it would be cool to get past them without being spotted. The photographs may pick up people passing in the opposite direction who would have no apparent relevance but who may when questioned be able to help us sort out the direction taken by Jason and anyone who was with him.

'As you know, Tina, it is my belief that your son has been taken by someone who will want money for his safe return. Please concentrate on what I just said – I said his safe return. You need to focus on that as it will be what will help you through the next hours or even days before we get Jason back.'

Tina freaked out. 'What do you mean days? Are you serious? Do you really mean days? Jason has never been without me for one night of his life – he will be terrified and he doesn't even have Ron Weasley.'

She twisted the Lego figure around in her hands and Martin wondered if she was thinking that maybe Harry Potter and his friend would do a better job of finding Jason. He knew his carefully considered suggestion would go down like a lead balloon but he had to make it.

'Tina, we need to get you back to you home. If Jason's disappearance is the kidnapping I believe it to be then I suspect that you will be contacted there.'

'No way, no bloody way,' shouted Tina. 'I am not leaving here until I find Jason.' She leapt to her feet and made her way to the door. She was right about having long strides as she had almost reached the children's play area before Helen caught up with her.

'Tina, calm down, just wait a minute. Let me try and explain why we need you to go back to your house. It doesn't mean that people will stop looking for Jason here, in fact there are already experienced search officers conducting a much more organised and thorough search, and it's best we leave that to them.'

Tina did slow down a bit and Helen was able to keep up with her. 'I can't possibly imagine what pain you're going through but what I do know is that if ever there was a crisis in my life I would willingly put its resolution into the hands of DCI Phelps. He is the best person you could possibly have on the case and he will work around the clock and get others to do the same until Jason is found.'

Tina came to a full stop and instinctively reached into her pocket for the one thing that would be of some help to her but realised immediately that she had left her cigarettes on the table when she had walked out.

There were lots of people staring at her and Helen asked if anyone of them could spare Tina a smoke. Instantly a cigarette was lit and Tina broke off the filter tip before taking several puffs in quick succession.

'Thanks,' she said, not even knowing who had been her benefactor but turned away as some people she did know started to ask questions about her son.

The situation helped Helen, who quickly explained that if they walked around outside they would be bombarded with questions and expressions of sympathy that although well-meaning would be distressing.

Tina walked more slowly back toward the room she had left less than ten minutes ago and Helen took the opportunity of telling her about the team that would be put in place to find Jason.

By the time they got back to the room Helen had managed to convince Tina that she would be more use to Jason if she went back home and waited to hear from whoever had taken him.

Martin expressed his gratitude to Helen and suggested that she drive with him and Tina to her house and that Matt continue the investigations at St Fagans. Matt nodded in agreement and then diverted his attention to Charlie, who had just wheeled herself into the room.

Martin caught sight of Charlie as he was leaving and wondered how she would cope with a missing child. She was the best they could ask for in terms of interrogating all forms of modern-day technology and he watched her manoeuvre her wheelchair to one of the tables and set down her laptop.

There were no outward signs of her pregnancy, it was still early days, but Charlie and Alex had been unable to keep their secret for long and everyone who worked in Goleudy knew that around next Easter time the couple were going to hatch an egg of their own. It was business as usual for Charlie apart from having to fight off uncharacteristic bouts of overwhelming tiredness but these moments were becoming less frequent and she was determined to carry on regardless.

Being confined to a wheelchair since her early teens had not held her back and something as normal as a pregnancy was certainly not going to get in the way of her life. What concerned Martin as he saw her getting down to the business of transferring images from a variety of gadgets was that she would be more vulnerable than usual to the feelings of a mother who had lost her son.

He allowed himself to consider for a moment the possibility

that Jason had not been taken to satisfy someone's love of money but to satisfy a more sinister love that some men have for little boys. It was not impossible that Jason had been stalked and snatched for this sick and disgusting purpose but Martin was convinced it was a well-planned kidnapping and that the perpetrator would soon be in touch with his or her demands.

As he directed Tina to where he had parked his Alfa Romeo Martin reminded himself of the need to keep an open mind and to consider every possible reason for Jason's abduction. To close his mind to anything at this stage could lead to the loss of vital time and possibly unspeakable consequences. If Jason had been taken for any form of sexual gratification he could be in immediate physical and psychological danger. He let Tina and Helen into the car and phoned Matt before getting in himself.

'Check on the list of sex offenders, in particular the addresses of any known paedophiles. If anyone has served time and recently been released we will need to pay them a visit today, along with anyone with a history of taking small boys.'

In response to Matt's question Martin continued. 'No, I haven't changed my mind, I still think that Jason has been snatched for money, but for now we have to consider every possibility. The chance of Jason still hiding is virtually nil, and like you I believe he is no longer at St Fagans. What we need to discover is how he was taken. Check all vehicle movement out of the site after the time his mother left him; there are some CCTV cameras. See if anything Charlie gets from the phones ties up with anything from the surveillance equipment.

'I don't need to tell you how precious time is in these situations, so pull all the stops out. I'm taking Tina to her house and we could find a clue already waiting for us there, or it may still be a question of waiting for a kidnapper to show their hand.'

'Finally, Matt, get everyone geared up for a two o'clock briefing and make sure everyone is aware that no comments must be made to the press other than through me. A child's life could be at stake and I don't want the media antagonising whoever has got Jason by printing some off-the-wall headlines.'

71

Twenty minutes after leaving the museum Tina pointed out a housing estate to Helen. 'That's where we lived when I left home. First of all I stayed with a woman who worked with me at the supermarket. Peggy was kind to me but the house was chaotic and I had to share a bed with her eldest daughter. Still, the overcrowding worked in my favour, and what with being pregnant and everything it wasn't long before the council and the welfare found me somewhere to live.

'I got away from my father because he wanted me to abort my baby and then I was terrified that the social service busybodies would think I couldn't look after him, and now this ... and now this. Maybe someone up there thinks I'm a rubbish mother and that Jason will be better off without me.'

Helen had been very impressed by the way that Tina was holding herself together, but now Jason's mother was filling her own mind with self-doubt and the tears were returning as she squeezed Ron Weasley almost to the point of destruction.

Quickly Helen gave her something else to think about, indicating that neither she nor Martin knew this area of Cardiff very well and needed her help with directions to her house. Tina lifted her head and looking through the window told Martin that he needed to take the first left.

In terms of distance Tina had not moved far from the small maisonette that she and Jason had called home, but in terms of perceived social standing she had jumped over the moon. An imposing red brick wall surrounded a prestigious development of just eight houses. There were no gates at the entrance but there was what looked like a state-of-the-art security system and as they drove towards the house that Tina was indicating Martin had the feeling that he was being caught on camera.

Each of the eight houses was individually designed and each protected its owner's privacy by the use of strategically placed trees, hedges, and walls. From Tina's drive it was only possible to see a tiny section of the side wall of her nearest neighbour's house and apart from that there was no sign of another building. Helen looked around and mentally applauded the architects and builders who had produced such an elegant arrangement that only very serious money could afford.

As they followed Tina to the front door Martin noticed an arched gate that presumably led to the back of the house and catching his eye Tina explained that she had been standing just the other side of that gate when she had taken Jason's photograph that morning.

'Mind if I take a look?' asked Martin.

'The gate's not locked,' confessed Tina. 'I'm not the most popular person around here as apparently my lack of security puts everyone at risk. There's an association that manages the security of these houses and we all pay an annual subscription, but as far as I can see that's all these people think about. Their houses, their cars, and their golf clubs are their gods. I'm the only one with a child who doesn't go to a private school and quite frankly I hate them as much as they hate me being here.

'This house came on the market when the person for whom it was being built apparently went on holiday to Turkey and was picked up as part of an international group bringing drugs into this country. The press called him the "careless leftie" but I can't remember why, it was probably something to do with him wanting to stand as a Labour candidate.'

Helen interrupted. 'No, it was a big case and I remember it well. He was the main UK man and his network was getting heroin from Afghanistan via Kazakhstan and refining it in Turkey. He was checking out the part of the organisation that transported it from Turkey to Greece when he reverted to his British way of thinking and was caught by the traffic cops in Athens driving on the left-hand side of the road.

'It was such a simple mistake but it led to the closing down of the whole operation – and the man who could have been living here is confined to a cell somewhere.' Helen considered the differences between the two styles of living and gave a mental thumbs-up to the Greek traffic police.

The scene they were now looking at was the exact one from Tina's phone – minus Jason. 'I'm surprised you could drag him away from here,' said Helen. 'I remember being excited about school trips but if there had been a choice between my own swimming pool and a bus ride I know which one I would have taken.'

'Jason hates the water,' said Tina. 'The gardener keeps it clean and at the right temperature but it's money for old rope for him because it's never used. When we first moved here some of Jason's school friends came round, but their clapped-out cars weren't welcomed by my snooty neighbours, and anyway I rowed with their parents about money.'

Martin wanted to hear more about these rows and to get details of the people Tina had quarrelled with. They may well have decided to get the money they wanted from Tina via a different route, and he would need to speak to all of them.

They followed Tina back towards the front door that opened onto an imposing hall and then through into a very modern spacious kitchen. Everything looked new, clean, and expensive but nothing looked like the sort of home in which Tina and Jason would have been happy.

Tina made for the corner of the kitchen where a surprisingly modest wooden table and chairs stood and sat down. She had already had one cigarette in the garden but as she was now in her own home and could smoke as she pleased, so she lit up again.

'What did you expect, Inspector? Did you think the kidnapper would be here waiting for me or what?'

Martin shook his head. 'No I didn't think that but I thought there could be the possibility of some sort of message being left here. If the kidnapper knew the day he was going to take Jason he could have sent a letter the day before so that you would find it today. I didn't notice any mail in the hall when we came through – was there anything before you left the house this morning?'

'We left before the postman had been,' Tina replied. 'That was another thing that upset Jason, the postman is one of the few people around here who even bothers to speak to Jase and they play a game of peek-a-boo through the letter box.'

'Do you always have the same postman?' asked Martin.

'Unless he's on holiday or off sick,' replied Tina. 'Why do

you ask?'

Martin looked through the faint haze of smoke that surrounded Tina and explained. 'The next couple of hours are going to be very uncomfortable for you because we are going to ask you to think of everybody you know. Family and friends obviously but also people like your postman, hairdresser, gardener, anyone you regularly meet at the supermarket, teachers, dinnerladies, and so on. You will be amazed at the length of the list by the time we are finished and then will come the nasty bit of attempting to rule individuals in or out of the kidnapping equation.'

Tina looked horrified as Martin had suspected she would be. 'No way!' she whispered but it was said without total conviction. 'Surely no one we know would be this evil. Isn't it more likely to be a stranger just doing it for the money?'

Martin shook his head. 'I am utterly convinced that you will know the person who has taken Jason and it is very likely that someone as close as your father or Jason's father will be involved. Think about it, Tina. We haven't yet been able to establish how Jason was taken from the grounds of the museum but from what you tell us he wouldn't have gone with anyone he didn't know. I'm sorry to have to ask again, but it could be vital that we know who Jason's father is and I promise you that the information will be kept in the greatest of confidence and only shared within the team on a need-to-know basis.'

Before Tina could respond they were interrupted by the doorbell and Helen went to answer it. Realising who it might be Martin explained to Tina that they were going to have to place taps on her phones and install a direct link between the house and Goleudy.

Tina nodded but her thoughts were on the question Martin had raised about Jason's father. She knew she would have to tell the inspector but there was something about actually speaking his name that for her was too real. Tina had always known who had fathered her son but she had never spoken his name, and she knew that once the secret was out it could never be totally put away again.

For years she had considered what to tell Jason but ironically today had been the first time he had really broached the subject. She remembered almost the last thing he had said to her. 'Have I even got a dad? I didn't know I had one. Have I got a dad?'

It was, as expected, the technicians who had arrived, and they needed Tina to show them where all the phones were. They also asked about computers and email addresses, but Tina told them she only used her computer for Facebook, and then only to play games and not for keeping in touch with people.

She showed them where the phones were situated and then, lighting the inevitable cigarette, re-joined Martin and Helen, who were sitting at the table discussing strategy.

'I've just asked DC Cook-Watts if she will remain with you for the time being and she has agreed. I would prefer to have someone from my team here and she seems to have gained your trust.'

'Thank you,' said Tina, and then she took a deep breath. 'In answer to your question, Jason's father is a man called Dan Painter but he doesn't know about Jason. He's old enough to be Jason's grandfather and in fact he is the grandfather of Megan, one of Jason's friends at school. Dan and my father used to go to the pub together and then come back to the house. He's a decent enough bloke and I don't blame him for getting me pregnant – it was me who made a play for him. But there is no way he will have had anything to do with this and that's a fact.'

Chapter Six

It was coming up to two o'clock and the team that were now heading up the search for the missing seven-year-old Jason Barnes had assembled in one of Martin's preferred venues – Incident Room One. It was certainly one of his most successful venues and he could easily think back over the past few years when some seriously deranged criminals had been brought to justice as a result of the soul-searching and the good old-fashioned teamwork that had gone on within these walls.

The beauty of the set-up at the South Wales Police Headquarters of Goleudy was that the setting seemed to retain the best of the past methods of policing whilst offering the opportunities of the most advanced modern detection. Martin hoped it would once again work its magic and inspire the team to work out what had happened to Jason and find him quickly.

If the kidnapper asked for money then as far as Martin was concerned that money would be handed over, and only when Jason was returned safely would the team concentrate on getting the kidnapper and retrieving the cash. Not everyone agreed with this strategy and there had been a great debate about it at one of the workshops Martin had attended. Most of the officers there had believed that once money was handed over the kidnapper had all the trump cards and may not honour any previously agreed arrangements to hand over the child.

It was a gamble, but for the moment Martin told the team that whatever the kidnapper demanded in terms of a ransom they would get it to him as quickly as possible.

Martin had agreed this strategy with Tina Barnes before leaving her home and had left DC Cook-Watts with the responsibility of helping Tina speak to her bank. He had no idea what amount of cash would be demanded but he didn't doubt for one moment that Jason had been taken for money and he didn't want any delays in getting hold of the asking price.

'OK, let's get down to business. The little boy, Jason Barnes, aged seven, was separated from his mother just after ten thirty this morning and has not been seen since. They were part of a school trip comprising three coaches that left Holly Road Primary at nine thirty and arrived at St Fagans National History Museum just about ten.

'The official adults involved with the organisation were six teachers and three coach drivers, and Matt has interviewed all of them and will give us an update in a moment. There was a parent or guardian responsible for each of the children and the school has provided us with their names.

'All of those people would have known weeks ago that the trip was planned and could have seen it as an ideal opportunity to snatch the boy. Even for the most vigilant of parents a school trip must be a bit of a nightmare, with the dilemma of allowing your child freedom to run about and mix with their friends versus the need to keep an eye on them.'

Matt nodded. 'I've been roped into a few of these outings and needed a stiff drink at the end of the day to get over the experience.' There was a bit of friendly banter about how little it took for Matt to need a pint after a day's work and then Martin continued.

'It's important that we are all aware of the recent history of Jason's mother, Christine Barnes, though she prefers Tina. In April this year she won more than eleven million pounds on the Euromillions.'

There were whistles and some expressions of envy as a few officers imagined themselves winning that sort of prize. Martin banged the table. 'From what I've seen and heard she hasn't had a great deal of happiness from her fortune. True, she has a magnificent house, but she has fallen out with her old friends and finds herself amongst people who are not willing to accept a single parent from a council estate as one of their neighbours.

'Her lottery win has never been a secret and so there will be plenty of people who are aware that she is more than able to pay a hefty sum of money for the return of her child. What we have to do and do quickly is to narrow down those numbers and concentrate on people who knew her circumstances well enough to capitalise on her day-to-day plans.'

'We need to look hard at the list of the people who knew that she and Jason were going on the school trip this morning. There will be others apart from those we have already mentioned. Do what we have done so successfully in the past and put yourselves into the mind of the criminal. I think he or she, but for the sake of simplicity let's say he, had this well planned and so will definitely be someone who knew that Holly Road School were visiting St Fagans today.'

'What we don't know is how the kidnapper persuaded Jason to go with him and why no one saw him walking off with the boy. That bit is a big puzzle and if we can solve that puzzle it will be an enormous step forward.'

'Any ideas?'

Matt jumped in. 'I've been to the spot where Jason was last seen, and he sat on a grass verge with his mother ahead of him and a number of people from his school walking towards that spot. His mother says there is absolutely no way he could have passed her without her seeing him and having put myself in the place that she was waiting, I have to agree.

'Whatever happened to Jason happened in the space of a couple of minutes and must have been well-planned. A group of people speaking Welsh were the only ones to pass her and she didn't say anything to them. She said that if they had been from Jason's school she would have asked them if they had seen him but at the time she had no real reason to worry. As far as she was concerned at that time he was still sitting on the grass having a strop.

'Tina has been asked if she remembers anything about the people and her recollection is quite good. There were two women, one man, and three children – she thinks one boy and two girls. The two girls caught her attention because they were riding very girly pink scooters and she wondered what Jason would have thought of them.'

Martin interrupted. 'It's vital we speak to those people. Do we know if they are amongst those who have been looking for Jason? I have agreed with the Chief Super that we get a press conference set up as quickly as possible and it's been arranged for four o'clock. I know that might seem pretty soon to some of you but given the unusual circumstances we believe it's the right thing to do. Helen is bringing Tina Barnes in for it and we will use it to appeal to the public in general and in particular to get that group to come forward.

'Always supposing they had nothing to do with Jason's disappearance they will have been the last people to see him before he was taken. Maybe they saw him talking to someone and will be able to give us some sort of clue as to how he was moved from that spot without anyone seeing him. They are our best lead at the moment – there's nothing else of any help.'

Charlie responded. 'Maybe there is, although at the moment we are still trying to put the pieces together. You will remember that you asked everyone who had been in the area at the time to give us access to all the photographs they had taken on their cameras and phones, and amazingly there were hundreds of them. That's the thing with digital technology: you can keep snapping away and then just delete any photos that are rubbish.

'As you would suspect most of the pictures are of seven-year-olds pulling faces and posing with their friends but inevitably there are bits of people in the background. Individual photographs would tell us nothing but we have been able to link a number of shots and have come up with a partial image of a person walking away from where Jason was last seen.'

There was a brief moment of excitement but Charlie quickly defused it. 'I don't want to raise your hopes, because from what I've seen so far there's no way we'll be able to identify anyone from the images we have. At first our technicians suggested we had picked up the ghost of St Fagans but we now think that the image is of a man wearing some sort of white jacket. There are still photographs for us to process and everyone is working hard to get the job done as quickly as possible.

'There's a clear shot of an elderly couple looking somewhat disdainfully at a little boy attempting to balance a can of Strongbow on his head. With the amount of gel that he has used to shape his hair I'm surprised the can didn't just stick there, but the boy's father has videoed it on his phone and everyone appears to be laughing hysterically at the boy's unsuccessful efforts not to drop the can.

'The man who offered that particular phone is a Mr Ponting, and he and his two sons travelled to St Fagans on the same coach as Jason and his mother. He is pretty sure that the last he saw of Jason was when his mother pulled him away from the park and he doesn't have a clue who the elderly couple are.'

Martin summed up. 'There are three sets of people that we need to identify and speak to without delay. The party of Welsh speakers, the elderly couple, and the person in what we think was in a white coat or jacket. I will use the press conference to persuade those people to come forward and hope they will be able to add just a bit more to the picture.

'Someone must have seen Jason after his mother left him and for the moment let us assume that the only person that did was the person who took him. What does that say to us?'

He answered his own question. 'Well Jason is a skinny little boy and of average height for his age. I could pick him up and carry him quite easily and I'm not exactly Mr Universe.' He pointed to one of uniformed officers who was well over six feet tall and built like Atlas. 'Ian could tuck him under his arm and walk away with him in an instant.'

Matt jumped in. 'Only problem with that suggestion is that Jason would have kicked and screamed if some stranger had suddenly grabbed him.'

'But if it wasn't a stranger?' questioned Martin.

'Even so they would have presented an unforgettable image as they walked back towards the museum – someone would have noticed them surely.'

'I guess Jason could have been wrapped up in a blanket or something.' Matt made the suggestion even though he felt that

81

it was slightly ridiculous but Martin wasn't throwing anything out at this stage.

'What about the fields? Could they have gone across the fields?' he asked another question and this one was directed at the man who headed up the local SOCOs.

Alex Griffiths had joined the briefing session and now took the opportunity to give some input. 'There's not much I can tell you from the scene of Jason's disappearance as the area has been well trampled over and I can't even tell you if there were ever any signs of a struggle. On a positive note there is no evidence of blood so hopefully the boy has not been hurt. Perhaps the most significant thing I can tell you is that no one has walked across any of the fields surrounding the path this morning. We have examined every piece of hedge and fence between the park and where Tina Barnes was waiting for her son and there is no sign of the grass being disturbed in any of the adjoining fields. They are not fields that are open to the public and it would not have been difficult for us to pick up any recent footfall. Sorry I can't be of more help.'

'On the contrary, being able to eliminate the fields brings us back to the paths, and with the certainty Jason did not pass his mother we now have only one exit to consider,' replied Martin.

'It still doesn't explain how no one saw Jason either on his own or being carried by his abductor … unless of course he was hidden in some way,' Matt shared his thoughts. 'That's the only thing that makes any sense. It seems unlikely that he was wrapped in a blanket but he could have been persuaded to get inside a box or a bag of some sort.'

'Would have been one hell of a big bag,' returned Martin.

'Not necessarily, you'd be surprised at what small spaces kids can squeeze themselves into.' Matt had a sudden mental image of rescuing one of his nieces from a hole she had crawled into when they were exploring some old ruins on holiday in France.

'A bag, some sort of container, is the only thing that's making any sense to me,' said Martin. 'If the boy had been wrapped up in anything he would inevitably have wriggled even if he had been persuaded that it was some sort of game. He wouldn't have gone unnoticed. As Matt indicated, it needn't have been a huge bag – but what would have persuaded Jason to get inside it? He could have been rendered unconscious but there is a serious level of risk involved with that.'

'Too true,' said Matt. 'A blow to the head would probably knock him out, but could also kill him and chemicals such as chloroform could have the same result in the hands of someone who didn't really know what they were doing. We are all convinced that the boy has been taken for the love of money and so the last thing his kidnapper will want is a dead hostage.'

'All this brings us back to the possibility that Jason knew the person concerned and, maybe as part of a game, agreed to get into the bag. It would then have been easy for the kidnapper to walk back towards the car park and drive off with the boy.'

While Matt was talking Martin had concentrated his efforts on setting up one of the large whiteboards in the room and drawing his well-known columns. He headed the first one 'Absolute Facts' the second one 'Facts to be Considered' and the third one 'What Ifs'. It was his tried and tested way of coordinating all the many and varied strands of any investigation and he had found on many occasions that by keeping the focus in one place, nothing was left to chance.

He asked his colleagues to recap on the known facts and within minutes his first column was unusually crammed. Quite often at this stage of an investigation there was little information but in this case every detail of the young victim was known. He wrote down the boy's name, age, height, and weight and used a magnetic strip to attach a photograph of Jason to the edge of the board.

Although he was convinced of the motive for the kidnapping there was no actual evidence to back up his belief. There had been no phone calls either to Tina's home or to her mobile, and no ransom note had been delivered; for this reason 'kidnapping' was placed in Martin's second column.

Charlie had looked at the laptop that had been brought from the boy's home. Yes, Tina did have an email address but it had only been used by the technician who had set up the system for her. Tina couldn't even remember what it was and she certainly hadn't given it to anyone. So the likelihood of a ransom demand being made via an email or any other electronic method was dismissed. That left a phone call, the usual postal system or a courier service.

There was a general discussion and everyone agreed that any type of special delivery service would be too risky, but as it looked as if the crime had been thought out in advance there could already be a note on its way to Tina.

Intercepting the mail had played an important part in the last case Martin and his team had solved, and Matt picked up the phone to speak to the Royal Mail staff in the Penarth Road sorting office, who had previously been so helpful.

'If I was sending a ransom note I would do it through a text message. It's easy enough to pick up pay-as-you-go phones, use them once, and then dump them. You wouldn't be expecting a reply, just compliance with your demands.' The suggestion came from Charlie, and as she spoke a number of officers were nodding in agreement.

Matt gave Martin the thumbs up as he ended his call to the sorting office and announced that the staff would pull out all the stops to look for anything in the system en route to Tina's address.

There was now a mass of things to do in Martin's second column and he checked his watch. He hadn't even thought about lunch and realised that it would now be out of the question to grab anything to eat before the press conference. He decided to spend the remaining fifteen minutes concentrating on column three and debating the 'what ifs' of the case.

This was always the column that stimulated the most discussion, as always Martin encouraged off-the-wall ideas, and the biggest debate was about who would turn out to be the kidnapper. If Martin had been a betting man he would have made easy money guessing who quickly came to the top of the list.

Sergeant Evans, who was used to galvanising the uniformed

staff whenever Martin was heading up a CID investigation, had joined the meeting and been listening to the conversation unfold. He had arrived at St Fagans just after Martin had left and between them he and Matt had organised continued searches and interviews.

He knew from past experience that the way in which he could organise officers to be of maximum support was by knowing what was going on with the thinking process of Martin and his team. There was a mutual respect between a man who coming towards the end of a long career as a front-line officer and a much younger man who was undoubtedly carving out a position somewhere near the top of his profession.

Like everyone else at Goleudy, John Evans knew that a big re-organisation was in the pipeline and wondered if what most people believed would be inevitable promotion would take Martin away from something he did so well.

Knowing that his input would always be welcomed Sergeant Evans said what most people were thinking. 'The boy's father has got to be near the top of the list of possibilities – have you spoken to him yet?'

'Not yet,' replied Martin. 'His identity is not common knowledge, in fact until today it was only Tina who knew it, but she has now given us his name and we will be bringing him in for questioning.'

'What about the little boy, does he know who his father is?' questioned Sgt Evans.

'No, and when I said his identity was not common knowledge what I should have emphasised that Tina was the *only* person who knew it – not even the man himself did.'

Martin listened to a ripple of general discussion about how possible it would be to father a son and be unaware of the boy's existence. The general opinion was that even in the days of youthful over-indulgence most men knew where they had sown their oats and could do the maths if one of their conquests had suddenly started attending ante natal classes.

The exceptions that were considered included holiday romances with subsequent loss of interest and contact, and that thought prompted another question from Sgt Evans.

'Is he still around? If he is he may have worked things out for himself and not wanted anything to do with his son until Tina got that lottery win.'

Martin replied. 'He is still around and he would have had the opportunity of knowing about the school trip today Tina doesn't want him to be told that he is Jason's father and so for the moment we're bringing him in as part of a general trawl of anyone who knows the boy and had reason to know about the school trip.

'If he has a water-tight alibi for this morning and can satisfy me on other fronts we can simply eliminate him from our enquiry and whether or not he ever gets told about his son will be up to Tina. It will be for us to upset that particular apple cart if we have to.'

Matt had received a phone call and he told Martin that Helen Cook-Watts had arrived with Tina Barnes and that the press conference was due to start in five minutes.

'They aren't waiting in your office as you suggested because Tina wants a cigarette before facing the cameras. Helen tells me that Tina has been briefed by our media people and she may or may not make a personal appeal for her son's return. She has told Helen that she will be led by you and if you think it will help she'll give it a go. They're in the car park but ready to come in as soon as we make our way down.'

Martin's relationship with the press had been strained during the past few months, to put it mildly, but he pushed aside memories of some possible career-breaking reporting and walked down the back stairs to enlist the help of a diverse bunch of people. A missing child would put everyone on the same side and Martin had a duty to ensure that the strength the media could bring to such a situation was used to maximum advantage.

Helen and Tina met them just outside the side entrance of the large ground-floor room that was used for high-profile press conferences, and he positioned her between himself and Helen before they made their way to the seats at the front.

The room was not as jam-packed as it had been on a recent occasion and Martin noticed that it was mainly local press, radio, and television people that he had seen before. The nationals obviously hadn't caught up with the story yet. Nevertheless there was a high level of noise and flashing lights and unsurprisingly Tina looked terrified.

In a no-nonsense way Martin made the necessary introductions and gave an account of the way in which Jason had disappeared. He followed it up with details of the searches and briefly indicated the lines of enquiry that were being followed before opening it up to questions.

It was obvious from the questions that the majority of the reporters had done their homework and knew all about Tina. They knew about her lottery win even down to the exact sum and the names of the people she had given hand-outs to. They knew where she lived and about her relationship with her neighbours. They knew about the way in which Tina had fallen out with some of her old friends. They knew where Tina's father lived and about the fact that he had never seen his grandson.

They knew nothing about Jason's father and within a few minutes it was a desire to find out about this missing link that inspired all their questions.

Laura Cummings had the ability to take centre stage whenever she asked a question and was easily the most recognisable figure in the room. She was a correspondent for local TV and was setting the scene for the behaviour her press colleagues would be obliged to follow.

'Tina,' she said in a voice that was intended to demonstrate concern and one she believed would generate more information than her usual forceful manner. 'We are all here to help DCI Phelps and his excellent team find your son. The more you are able to tell us the more we will be able to enlighten the public and get them on board. Is it possible that Jason has just decided to visit his dad and they are just having some boys' time together?'

Ms Cummings was looking directly at Tina as she spoke but

Martin could see the distress Tina was under and stood up to respond to the question.

Tina beat him to it. 'My Jason doesn't know who is father is, you stupid cow. You pretend you want to help but you really just want to dig for dirt. Somebody has taken my boy and I just want him back … I don't want to talk to you lot … I just want Jase back. If whoever has him wants my money they can have it … I just want my Jase back.'

Tears streamed down Tina's face and she manically ran her fingers through her hair, causing it to stick up in some bizarre fashion. She looked dreadful and so Helen helped her out of the room, leaving Martin to bring the press conference to some sort of order.

For the first time that Martin could remember, Laura Cummings looked a bit shocked and he felt a tiny bit sorry for her. True she had tried to get Tina on the back foot, but she hadn't bargained for that response and it was obvious that some of the other reporters had been amused to see her put down. What a bunch!

Speaking as if nothing had happened Martin made the appeal that had been agreed. He spoke of the group of Welsh speakers who must have walked past Jason and drew particular attention to the two girls on pink scooters. There were photographs shown of the elderly couple, and finally he mentioned the person who was seen at the time wearing a white jacket or coat. He emphasised that those people were not necessarily suspects, but may have seen Jason before his disappearance, and were urged to come forward.

Martin finally mentioned the fact that Jason may have been taken from St Fagans in something like a strong bag and ended on a general appeal for the public to be vigilant. 'Jason is a small seven-year-old boy. He has ginger hair and lots of freckles and when he was last seen he was wearing a Stone Island blue sweatshirt and jeans. His jacket is light brown with an all-over Zucca logo and four pockets at the front with stud fasteners. He was wearing black leather Kickers boots and the photograph that we are circulating shows him in the clothes I've just mentioned, as it was only taken this morning.

'We are expecting to hear quite soon that Tina Barnes has received a demand for money in return for her son and if, as I suspect, the kidnapper is watching this news item I have a message for him. Our primary objective will be to get Jason back to his mother safe and well and if there has to be an exchange of money to secure that objective then so be it. We will do nothing to put Jason at risk but kidnapping is one of the most serious crimes and I will personally do everything I can to bring this callous perpetrator to justice.'

Hands shot up all over the room and journalists loudly questioned the legal position of the police when it came to negotiating with people demanding money with menace. Martin ignored them and joined Matt, who had been standing near the side door, and they both walked out.

It didn't take a world-class detective to guess the likely whereabouts of Tina Barnes, and she was indeed in the car park taking refuge in large quantities of nicotine.

'She's beating herself up about her outburst back there,' Helen told Martin. 'She seems to think the press will now be more interested in making her look a fool for calling the television presenter a stupid cow than getting the public engaged in looking for Jason. I've told her that it was completely understandable and it's unlikely to be featured in any appeal for Jason's return, but she doesn't believe me.'

Martin smiled at Tina. 'Helen is right, no one knows better than I do what a pain in the butt the media can be, but they know their business and their focus will be on helping to find Jason. That's what'll engage the public, up their rating figures, and sell their newspapers. No one outside their own little network is going to be interested in your opinion of one of them. I suggest we get you back home. Helen will remain with you and there will be a couple of other officers staying at the house, keeping an eye out for any movement from the kidnapper and manning the phones.' Martin saw that Tina had reached yet another stage in her rollercoaster of emotions. Initially she had been devastated and terrified, and then focused and determined, but now she looked like someone who had just had all the stuffing taken out of her. She looked totally helpless and Martin watched as Helen took her hand and urged her into a waiting squad car.

'Poor thing,' remarked Matt, as the two men watched the car pull out of the car park and caught sight of a number of photographers flashing away as the police car slowed down before joining the main road.

'There'll be more of the same waiting for her at her home, you can bet on that, but for now the media will play a major part in this enquiry and we need their help.' As the two men walked back into the building Martin asked if there had been anything from the sorting office and if Dan Painter had been brought in for questioning.

'Nothing from Penarth Road as yet but everyone there is aware of the urgency of the situation. The manager told me any letters posted today may not get to them until much later. Lots of post-boxes only have a late afternoon or early evening collection and if our kidnapper is using the Royal Mail I doubt he would have risked sending it yesterday in case Tina got it before she left home this morning. Even if there is a letter it will be amongst thousands of pieces of mail from all over Cardiff, and although the system is slick it's not instantaneous. It's not like the last time when we were looking for a particular coloured envelope – this time we don't even know if the kidnapper has actually sent a letter and if it is correctly addressed and with the proper postcode.'

Martin nodded. 'What about Dan Painter? Have we located him yet?'

'I think Sgt Evans wants to speak to you about that,' said Matt. 'His officers have been all over the place bringing in everyone and anyone on Tina's list of people who know her and her circumstances. Dan Painter is on that list but I don't think he's been brought in yet. ·

'OK,' said Martin. 'Though I must get something to eat before I speak to Sgt Evans – what about you, have you eaten?

Matt shook his head. 'I had just had a sandwich and a coffee with my niece when I got your call, but that was hours ago and my stomach thinks my throat's been cut.'

Martin grinned as Matt's response to the offer of food had been exactly what had been expected, and the two men made their way to the staff dining room.

Although the incident rooms were the places where the detailed work on cases was carried out there was no doubt that discussions over coffee, with the help of Iris' home-from-home cooking, were often key to solving crime. Iris was responsible for the catering in Goleudy and it was rumoured that some officers even came to work on their days off if it was one of her famous curry days.

Today the lunch session was well and truly over but after a few minutes discussion the two detectives opted for a simple cheese and ham toastie. 'Any news about the little boy?' asked Iris when she brought the food to the table. The dining room was the hub of the building and there was very little that went on that wasn't debated there, but it was unusual for Iris to ask a direct question about a case. 'We had the Red Dragon radio station on earlier and the presenter mentioned that a young boy had gone missing on a school trip to St Fagans. Then I heard some of the officers over lunch saying you were at the museum and so I guessed you were involved with the case.'

'We'll be recruiting you to CID,' teased Matt.

'No news, I'm afraid,' answered Martin.

'Poor little bugger. I don't know how I would have coped if one of my kids had been taken and it would be the same with the grandchildren – it doesn't bear thinking about. Please God he will be alright and not abused in any way. The poor mother must be going out of her mind with worry just thinking what someone could be doing to her little boy. There are some evil bastards in this world.'

Chapter Seven

How the hell had he got to this point? It was the stuff of anyone's worst nightmare, but he knew he wasn't having a terrible dream.

He wasn't on his own but the other two people were not wide awake with their minds full of confusion and fear. One would never be wide awake again and was growing colder with every hour. Susan had driven him mad with her tormenting and her foul mouth but he would never have believed himself capable of actually killing someone. It had been so easy and in some ways that was the thing that scared him most. He obviously didn't realise his own strength. But or maybe there had been something wrong with her? Maybe she'd had a heart attack or something and the fact that he had his hands around her throat when she died was just a coincidence?

He wasn't convincing himself and he knew he wouldn't have a hope in hell of convincing anyone else. If he could say it had just been a bit of a domestic that had got out of hand he might have stood a chance, but there was another body in the caravan that would make that line of defence impossible.

The other body was not cold but was very still. Jason had wrapped himself in a faded blue blanket and all that could be seen of him was a mop of ginger hair and a very red face. There was something about the colour of his face that made Dan Painter take a closer look.

He bent down and even before his hands had touched the blanket he felt the heat coming off the small body and there was something about the boy's breathing that terrified him.

Dan had daughters of his own and he remembered one of

them, Lucy, having something the doctors called a febrile convulsion when she was just four years old as a result of a high temperature when she had tonsillitis. It had been one of the scariest moments of his life when his daughter had lost consciousness and began jerking and twitching. He had thought she wouldn't recover and now he was scared that Jason was going to die.

Something at the back of his mind told him that he needed to stop Jason overheating and Dan carefully removed the woollen blanket. The boy's skin felt hot enough to fry an egg and each intake of breath was accompanied by a sort of high-pitched grunt.

Dan got to his feet and paced backwards and forwards in the small space between the collapsed table and the bedroom door. He was caught between one dead body and the even more terrifying sight of a very sick child. Jason stirred and opened his eyes.

Not wanting to scare the boy any further Dan desperately tried to raise a smile but although Jason's eyes were open he didn't seem to see him at all. With eyes wide and glazed violently pawed at his limbs, as if trying to brush off crawling things that only he could see.

His behaviour terrified Dan, and not knowing what to do he threw open the door of the caravan and almost fell down the single metal step.

It wasn't a cold afternoon but there was a marked difference between the outside temperature and the cloying atmosphere of the caravan, and the change came to Dan's rescue. He walked around the perimeter of what had been the building site and began unravelling the mess inside his head.

In the plans that he and Susan had considered for weeks this should have been the time when they would just be sitting back and waiting for the money to come to them. They believed that the most difficult part would be getting Jason to cooperate – but that bit had been easy.

The idea of using the Holly Road school trip had come when Dan's granddaughter, prompted by her mother, had asked him for some spending money. She told him that all the kids in her class were going to a place where there were houses from the olden days and you could buy sweets like old people had had when they were little.

When he mentioned the trip to Susan she immediately saw it as an ideal opportunity to kidnap Jason. Up to that point Dan had not really taken their plans seriously but had seen them as a way of keeping Susan's interest. He wished he hadn't told her about the school outing but she was really fired up and her imagination ran wild. He remembered her considering the possibility of setting fire to one of the buildings and seizing Jason in the confusion that would result, and that was one of her less crazy ideas.

Realising that she was serious about a kidnap and ransom scheme Dan forced himself to come up with a more rational plan. His brother Will had played cricket in his younger days and from the back of a wardrobe Dan fished out a white sweater and trousers and a bat that hadn't been used for years. Will had disappeared off the face of the earth more than fifteen years ago and Dan didn't know if his big brother was dead or alive.

Will's cricket bag had fallen to pieces but a visit to Sports Direct had provided Dan with a new one, together with a white floppy hat and sports shades. Not even Dan's mother would have recognised him in his cricket gear as he parked Susan's sister's car in the St Fagans car park.

Something they hadn't considered was the need to pre-pay for parking. He had no coins and didn't want to attract attention to himself by asking anyone to change a note for him. Cursing that they hadn't thought about parking charges, Dan decided to take the risk that security staff wouldn't notice his car without a ticket and went in search of Jason.

He saw the three coaches from Holly Road School pull into the car park, and the skinny woman with black and blue hair – accompanied by a red-headed kid – was not difficult to pick out. Dan kept his head down when he caught sight of his own daughter and the granddaughter he had provided with pocket money for the trip. He knew that there was no way they would give some aging cricketer a second glance but that hadn't stopped his stomach taking a tumble when they appeared to be looking in his direction.

As he had suspected Jason and his mother took off on their own and Dan hung back just watching from a safe distance as they made their way to the nearest public toilets. It was a possible opportunity and Dan considered risking it when he saw that Jason was playing around, on his own, outside the ladies' toilets. With his heart beating nineteen to the dozen Dan took off his dark glasses and began walking towards the boy.

He did a sharp about-turn and quickly put his glasses back on as he realised he wasn't the only person walking towards Jason. Leaning against a wall and pretending to look for something in his bag, Dan watched one of Jason's teachers as she waited with him until his mother came out of the toilets.

He wasn't close enough to hear their conversation but Tina didn't seem too pleased as she yanked Jason off and Dan followed, at a distance but keeping them in sight. Tina was walking at top speed and it was not only Jason's little legs that were having difficulty keeping up with her. Dan had to increase his stride but then stop abruptly and stared out over the fields as suddenly Tina stopped and bent down to speak to her son. As before he was too far away to hear what was being said, but he picked up from the body language that mother and son were having an argument.

He watched Jason throw himself on the grass and could hear him shouting at his mother, who had lost patience with him and was walking away.

It had to be the moment. Dan pulled off his hat and dark glasses and with a wink and a smile walked up to Jason. He wanted the boy to be able to see who he was and not to feel frightened by his approach and he needn't have worried on that score.

'Hi, Megan's grampy!' said Jason. 'I didn't know you were on the bus, I only saw Megan and her mother.'

Dan had no time for chit-chat and he quickly sat next to Jason and asked him where his mother had gone.

'For a fag most likely,' replied Jason.

Not wanting to waste precious seconds Dan immediately suggested that they play a trick on her and he watched as with a grin from ear to ear Jason snuggled down inside the cricket bag, eagerly drank the apple juice, and quite simply allowed himself to be carried away.

From start to finish the plan had taken no more than a minute to execute, but it had been the longest minute of Dan's life. As he carried the now somewhat heavier bag back towards the car park he struggled with the sound of his heart thumping loudly and a considerable degree of nausea.

Jason played his part well, although Dan had to tell him to stop giggling especially as they passed members of the school trip. Dan had remembered to put his dark glasses and hat back on and the disguise would probably have been enough, but whenever Dan noticed any of the Holly Road school group he kept his head well down and whistled loudly to drown any possible noise from Jason.

Thinking back over the whole thing Dan couldn't believe that he had actually gone through with it and how easy the actual business of abduction had been. He swallowed hard as he remembered his near miss with the traffic cops but that problem had been averted and from then on things should have been plain sailing.

He certainly hadn't anticipated ending up with a dead woman and a sick kid and he kicked against a large stone, dislodging it and causing it to fall into a pile of discarded building material. It surprised him to see how the stone disappeared and so did half a bag of sand and several pieces of timber, and he almost lost his footing and disappeared himself.

Taking a good look he saw that several long planks of wood had been placed across what was basically a hole in the ground and into which a lot of rubble and rubbish had been thrown. He remembered the bunch of builders who were involved with this project and was not surprised at their sloppy habits. Dan guessed that they were trying to avoid the cost of transporting waste away from the site and would probably have put a thin layer of top soil over their mess before the house was handed over.

Maybe he had reason to be grateful for their slipshod practices as he realised that the bottom of their little pit was about four feet down and would be an ideal place to dispose of a body. Even as he thought of it he didn't know if he would be able to do it and racked his brain for another way out. Dan was not normally a violent man. True, he had been involved with a number of pub brawls during his lifetime – but he had never struck a woman, and he couldn't get his mind around the fact that he had now killed one.

Desperately trying to think of what he should do next Dan narrowed down his options. He could bury Susan a few inches away from where he was standing and cover her body very easily with all the stuff that was scattered around. He knew that no one came to the site because he had staked it out over the past few weeks. It had been their plan to bring Jason to the caravan and for Dan to phone Tina giving her the location of the caravan – but only after the money was with them and they had boarded their flight to Mexico.

Could he still get away with that plan? Dan shook his head because of course he couldn't risk the police coming to the caravan. Other people like the press would invade the place and there would be too great a chance of Susan's body being found.

He considered handing Jason back to his mother and confessing to the kidnapping. Yes, he would face a jail sentence but he could say he had done it to have some time with his son. That would mean him getting his hands on the letter that he knew was destined to arrive at Tina's house the next day and there was no way he could do that.

In any event, handing Jason back and him staying to face the music was not an option as the boy had seen Dan strangle Susan. Even at the tender age of seven he would be able to tell the police exactly what he had seen.

Although Dan was thinking through his options it was becoming increasingly obvious that he didn't really have any. He would have to dump Susan's body and it would have to be here as he couldn't risk taking her anywhere else, but leaving the body here would mean he would have to take Jason somewhere else for the handover and he didn't have anywhere in mind.

Dan persuaded himself to take one step at a time. He returned to the caravan and steeled himself to pick up Susan's body and carry her to what he hoped would be her final resting place. He remembered the ease with which he had carried Jason but Susan was a different kettle of fish and the term dead weight came to his mind. Once he had geared up the nerve to touch her he became more resolved and by the time he had reached the hole in the ground he had convinced himself that she was responsible for the whole bloody mess and felt no remorse as he heaved her into her makeshift grave.

For the next fifteen minutes Dan picked up every piece of stone, metal, and wood he could lay his hands on hurled them on top of Susan's body. When he had finished the hole in the ground had been filled and there were several inches of discarded building material standing proud of the surrounding area.

Dan wondered if he should flatten it by jumping on any protruding bits but the idea seemed a bit too much like dancing on someone's grave and he didn't have the stomach for that. He turned his attention away from the burial mound he had created and looked at the area beyond the confines of the building site. It was easy to see why the location had been chosen and in the cool clear October air he could see for miles over fields and trees and the parting of two low hills revealed the line of the coast.

It was so quiet, so deathly quiet.

A call of nature hit Dan and he satisfied it by relieving himself over one of the front wheels of the caravan and watching the warm stream of urine settle into a pool before it too disappeared into the ground. He was surprised to find that he was hungry and wondered if the boy could stomach something.

He hadn't looked in Jason's direction when he had carried

Susan's body out and he didn't even know if the boy had seen him. Dan was afraid now as he returned inside. He was worried that the boy was even more sick than he had first thought, but it was something he had to face and he summoned up the courage to look at his young captive.

Dan's heart almost stopped beating at the sight of a motionless child who was no longer the florid colour he had been an hour ago. Jason's face was now bereft of any vestige of colour. His ginger hair accentuated the pallor of his cheeks and his breathing was no longer audible but was extremely shallow and rapid.

This wasn't part of the plan either. Dan realised that the kid was sick but he didn't have any idea what had caused this sudden onset of symptoms. Jason had seemed fine when they had spoken at St Fagans and surely his mother wouldn't have taken him on a school trip if he had been unwell.

Kids did pick things up very quickly and in Dan's limited experience they also got over things much faster than adults. He convinced himself that Jason was sleeping off some sort of bug and was supported in his hopes by the fact that the boy was not as hot as he had been.

Dan boiled the kettle and used the first lot of hot water to wash his face and scrub his hands until they felt like they had been scoured to the bone. He was ritualistically washing himself clean of recent events and by the time he sat down to eat a plate of beans on toast he felt able to think more clearly than he had done for hours.

It had always been the plan to follow the unfolding story of Jason's disappearance on the radio and television, and Dan turned on the small portable television set that he had brought from home. The radio had been Susan's, and he couldn't bring himself to touch that, so he concentrated on the TV, switching from channel to channel searching for news programmes.

He marvelled at the clarity of the picture and sound, remembering that one of the things Susan had complained about was that they may only get a limited reception for the television coverage.

He actually jumped when Jason's face filled the whole of the small screen. How the hell had they got a photograph of the boy wearing exactly the same clothes that he was wearing now? The image stayed in place for the whole time that the presenter told the public about the school trip to St Fagans and Jason's disappearance.

The cameras then followed Tina going into the press conference and Dan listened as someone called DCI Phelps appealed to the public for help. He couldn't quite work out what had happened to Tina halfway through the session. She had obviously said something but her words had been spoken over by the newsreader. Dan could just make out the words, 'I just want Jase back. If whoever has him wants my money he can have it … I just want my Jase back.'

This encouraged Dan, who would be more than happy to return the boy in exchange for a chunk of her fortune. It sounded as if she would hand it over willingly and maybe that part of the plan would go off without a hitch and his hopes were raised. A few seconds later they were dashed again as he listened in amazement to the facts that already seemed to be at the fingertips of this young detective.

Dan remembered the group of people the DCI was asking to come forward and he knew that one of the girls on a pink scooter would be likely to recall him as she had run over his foot and the bag carrying Jason had lurched forward. That had been when Jason started giggling but Dan didn't believe the girl could have heard that.

He put his own thoughts on hold and listened intently to the rest of the appeal. Dan had also seen the elderly couple whose photograph was being shown but he had no worries about them. They hadn't noticed him he was sure because they were far too busy expressing their disgust that a little boy was being encouraged to balance a can of cider on his head.

The final words of DCI Phelps' appeal caused a renewed bout of nausea as Dan was shocked to hear that the police were looking for a man dressed in a white jumper or jacket and had already figured out that Jason had been taken from the museum in some sort of bag. In other words, they were looking for him!

That meant that they would be looking at the CCTV cameras around the car park and could pick him up putting the bag into Susan's sister's car. Panic set in and he was in danger of seeing the immediate return of his beans on toast as he fought the feeling of sickness that was getting the better of him.

He walked back outside but the first thing he saw was a recently established pile of debris. To most people that is all it would have looked like but in Dan's eyes it was so obviously a grave that he could easily envisage a cross and some floral tributes adorning the top of the pile.

His brain was racing and he could not make it stop long enough in one place to allow any rational thinking, but he would have to attempt to put the brakes on his over active imagination. In his mind's eye he could already see the blue flashing lights taking the coastal road up towards the caravan. He sat down on the grass and rubbed his face and the side of his head and it seemed to have the desired result of erasing some of the demons and bringing common sense to the surface.

Even if the police did pick him up putting a bag into the boot it was Diane's car, not his, that would be identified. They wouldn't recognise him, as he was certain that he had never looked up and the best image the police could get would be of an averagely built man dressed in a white sweater and trousers. That wouldn't lead them to him. Diane didn't even know her car had been 'borrowed' and would have a rude awakening when the police rang her doorbell.

He had to think what to do with Jason, but all he could decide was that the rest of the plan would have to stand. Tina would get a letter tomorrow morning telling her that Jason was safe and would not be harmed if she complied with the demands.

Dan was certain that she would do that and that he would have no problem picking up the ransom. The police would not interfere because at that point in time they would not know the whereabouts of Jason and would not risk his safety.

After that the plan would have to change as Dan would no

longer be able to give the caravan as the place for Tina to find her son. He would have to think of somewhere else to take the boy and it would have to be somewhere he wouldn't be discovered until Dan was several thousand feet in the air.

Things were entirely different now. There had never been any question that having picked up the ransom and been safely boarding the plane to Mexico that Dan would phone Tina and give her directions to find her son safe and well. But now Jason had witnessed a murder ... so what did that mean for the boy's chances of being found alive?

Chapter Eight

It was coming up to 11.30 when Martin pulled up outside the large steel gates of the Royal Mail sorting office. Matt jumped out of the car. There was no need for him to walk very far as the shift manager, Timothy Crowe, was waiting on the pavement and they recognised one another immediately.

'This is getting to be a habit,' he smiled briefly as he handed over a white envelope that had been put into a plastic bag. 'It's the only piece of mail on the premises addressed to Tina Barnes and it's taken us a bit longer than we had hoped to find it because there's no post code and our systems scan that first. We've all guessed that this has something to do with the missing school boy and we've got our fingers crossed that nothing bad has happened to him.'

Matt remembered the system from the last time he had asked for the help of the sorting office and asked Tim to thank the staff for their cooperation and thoughts. Minutes later Martin had turned the car around and they were heading for Tina's home.

'It's strange the way life throws things up in batches,' said Martin. 'I'd never sought the help of the postal system in any case during the whole of my career before last month, and now we've used it in two consecutive investigations. Is the address handwritten?' he asked Matt.

'Yes, I could see it clearly under the security lights back there. It's written in blue ink and it looks as if there has been an attempt to disguise the writing, because it's all over the place.'

'Of course it may not be a ransom note and could just be a run-of-the-mill letter from someone Tina knows.' As he spoke

Martin put his foot down harder on the accelerator and nothing more was said until he turned the corner into what had previously been Tina's well-ordered development of expensive houses but now resembled a circus ring. The first figure Martin recognised was that of John Evans coming down the drive of the biggest and most expensive-looking house of the group.

John Evans looked decidedly rattled and Martin pulled up alongside him and asked him what he was doing there.

'You wouldn't believe the number of calls we've had from these people,' he said waving his arms around as he spoke to take in all the houses adjacent to the Barnes' home.

'Not one of the calls had been an offer to help with the search for a missing child. All of them are just hell bent on complaining to the police that there are people trespassing onto their property. Can you believe it? The man in the house I've just come from didn't even enquire about the boy and when I tried to reason with him he said that the boy and his mother should have stayed on the council estate they came from. He almost spat out his distaste when he suggested that her sort of people are good at piling up flowers and teddy bears to ease their guilt when one of their kids gets killed. He wasn't even interested when I explained that as far as we know Jason has not been killed and he slammed the door in my face after bellowing that the sort of media circus that was outside his house had better be moved – or else.'

Martin had witnessed his favourite sergeant express a number of emotions over the years but he had never seen him so angry.

'If having pots of money turns people into uncaring, self-centred pieces of shit I'll just be happy to stick with my pension.'

John was calmer now that he had got that off his chest but was also a bit ashamed as he asked Martin if there was any further news of Jason. 'See what I mean?' he emphasised. 'Normally that would have been my first question. They say behaviour breeds behaviour and there was me putting my own moans first before asking about the kid.'

'We possibly have some news and if you follow us to Tina's house we may need your help,' said Martin as he drove on just a few yards before turning into Tina's drive. It hadn't escaped his notice that the media had witnessed his conversation with Sergeant Evans and there were flashes lighting up the darkness at an increasing rate as he and Matt left the car and made their way to the front door.

Lessons in how not to annoy the neighbours obviously didn't feature in the media training manuals and as if to prove the point several reporters shouted questions and spoke loudly into microphones.

'What are you doing here, DCI Phelps?'

'Have you found the kid?'

'Is he alive?'

'Have you come to tell his mother he's been murdered?'

'Must be bad news for you to be here at this time of night – come on, what can you tell us, you must be able to tell us something.'

Martin was inclined to use the two words that annoyed him more than any other two in the English language, but refrained. He was always frustrated when suspects relied on the 'no comment' card but on this occasion he would have liked to use it himself. Instead he said quite truthfully that at that moment there was nothing he could tell them but he hoped that position would change very soon.

He suddenly realised that he was no longer the focus of the flash photography, as the subject that now took their attention was Tina Barnes, who had opened the front door and was standing next to DC Cook-Watts. It was no surprise that she held a cigarette in her hand, but what was a surprise was that she was soaking wet. Her multi-coloured hair was flat against her face and although she was wrapped in a gigantic white bath towel she was still surrounded by a small pool of water.

Matt ushered everyone inside and shut the door. It occurred to him that Tina must have taken a swim but he didn't want to give the press the opportunity of saying that she had been chilling out in her personal pool when her son's life could be in danger.

The reality was very different as Helen explained when they were all standing in the hall.

'Tina was fine until about ten minutes ago when the phone rang and someone demanded to know where she was. I picked up the phone put in by our technicians and could hear the conversation. The man on the line was obviously drunk and kept insisting that he had been waiting for half an hour for her. It was difficult to make much sense of what he said and I told Tina to ask if Jason was with him. That seemed to confuse him totally and we thought he was going to hang up.

'That freaked Tina out and she yelled down the phone demanding that she be allowed to speak to her son. It must have been the tone of her voice because the guy seemed to sober up a bit and asked her what the hell she was on about. It turned out that he was someone out on a stag night and whose girlfriend had promised to pick him up. I took over the call and asked him to give me his girlfriend's number and as I suspected, in his drunken state, he had dialled 02 at the end of the number instead of 20.

'I think it was partly relief and partly disappointment that sent Tina on a bit of a rampage and she smashed up a number of ornaments and pots in the garden. I should have seen it coming but I didn't and she didn't even make much of a splash as she jumped into the pool. My first instinct was to jump in after her but even before I got to the pool she was pulling herself up one of the ladders.'

Tina was no longer dripping and she pulled the towel tighter around her fully clothed body. 'It wasn't Helen's fault,' she explained. 'I actually don't swim and I don't know what made me jump in, but it was the shallow end and I was right next to the ladder so I was OK – it was that phone call. As it was so late I just expected it to be the person who took Jase.'

'Do you want to change out of those wet things?' asked Martin. 'We have a letter that we suspect may have been sent by Jason's kidnapper and as agreed we've brought it along for you to open.'

He held out the plastic bag and half expected Tina to snatch it from his hand. Instead she hesitated before surprising everyone and saying that she would change first.

'God only knows what will be in that letter,' she said. 'I owe it to my Jase to be prepared to do whatever is necessary to make him safe and I think I'll be able to do that better in dry clothes.'

She headed for the stairs and Helen decided not to follow her. 'I think she'll be alright, and she should be capable of doing almost anything if there is a chance of getting Jason back. I must confess that initially I thought she was a bit of an airhead, but my opinion of her is changing. Yes, her jumping in the pool was totally erratic, but bloody hell – I don't know how I'd behave in her position.'

'I wish she would hurry up,' suggested Matt. 'I'm desperate to know what's inside that envelope.'

'I'm desperate, too,' said Tina as she returned dressed in black trousers and a pale pink sweater with a darker pink smiley face super-imposed on the fabric. 'This is Jason's favourite top, and I'm wearing it for good luck so let's get on with it.' She stretched out her hand for the envelope but Martin gave her a pair of disposable gloves before she touched anything. They wanted to get as much in the way of forensics from the letter as was possible and so with gloves already on Matt used a knife to slit open the envelope and handed the folded notepaper to Tina.

She visibly steadied herself before unfolding the sheet of white paper and reading the same style of writing that had been seen on the front of the envelope. Matt had said that it was all over the place and it was. There was a mixture of block capitals and joined up writing and almost every letter produced in a different style, but stripped of all the bizarre creativity it read:

Jason is safe.
You will get him back if you follow these instructions.
Put one million pounds in used notes in a lightweight suitcase.
Half the notes must be £20s and half £50s.
Leave the case in the red telephone box opposite the church on Wentloog Road.

TODAY, THURSDAY at 2 p.m.
If I am picked up by the police Jason WILL be killed
*You will be told where to find your son when I have the money
and I am sure you have not had me followed.*
*I repeat, Jason is safe at the moment and it is up to you to keep
him safe.*

They all read the note several times with each of them picking
out different elements of the message. For Tina the only point
of focus was the first sentence and she read that line over and
over – Jason was safe and the kidnapper had even said the same
thing at the end of the note.

Before anyone else had a chance to speak Tina laid down the
rules.

'We will do exactly as he asks,' she said quietly but firmly.
'I will get the money as requested and I've already got a blue
lightweight suitcase ready for when I take Jason to Disneyland
at half-term.' She had a new resolve in her voice and seemed
totally convinced that all she had to do was get the money and
her son would be found; she could not or would not
contemplate anything that would change that situation. 'To be
honest I thought the man that took Jason would ask for much
more than a million – I would have given him every penny I
have.'

Matt had read the note and was considering the logistics of
the demand. He struggled to remember an amusing training
session he had attended when the presenter had posed as a
blackmailer and demanded a payment of three million in £20
notes.

Apparently a million pounds in that denomination weighs
about eight stone and the blackmailer had wanted that
multiplied by three stuffed into a briefcase! One of the course
participants, Carl, had confessed to weighing in excess of
eighteen stone and so the comparison was made suggesting that
the blackmailer would have had to be able to lift Carl plus the
weight of a small child in order to get away with the money.

Matt considered the demand of a million pounds being half

in £20 notes and half in fifties, and based on what he remembered guessed that the weight of that bundle would be somewhere around six stone. He looked at Tina and wondered if she would be capable of lifting that much, then dismissed the thought. She would carry it until she dropped if it meant getting her son back but Matt didn't share her belief regarding the honour of the kidnapper. Once he had the money there was no knowing what he would do.

Martin read the note for the third time and he too had thought about the actual physical volume of the money but the other thing he picked up was the fact that there was more than one person involved with Jason's abduction. Whoever had written the letter was going to pick up the money but there was the threat that Jason would be killed if he was apprehended.

Did he mean Jason would actually be murdered or did he mean he had been left somewhere without food or water and would die if the kidnapper was arrested before he had revealed the child's whereabouts? Supposing the plan was to kill the boy if the kidnapper was caught then there had to be someone else involved, and it was this thought that was taxing Martin.

Helen had busied herself with making some coffee that was welcomed by the men, but Tina ignored hers and lit a cigarette.

'The kidnapper will be unaware that we already have his ransom note in our hands and normally it would be at least eight hours from now before the postman dropped it on your doormat. There are things we can put in place like cameras around the area of the post box and we could put a tracker on the suitcase.'

Before Martin could say any more Tina interrupted. 'I don't want you to do anything. If this man thinks I'm helping the police God knows what he'll do. Don't ask me why, but I trust him and I believe that if we just do as he wants then he will tell me where Jason is and that's all I want.'

She stubbed her cigarette out in an overflowing ash tray and still clutching the Lego Ron Weasley she surprised everyone by announcing that she was going to bed. 'I know what I have to do tomorrow and I won't have the strength to go through with it if I don't get some sleep.'

'I wasn't expecting that,' said Helen. 'I've been trying to get her to get some rest for hours and she's had nothing to eat or drink. She just lives on cigarettes. The fridge is full of milk and strawberry milkshakes but I can't see those being for Tina. If she does manage to get to sleep I'll try to get her to eat something when she wakes up.'

'Are you OK to stay?' asked Martin.

'Yes, my brother brought a few of my things around earlier. There are a number of bedrooms but I think I'll just use the sofa – it's bigger than my bed. What are you going to do?' Helen cleared the coffee cups as she spoke.

'In spite of what Tina said we will still set up some cameras around the phone box. They can be done while it's still dark and will be positioned so as not to be noticeable. I'll speak to Charlie about the feasibility of using a tracker without drawing attention to the operation.' He sighed.

'It's a fine line to be walking, Helen. There is every chance that the kidnapper will renege on his promise to let Tina know where her son is once he's got his hands on the money. The only thing that is keeping that woman together is her belief that a million pounds will buy her son's freedom, but unfortunately we have good reason to be cynical. There's enough case-history around to tell us that things can go badly wrong.

'If we interfere and the kidnapper finds out he may be forced to step outside any plan he currently has and that could endanger the boy's life. But if we do nothing and allow Tina to simply hand over the money we are completely at the mercy of a man we know nothing about other than that he wants to be an instant millionaire.'

Helen nodded. 'On that count I can tell you that Tina's bank is already in the picture and I have a direct contact who is waiting to hear how much money is needed and if there are any specific requirements. The manager sounded really young but took the whole thing in his stride. It appears that even if used notes are requested they will be able to use electronic scanners to record the serial numbers on all the notes in next to no time.

My initial thought was that this meant we could pick the man up as soon as he started spending, but of course that wouldn't be the case. If he used a £20 note to pay for anything it could be given to the next customer who wanted change or used by the shopkeeper to buy stock. We could hardly circulate what would amount to thirty-five thousand serial numbers and ask the public to keep an eye out for them.'

Martin smiled and said that the serial numbers would only be useful if the kidnapper was apprehended and the ransom money found somewhere connected to him. At that point it would secure a conviction, but for now the numbers were just a small weapon in the armoury needed to catch this man.

Sergeant Evans had followed the detectives as requested and had witnessed the opening of the ransom note and the subsequent conversation. 'Is there anything you need me to do?' he asked.

'Just stand down all those involved in the search at St Fagans and be sure that everyone, especially the museum staff and the public, is thanked for their efforts. I think all we need to tell people at the moment is that we have reason to believe that Jason has been taken off the premises, obviously nothing about the ransom note.

'It's now well past midnight and I suggest we all try to get a few hours of sleep and then meet up at eight in the morning.'

The press seemed to be prepared to be mown down as they congregated around Martin's car when it left the drive but slowly edging forward he managed to avoid gathering any trophies and drove off without a word.

En route to Goleudy Matt made a number of calls and initiated action on some of the safeguards that had been suggested and hoped that they were doing the right thing.

Neither of the men went into the office and Martin's car only stopped long enough for Matt to jump out and get into his 4x4.

Martin suddenly realised that he was both tired and hungry and couldn't wait to get to the cottage. It was now the early hours of Thursday morning and there was virtually an empty road ahead of him. The significance of the fact that it was

Thursday suddenly dawned on him and for one of the few times in his career he cursed his job.

This wasn't just any old Thursday, it was Thursday the sixth of October – Shelley's birthday.

He had planned the day. He was always the first to wake up and would introduce her to her birthday by gently tickling her belly. From past experience he knew that his delicate touch would lead to an hour or so of passion, as they both agreed that the best time for sex was immediately after sleeping together all night.

Next on the agenda he had planned was breakfast in bed and watching her open the card and present he had hidden away in the spare room. He realised with regret that most of his plans would now be put on hold.

He quietly let himself into the cottage and having forgotten about his need for food he made straight for bed. Shelley was fast asleep when he entered the bedroom but she stirred as Martin snuggled up close to her. An hour or so later they were both considering whether or not to change their minds about the best time to have sex but fell asleep before they had reached a decision.

Chapter Nine

The boy wasn't nearly as hot as he had been and he looked a bit better this morning. A quick glance in the mirror told Dan that the same couldn't be said about him. He had barely slept a wink and in some ways he was grateful for that because every time he did doze off it was only to be confronted by images of Susan rising from the rubble and coming in search of him.

She had metamorphosed into a monster with two heads and as only one of the throats had been strangled she was half dead and half alive. The body parts that were still living dragged along the rest and with a sneer and an evil wink she held out a decomposing hand.

He didn't even need to fall asleep to see this vision from hell – all it took was for him to close his eyes and with each blink she grew more grotesque as bits fell off her and Dan wished the boy would wake up and speak to him. He craved for the sound of a living human voice to blot out the whines and groans that his imagination was creating out of the mouth of the woman he had so recently murdered.

He stared hard at Jason and the boy seemed to sense his gaze and slowly opened his eyes. They still had the glazed-over appearance that had worried Dan last night but they were showing signs of recognition.

'Where's the lady gone?'

The words were spoken in a whisper and to Dan they brought the first glimmer of hope he had dared to have for hours. Perhaps Jason didn't remember what had happened to Susan. Perhaps he was already feverish when the fight had started and had no recollection of seeing the life squeezed out of her. Jumping at the possibility and turning away from the boy Dan picked up the neck of the gin bottle he had missed when clearing up earlier. If there was a chance that Jason did not remember what he had seen then nothing should be left around that could jog that little mind of his.

With an exaggerated shrug of the shoulders Dan replied. 'You know what women are like, don't you? Change their minds from one minute to the next. She wanted to come with us but now she's gone off to see her sister.'

Before he could say any more Jason interrupted. 'Where's my mum? I want my mum. You said we could play a little trick on her, that's all. Where is she and where's Ron Weasley?'

The questions were causing Jason some distress and Dan feared the boy would suffer some sort of relapse as his face was returning to the washed-out pallor of the previous evening. He handed Jason a glass of water but it was refused and then the same questions were asked but this time with the sound of terror in the little boy's voice.

Dan sat down beside Jason and tried to reassure him. 'I promise you that you'll see your mother later and be able to go home with her, but for now I need you to calm down or you'll make yourself ill again.'

'Is she coming to get me? Where are we? Does my mother know where I am? I can't hear any cars.' Jason hesitated and then continued. 'Is Megan here? I know you're Megan's granddad. Does she live here with you or with her mother?'

Realising that the only way to keep the boy calm was to give him answers Dan decided that honesty, partial at least, was the best policy. 'Yes, I'm Megan's granddad, but you're a big boy so you can just call me Dan.'

Jason seemed to like the idea of being able to call a grown-up by their first name and raised his head slightly.

Encouraged, Dan continued. 'What I said just now is true. You will be back at home with your mother later today but I can't answer for Ron Weasley – is he a friend of yours?'

The first faint vestige of a smile appeared on Jason's face and must have arrived with a small portion of courage. 'Don't you know nothing, Mr Dan? Ron Weasley is Harry Potter's friend – I've got them all.'

Like most other people on the planet Dan had heard of Harry Potter, but the antics of young wizards and schools of magic was not really something that grabbed him. Still if it was something that Jason liked to talk about he would become an instant fan.

'What do you mean you've got them all?' he encouraged.

'I've got all the Lego figures, of course, and lots of the places in Hogwarts, but I haven't put them together yet and my mother says it will take us for ever to do them all.'

The mention of his mother was a trigger and Jason's mouth turned down and any sign of a smile disappeared. 'I don't want to wait until later. I want my mother now. Has she gone back on the bus without me?'

Jason's young mind struggled to remember what had happened since the time Dan had approached him in St Fagans. He had been cross with his mother and had told her that he didn't want her stupid ham sandwiches, but she wouldn't take him to McDonalds. They often quarrelled about food, and according to all his schoolmates refusing to eat proper food was the best way in the world to wind up adults.

He hadn't noticed the man in the white jacket coming towards him but as soon as he had removed his hat and dark glasses Jason recognised Megan's granddad. He remembered the time Dan had spoken to him in the schoolyard and he knew that Megan loved her granddad so he had no reason to be afraid.

He thought it was a great idea when Dan suggested they play a trick on his mother and he had hopped into that big bag willingly. The drink Dan had given him was very sweet, and he'd drunk it all but remembered a somewhat bitter after-taste and had wished he had some bubble gum in his pocket.

At first being carried in the bag had been fun and he had giggled a lot but it was dark and cramped and then it had become even darker as Jason felt the bag being put down and heard a thump. He had no idea that the sound he had heard was the boot of a car being closed or that he and the bag were in that boot.

No matter how much he tried, Jason could not remember what had happened after that, being in a drug-induced sleep – and unbeknown to his kidnapper incubating a potentially serious viral infection.

He remembered seeing a woman when he woke up and she wasn't very nice. Everything else was a bit of a jumble in his head and he had felt so hot and stiff and sick. There was something else about the woman that he struggled to remember but nothing came back to him. All he knew was that he was glad she had gone but he didn't really know why.

The headache he had experienced earlier was coming back and he was starting to feel hot and shivery again. Not as bad as before but enough to make him want his mother. He wanted a cuddle more than anything in the world, and despite what Dan had said about him being a big boy he couldn't stop the hot tears running down his now very pale cheeks.

Dan once again offered him a drink of water but Jason didn't even want a sip. He put his head back on the pillow and his eyes rolled around in their sockets before he held his hands in front of them, protecting them from the shaft of watery sunlight that had emerged from behind a grey cloud.

His breathing had returned to the rapid shallow type and Dan didn't need anything as sophisticated as a thermometer to know that the boy's internal kettle was on the boil again.

He didn't want the boy's death on his conscience; after all, Jason was his son, even though he had only realised the fact quite recently. Perhaps it would help if his son knew that he was with his father, but Dan didn't think so. The Harry Potter-loving kid probably had fantasies about his father being a powerful wizard and the reality would be enough of a shock to finish him off.

What the hell was he going to do with the boy?

He tried the cold water treatment on his face and head in an attempt to get his brain into gear but the instant he closed his eyes Susan reared her now almost fully decomposed head and he thought he would vomit. He retched and gagged but he didn't vomit as there was nothing in his stomach to throw up, but he needed air and he opened the door.

Seconds later he slammed it closed, as the outside had thrown up a picture of Susan that was beyond description and now he was even seeing her with his eyes wide open.

'Christ,' he shouted. 'What a fucking mess! How the hell did I get here?' There was no one to answer his question or to complain about his bad language as Jason was, at best, fast asleep.

After several minutes Dan found that he could close his eyes without the previous horror, and this was such a relief that he found himself able to start thinking more rationally. The big question for him was whether he could risk Jason being found at all?

Their recent conversation suggested that the boy had no recollection of him killing Susan but was it something he would remember when he was better. Dan had no doubt that the child was sick, but how sick he didn't know. Should he be in hospital? Maybe he wouldn't recover unless he received treatment.

One thing was certain, which was that he could not be found at the caravan. He racked his brains to think of a place he could take the boy. It had to be somewhere where he wouldn't be found until after the ransom had been collected, and Dan was en route to Mexico. He had made up his mind that he would follow that part of the original plan and hoped that it wouldn't be an issue if he turned up at the airport without the other half of his booking.

It was going to be known that it was he who had taken Jason, and so he could see no reason not to take the boy back to his own place and leave him there.

He debated with himself the question of Susan. If the police were directed to his flat they would soon gather evidence that she was living there. What would that mean? They would look for her and not be able to find her, and would assume she was with him. He couldn't see any flaws in his thinking but had no illusion about his current ability to get things wrong.

If, in the fullness of time, Jason was able to remember more detail of his caravan experience it would be no problem, because Mexico would have swallowed Dan and would be helping him spend his money.

Once he had made up his mind on a course of action Dan wasted no time in carrying it out. He didn't bother clearing anything from the caravan, still believing that he would be untouchable if and when anything was ever discovered.

After turning the car around Dan carried Jason to it and put him and the blue blanket on the back seat. He was really shocked by the heat that was being transmitted from Jason and hoped to God that the boy wouldn't die in the car. Somehow he would get through the procedure of picking up the money and driving to Heathrow airport with the knowledge that he had left Jason alive and told his mother, as promised where to find her son.

He wasn't sure how he would cope if he had to leave a dead kid in his flat, and not just any dead kid – his son.

His hands shock slightly as he put the car into gear and drove away from the building site with no sign of Susan either alive and smiling or dead and decaying sitting in the passenger seat. What he did have was some excess baggage on the backseat and he was anxious to get it moved as quickly as possible as it was now ten minutes to one and at two o'clock he had an important pick up.

The petrol gauge shot up to record virtually a full tank, so that was one thing he had managed to get right and it would easily get him to Heathrow. After that he would just dump his car in one of the long-stay car parks – it was well past its sell-by-date anyway but thankfully had always been reliable.

He pulled up outside his home and looking outwardly in control he began turning the key in his front door.

'Where the hell have you been?' a woman's voice shouted from the corner of the building. 'I've been phoning Susan all morning, and non-stop in fact since I got a visit from the bloody police. Where's my sister?'

The voice could have been Susan's, and the sound of it

almost made him throw up, but that was where the similarities between the two women ended because Diane was a tall shapely blonde and would have been Dan's sister of choice had she been available.

He realised who was shouting at him and struggled to compose himself, even forcing a false smile. 'What's up? Susan's not with me – I haven't seen her for a couple of weeks. I think she's traded me in for a younger model. What's this about the police?'

'Wish to hell I knew,' replied Diane. 'They were waiting for me when I got home from work this morning and asking questions about where my car was yesterday. Can you believe that they're linking my car with the disappearance of that kid that has gone missing from Holly Road School? They're off their heads. I told them my car was outside my house all day yesterday and I was tucked up in my bed but they wouldn't listen and they've just taken my car in for what they call forensic examination. They are nuts.

'It wasn't until after they'd gone that I wondered if Susan had borrowed the car, she's done it before without asking me, but I can't see her visiting a museum, can you?'

'Not in a million years,' replied Dan.

'Then just as I was about to go to bed a couple of detectives turned up and starting asking questions. They seem to think someone took my car when I was asleep and used it to kidnap that kid who was on the news. They didn't say that in so many words but you'd have to be completely thick not to work it out.' Diane raised her eyebrows and to Dan's horror her face suddenly took on a family resemblance to the woman he had strangled – more than he had ever noticed before.

He steadied himself. 'Well, it couldn't have been your sister, because she hasn't got a licence – as I found out when she wanted to borrow my car.'

'No, but that hasn't stopped her in the past, and if someone did take my keys and drive my car it would have had to be someone who could get into my house. And apart from me Susan is the only one with a key to the front door. She could have taken the car for someone else and they said on the radio that the police are looking for a man in a white jacket.'

The conversation was getting too close to the truth for comfort and Dan was becoming increasingly aware that time was ticking by. He turned his back on Diane and turning the key started to open the door.

'How about a cup of coffee and a lift back home?' Diane suggested. 'Maybe my sister will have turned up by then and be able to tell us what's going on.'

Dan froze at the suggestion and the only thing he could think of was to be as rude as possible. 'One fucking sister messing up my life is enough, so thanks but no thanks. I don't want coffee or anything else from you,' he shouted, and walked into his home slamming the door behind him.

He left a very bemused and angry woman on the doorstep. She'd always thought that Dan had a soft spot for her and was completely thrown by his reaction to her suggestion of coffee. Diane wasn't used to men rejecting her offers and she shouted through his letter box.

'In your dreams, mate! It's Susan who likes to do it with old men, not me, and looking at you this morning old is the operative word. I wouldn't do it with you for a million pounds!'

She crashed the letter box down and walked away unaware of the irony of her final words. Dan watched her until she was out of sight and then checked that their altercation had not attracted the attention of any of his neighbours.

There was no one around, and before losing his nerve he lifted Jason out of the car, carried the boy through to his bedroom, and placed him on the bed. The extra time spent in the car wrapped in the blue woollen blanket had done nothing to help his fever, and as Dan placed him on the bed Jason again had the same sort of fit that Dan remembered his daughter having years ago.

Life was throwing stones at him and it didn't occur to him to consider he could simply be reaping what he had sown.

Jason's convulsion had not been as bad as he remembered Lucy having and she had recovered and so he assumed that

Jason would do the same. He had nothing to feel guilty about as far as the boy was concerned. He hadn't made Jason ill, it was just one of those things with kids, they were up one minute and down the next and before you knew it they had bounced back.

Dan didn't risk a backward glance towards the bed as he headed for his front door. Images of a deathly white boy oozing heat and fitting were already etched on his conscience but at least, in his mind, the boy was twitching so must still be alive.

Now if Dan closed his eyes for just a second there was a fight for his attention and he wondered how long it would be before Susan and Jason stopped competing to ensure he continued to live in hell.

He anxiously realised that it was twenty minutes to two. Twenty minutes to the time he had given Tina to deposit the money. That was fine, he would get there with minutes to spare but with no need to hang around and let the nerves kick in.

Driving to the spot he had previously planned to park his car he was relieved to see that there were spaces available. Good, perhaps his luck was changing and everything else would go off without a hitch. He looked around nervously and could see nothing more than people walking and shopping. No one paid any attention to him. To his untrained mind and eye it looked as if Tina had listened to his instructions and an excess of adrenaline pumped through his veins as for the second time in two days he lifted a heavy bag.

Chapter Ten

Even before 8 a.m., and in spite of the fact that it was Shelley's birthday, Martin was in Incident Room One and was working on the columns of information he had set up the previous afternoon.

The detective had his mind firmly focused on the task of finding a missing boy and bringing in a ruthless kidnapper.

The man still basked in the memory of the love that he and Shelley had shared prior to the five hours' dreamless sleep that he believed it had allowed him.

It was not unusual at the start of a case for Martin to go for nights without sleep as his brain refused to shut down and insisted on analysing the smallest of details whenever his head hit the pillow. At a critical point during his last case he had discovered that a walk to the beach in his hometown of Llantwit Major, followed by a couple of pints at one of the pubs had provided the off-switch his mind needed. Now he had discovered another and it gave him a warm glow just thinking about it.

Thank God Shelley was not one of these silly women who would worry about her birthday plans being set aside to accommodate his job. With any luck the day would bring about the result that was needed and their evening with four friends at Llanerch Vineyard would still go ahead. For the moment Martin couldn't second guess that possibility and his mind was now firmly on the job.

Matt arrived with two cups of coffee and for a second Martin wondered how much longer he would be in his current post and Matt in his. He had heard whispers that the changes in the current review of services were going to be more draconian than had first been anticipated, but he didn't know for certain which of several options would be chosen. He did know that in all the scenarios he had been consulted on Matt would come out very well and he wished he could tell him so, but for now he could only thank him for the coffee.

'I've spoken to Helen,' said Matt. 'There have been no further developments at the house overnight but we didn't really expect there to be. As far as the kidnapper is concerned Tina would only about now be getting his ransom note through the post and having to make arrangements to comply with the demands.

'The reality is that there are now very sophisticated gadgets available and amongst the notes that will be delivered from the bank later is the tiniest but most efficient tracking device that has ever been made. According to Charlie, Q from the Bond films would have waxed lyrical about the device. She couldn't resist telling me that her grandfather had been friends with Desmond Llewelyn, the actor who played Q, and apparently the man himself was completely clueless with technology.

'I've had an email from Charlie and from what I can gather she was here most of the night and Alex stayed to help her. They have done as requested and much more – so no surprise there.

'All the photographs have been studied and by picking out bits and pieces from a multitude of backgrounds she has come up with the image of a man wearing a white jacket and possibly white trousers and carrying a large bag. I really believe that this is our kidnapper.

'We've had two good responses from your television appeal and the elderly couple who were identified on one of the photographs are on their way here now. They didn't see the news item last night but they heard the appeal on the radio this morning and remember being passed by a cricketer so that could be our man.

'The other response was from the group of Welsh speakers that were identified by Tina. Apparently they left St Fagans not

126

long after she had seen them. They had been planning to stay the day but had received a phone call to say that a family member, a grandmother I think, had been involved in an accident. She had been taken to hospital in Wrexham and so that's where they went.

'It took them over four hours to get there and then they were waiting for news of their relative so they also missed the evening television appeal. I believe they were in the hospital most of the night and must at some point have become aware of what had happened at St Fagans. Charlie says they rang here about 2 a.m. and she was asked to speak to them.

'They are adamant that they saw no one even vaguely resembling a cricketer, but they do remember a little boy with ginger hair sitting on the grass and they remember passing a woman with blue streaks in her hair who was leaning against a wall and smoking.

'Their relative is apparently in a critical condition but the family has said that if they can be of any help in finding the kid they will drive here later today. Charlie doesn't think they'll be able to tell us anything else, but as she says in her email she's not a detective.'

'Maybe not,' replied Martin, 'but she's a bloody good member of the team.'

'She certainly is, guv, and I've saved the best of her lengthy email until last,' said Matt. 'Every CCTV camera at St Fagans has been scrutinised and the man in white was picked up going back to the car park. Unfortunately the tapes are unable to pick up which car he makes for but do give us the time he entered the car park. Apparently there was some confusion with the wrong tapes being brought to Goleudy and Charlie was too tired to wait any longer. She left instructions with her team to look at every car that left after the point the kidnapper was spotted and to involve uniformed officers to follow up registration numbers or whatever.

'When I arrived I was confronted by a very excited Sgt Evans who couldn't wait ...'

As if on cue Sgt Evans stuck his head through the door.

'I can go away if I'm interrupting anything important but I thought you would want an update.'

Matt grinned. 'That famous nose of yours is as always on the right scent as I was about to tell DCI Phelps what you told me earlier. Over to you.'

'It's been a long night and I was just going to sign off and get my head down for a few hours but there have been some further developments that you will need to know about. Has Matt told you about the follow-up on the cars?' Sgt Evans asked Martin.

'Start at the beginning, John,' suggested Martin.

'OK, well when we eventually got the right tapes it was a relief to find that not many cars left the museum in the time span we were checking. I thought the kidnapper would have driven off immediately but just to be sure we looked at cars over a thirty-minute slot. There were only four cars in the whole of that time – lots coming in, but only four leaving.

'Not surprising really as most people would be arriving with the intention of staying a few hours at least.' John was about to give examples of how his family often spent the whole day at the museum but a raised eyebrow from Martin kept him on track.

'It wasn't difficult to get names and addresses based on the registration numbers, and we had officers knocking on doors at some ungodly hours. Two of the owners were easily eliminated. One was a woman in her early sixties who works as an early morning cleaner at the museum. She gave a lift to two other cleaners and they could all vouch for her.

'Anyway, she obviously doesn't fit the description of the man we are looking for, and neither does the owner of the black Audi that was the second car to be knocked off our list. That owner is a man and he was at the museum to deliver some plans for moving an historic pub to St Fagans. All he did was hand over the plans at the main entrance and leave. We checked the CCTV and his car is seen coming in and gong out in the space of a couple of minutes. He wasn't carrying a bag and he certainly wouldn't have had the time to carry out a kidnapping.

128

'The other two cars weren't that simple to track down and we were told a Mr Ashton, who owned the dark blue Ford Fiesta, had obviously not registered a change of address with the DVLA. What used to be his home is now occupied by a woman who seemed to be entertaining more than her fair share of gentleman guests and was not best pleased to get a visit from the law.'

'Did you get a new address for Mr Ashton?' asked Martin.

'Not as yet but we've got your people working on it. Also the fourth car, a silver Ford Focus, is with Alex and his lot and I understand he is getting excited about some possibly significant findings. It belongs to a Diane Evans and she swears that her car has been nowhere near St Fagans so obviously that immediately raised our suspicions because we know beyond any shadow of doubt that it was there.

'According to her she drove her car home on Wednesday morning after a night shift at Asda's and left it outside her house when she went to bed. She was back in work when officers knocked at her door, and they caught up with her when she got back home this morning.

'She thinks we've all lost our marbles, although according to the team that took the vehicle in they would have lost more than their marbles if she had carried out what she planned to do to them if they took her car.'

'What does Alex think he's found?' asked Martin. 'Does he think this is the car that was used to take Jason?'

'Don't know, but you can bet he'll let you know as soon as he has anything solid to tell. I'm off home for a few hours now, but all my lot know what is expected of them and I'll see you later.' Sgt Evans walked off in the direction of the bed he was eagerly waiting to occupy and Martin and Matt discussed what had been said.

Martin gathered his thoughts. 'I don't think it was a woman who took Jason, but Diane Evans could be an accomplice. Perhaps she handed over the keys of her car to the kidnapper and he used it whilst she slept yesterday. We need to check that she actually did her Tuesday and Wednesday night shifts at the supermarket and if any of her neighbours noticed any movement of her car yesterday. I want to speak to her and I'd like to do that at her home rather than here, so let's go. I need to pick up a couple of things from my office so will you get her address and meet me in the car park in five? Get the keys for one of the squad cars.' suggested Martin. 'I want this to look seriously official and that could rattle the woman if she has played any part in this.'

'OK,' called back Matt as he crashed through the door and disappeared down the stairs.

'Diane Evans lives in Gower Road, Ely,' said Matt as he punched the postcode into the sat-nav of the marked police car. 'If my memory is correct it's just off Cowbridge Road West and shouldn't take us more than fifteen minutes tops.'

Martin nodded. 'I spoke to Alex before I left and he's been busy. He says that the boot of the Fiesta is a bit of a mess but there is no doubt that a space has recently been created in the middle to accommodate a large object. If the boy was taken in a bag it's unlikely they'll find any of his DNA but it depends on the circumstances of the kidnapping and whether or not the bag was open or closed.

'Anyway he had obtained a sample of Jason's hair from his bed at home and is testing every item in the boot for evidence of the boy having been there.'

Matt turned the car onto the A48 and then negotiated a few side roads before pulling up at Diane Evans' address.

There were a few people hanging around and a number of parked cars. The towing away of Diane's car earlier would have caused a bit of a stir but the excitement was visibly mounting as neighbours clocked the appearance of the police car.

The houses had small front gardens and Martin and Matt could feel half a dozen eyes focused on their every move as they knocked Diane's door.

It opened instantly as she too had seen the patrol car pull up. 'This is turning out to be one hell of a day. Who are you and what do you want now? An apology for taking my car without my permission would be too much to ask for I bet – so what now?'

With the required ceremony the detectives showed their warrant cards and made the necessary introductions.

'Bloody hell, I've moved up in the world. Christ knows what I'm supposed to have done to get the CID camping out on my doorstep, but you had better come in before that lot out there risk their necks trying to see what's going on.'

'Do you live here on your own?' asked Martin as they moved from the short passage into a much larger room than he had expected. It would have originally been two smallish rooms but the dividing wall had been knocked down to create a decent-sized lounge/diner with a door at the far end probably leading to the kitchen.

'What's that got to do with you?' Diane said, turning to stand with her arms folded and a decidedly unwelcoming attitude. She did not sit down or offer the men a seat, and Martin could see that getting information from her would be tantamount to getting blood from a stone.

He came directly to the point. 'Our only real interest at the moment is in your car, and you, as the owner, obviously have access to the vehicle. If there are other people living here then they too may be able to use your keys and that's what we are trying to establish.

'You know from the officers who called previously that your car was seen at St Fagans museum yesterday morning and you seemed to think that was unlikely.'

'Not unlikely, bloody impossible,' began Diane but Martin stopped her.

'There is no point in you telling us that it was impossible because we have clear and indisputable evidence that your car was seen leaving the museum, and if you are saying that you weren't driving it we need to find out who was. It's unlikely that it was stolen as in my experience car thieves rarely take a car back to where they found it so maybe someone you know used your car. That's why I repeat the question – do you live here on your own?'

'I still say it's bloody impossible so maybe your cameras got

131

it wrong. I work six nights a week and when I get home I'm knackered. I usually park outside and just chuck my keys on the table and go straight to bed, and then I'm out of it until the middle of the afternoon.' Diane pointed to where her keys were on the corner of the glass-topped dining table. 'That's where I would have left my bloody keys yesterday when I went to bed and that's where they were when I woke up.'

Martin briefly wondered how many of Diane's 'bloody' adjectives would normally be of the effing variety, as she was, by her standards, on her best behaviour, but this was soon to change.

Martin wasn't sure if she had really only just thought of the possibility or had just then decided to share her thoughts. 'My fucking sister has taken my keys before, and if she's done it again I'll strangle the cow.'

Another thought she had was obviously more amusing and she shared it. 'The very idea of my sister paying a visit to a museum or anywhere like that is just too bloody funny. She only needs two things to improve her body and mind, namely sex and bingo. Add to that the very thought of her being in the land of the living before lunchtime and you're in fantasy land. I still say you lot have cocked it up and you've got the wrong car.'

Martin ignored Diane's assassination of sister's character and went back to what the woman had said about her sister having previously borrowed the car, presumably without permission.

'Too bloody true it was without my permission,' shouted Diane. 'She's taken her test a couple of times but never passed, and once when she took the car I ended up with three points on my licence. The stupid cow was doing over the odds in a thirty-limit area where everyone knows the speed cameras are always working. I was tempted to just drop her in the shit, but she had just had a decent win on the bingo and £500 for three points didn't seem like a bad deal so I went along with it.'

Matt shook his head, but they had other things to think about than her messing with the traffic laws and he pushed her on the possibility of her sister taking the car again yesterday.

Diane could see that the detectives were hell-bent on getting to the bottom of the car mystery and she sat at the kitchen table and indicated with her eyes two chairs for their use. 'When I went to bed I left the keys where you see them now, and as far as I know they hadn't moved but, Christ, I didn't look that closely. I gave the blokes who came for the car the spare keys because that set there has my house keys and the keys to the shed and I need those.'

Diane had still not answered Martin's question about who, if anyone, lived in the house with her so he tried another approach. 'Where is your sister now? Does she normally live here with you?'

'We've both lived here since we were kids. This was our parents' house but Mam died when I was seventeen and Susan just fifteen. Our father used to bring a lot of different women back here but as she got older Susan became more of a handful and used to cause some violent rows. Dad couldn't stand it any more so he buggered off with one of the women and we haven't seen him from that day to this.

'Susan's got a room upstairs but she hasn't been around much for a couple of weeks. That usually means she's shacked up with someone and she tends to stay with whoever is flavour of the month until the fun or the money runs out and then she's back here to sponge off me.' Diane shrugged her shoulders and stood up. 'Look, I'm working tonight and want to get some sleep so if you've finished I'm off to bed.'

Martin stood up and asked one final question. 'I don't suppose you know who your sister is with at the moment, do you?'

'Haven't got a bloody clue, she'll turn up sometime as per usual but even then she won't tell me where she's been.' Diane walked into the kitchen and switched on the kettle and the two men made their way to the door and said nothing until they were back in the squad car.

'Not much sisterly love to note there,' remarked Matt. 'Doesn't take us any further forward either, does it?'

'Not really,' agreed Martin. 'We need to get officers knocking on doors in this street to see if anyone noticed the car being moved yesterday, and more importantly if they saw who moved it.'

Before he re-started the car Matt made a phone call to get the house-to-house enquiries moving and Martin looked around at the number of people who were either openly or covertly watching the police car. If just a few of those who were now taking an interest had been just as nosey yesterday then they might get something but he knew from past experience that neighbours had selective memories when it came to giving information to the police.

'We might as well go straight to the Barnes' house and check that everything is in place for this afternoon. Unless Alex comes up with a miracle I can't see us discovering the whereabouts of Jason prior to the handover of the money, and after that we're at the mercy of the kidnapper regarding the boy's release.'

As Matt pulled away his phone rang and Martin picked it up.

The call was to report some progress regarding the route taken by Diane Evans' car when it had left St Fagans and as suspected it could be followed by a series of cameras back to the area of her home. A more significant piece of news was the fact that at some point the car had actually been the subject of attention from the traffic police. The car had been parked in a lay-by and the driver had pulled out virtually in the path of a police patrol vehicle. The two officers were just about to chastise the driver for driving without due care and attention when they decided that some young idiots driving recklessly were more deserving of their intervention.

Martin took a deep breath as he listened to the caller. If, as they now believed, Jason was being transported in that car those officers had come within a hair's breadth of discovering him. He always cursed the lunatics that drove like maniacs but now he wished them all in hell for having caused the diversion that had undoubtedly helped the kidnapper.

What was the car doing parked in a lay-by anyway? Martin

listened intently to the rest of the call and then relayed the information to Matt.

'At least the officers who saw the car are able to tell us that there was only one person in the vehicle and that person was a man. They are currently in Goleudy attempting to provide an image of the man but the fact that he has greying auburn hair fits in with it being Jason's father. My money is now definitely there.

'Let's change our plans and head back to Goleudy. I want to speak to those officers and chase up an address for Dan Painter.'

Diane had not gone straight to bed as she had said but waited impatiently for the two detectives to drive away before putting on her coat and picking up her keys. She had not been completely honest with her CID visitors and although there was little love lost between her and her sister she was after all family. Diane knew exactly who her sister was seeing and it would take her less than ten minutes to walk to his house. She would warn her sister that the police were looking for her but that would be it – after that she could go to hell. She could hardly know that her sister was possibly already there.

Chapter Eleven

Diane was wide awake and dismissed any thoughts of returning home and getting any sleep today. Her blood was still boiling as she headed off from Dan's home. All she had asked for was a coffee and a lift back home but he had assumed she wanted him. She thought back to the strange look he had given her before he literally slammed the door in her face, and recalled a mixture of fear and hatred in his eyes. He had looked a bit like an animal caught in a trap and his reactions had been way out of proportion to anything she had said.

Her instinctive reaction was to hurl abuse back at him and now she began to wonder if Dan and her sister had parted company following some sort of row. Susan was prone to fits of temper if she didn't get her own way, and if Dan had been the victim of one of those episodes perhaps he was getting some of his own back by being offensive to her sister.

No, it was more than that, and now she couldn't get the look on his face and the haunted expression in his eyes out of her mind. She slowed down her walking pace and her imagination went into overdrive. It was possibly the effects of lack of sleep, a visit from the police and the taking away of her car, a visit from real-life detectives, and a slanging match with Dan. Whatever it was she suddenly got the idea that all was not well with her sister and decided to risk some more abuse and go back and ask him if he knew where Susan had gone.

She walked more slowly on the way back and tossed over in her mind the questions she wanted answered. When was the last time he was with Susan, and did she have any plans when he had last seen her? Diane had no way of knowing the extreme reaction that such questions could produce in Dan.

Her thoughts came to an abrupt end as she turned the corner into Dan's street and saw him leaving his home. For some reason she couldn't explain to herself, instead of rushing towards him she moved into the side of some garden hedges and watched him without his seeing her.

She giggled at her own actions and was feeling light-headed from the lack of sleep, but couldn't shake off a strange feeling of unease as she saw Dan several times check that his front door was locked and look around anxiously before getting into his car. His behaviour didn't seem quite right to her and her stomach was churning over as she watched him drive off slowly. She headed towards the door he had just locked.

As far as she knew this was where her sister had been living and she could still be inside. It had suddenly occurred to Diane that if Susan had taken her car yesterday then she wouldn't want to be questioned about it. Not by her sister and certainly not by the police. Diane had set out from home with the intention of warning Susan that the police were asking questions, but Dan's behaviour had put some new thoughts in her mind.

The pair of them could have used her car, but what for?

The police had said her car had been at St Fagans and that was the place where that little boy had disappeared from. Nothing in her brain could work out any connections between Susan, Dan, and a kidnapped boy, but now she was determined to make her sister answer some questions.

As she approached the door she was becoming more and more certain that Susan was in the house and two possibilities entered her sleep-deprived mind that was probably well into the stage of malfunction. Either Susan had taken the car and was curled up in Dan's bed, hiding from its owner, or Dan had made her take it for some illegal purpose and they had subsequently fallen out.

Diane pictured her sister tied to the bed and in fear of her life, but it was not a well-formed idea and she made herself smile as she thought that it would take a very large roll of duct tape to strap up Susan's mouth. Nothing like that would be on the cards – but nevertheless there was an element of serious concern amongst Diane's thoughts.

She pulled herself together and hammered on the door causing a small shower of brittle paint to fall to the floor. The door was painted dark brown, but the latest coat was years old and was peeling off to reveal layers of red and blue that were trying to make a comeback. Diane hadn't noticed how shabby the place was until now, and she stopped knocking and looked through the letterbox.

When she had shouted at Dan she had been hopping mad and hadn't noticed that although the atmosphere inside was not fresh, there was something she instantly recognised. It was Susan's perfume, and if her sister wasn't there now she had been there much more recently than the couple of weeks Dan had suggested.

For her sixteenth birthday Susan had been given a bottle of Christian Dior's Poison and from that day it had been the only perfume she ever used. Even when she was skint she always found some poor sucker to buy it for her, and it always took a couple of days for the scent to leave wherever Susan had been.

Diane was now absolutely convinced that Susan was in the house, and banged the letterbox down hard several times. She then knelt down to get a better look inside, listening for any sound, but there was nothing.

She was unaware that the only person inside who could have made a sound was Jason but there was no sign of life from him.

Undeterred she thumped on the window and then went back to clashing metal against metal and shouting through the letterbox. 'I know you're in there, Susan, and I know you took my car so open the door. I'm going nowhere until you do so just open the fucking door.'

There was still no response from Dan's house but two of Dan's neighbours flung open their doors and asked what the hell was going on.

Diane instantly recognised one of the men who also worked the night shift at Asda and had probably been asleep. Before he

139

could say anything Diane greeted him and apologised. 'Hi Mark, I didn't know you lived next to Dan, and look, I'm sorry if I've woken you, but I'm looking for my sister.'

Because he knew her, Mark Davies was prepared to listen, but the other neighbour was far less accommodating. 'You've been hammering and shouting for ten minutes now and if you don't shut up I'll come out there and shut you up.' He had partially closed his own front door and Diane could see that he was dressed in just a grubby string vest and a matching pair of Y-fronts. Although his words were threatening, his appearance was laughable, and realising this he went back inside and slammed his door.

Mark, who wore a pair of crumpled black jogging bottoms, was suddenly aware of his own lack of style and cursed the fact that Diane had caught him off-guard because he had been trying to get up the nerve to ask her out. Still, he thought, she was obviously in some sort of trouble and this could be a God-sent opportunity for him.

'What are you doing here? Did you say you're looking for your sister? Why don't I make you a cup of coffee and you can tell me what's up.'

Diane didn't really fancy sharing a coffee with someone she wouldn't normally give a second glance, but she suddenly felt very tired and sitting down seemed like a very good idea. 'OK,' she nodded and followed Mark into his house.

To call the properties 'houses' was pushing it a bit, she thought. It was more as if one building had been divided into four. Dan and Mark's front doors were set in the middle and they occupied equal halves of the ground-floor space. At the back of the property were stone steps leading to two similarly placed front doors belonging to the people who lived on the first floor. There were ten such structures, making it possible to house forty single tenants or couples and Diane remembered that the development had been created to help first-time buyers get a foot on the property ladder, but that hadn't worked and now the buildings were used for social housing.

Mark lived alone and Diane was surprised to see how neat

and tidy everything was as she plonked herself on a two-seater canvas sofa and closed her eyes. 'Better make my coffee extra strong,' she called out to Mark. 'Lack of sleep is catching up with me fast and I just need enough of a boost to get me home and then I can crash out for a few hours. It looks as if I've been wasting my time here anyway.'

She looked up as Mark put a mug of coffee on the small wooden table and even though she worked with the man she noticed him for the first time. She had always thought he was just a kid but actually he wasn't as young as she had always imagined, and was probably only a couple of years younger than her. He was one of those people whose school photos and retirement photos would show very little changes and he had probably never even changed his hairstyle.

He smiled at her and she realised that it was his silly lop-sided grin that made him look like a big kid, but through her droopy eyelids she saw a very likeable face and smiled back.

'I thought that someone was being murdered when I heard all the banging and shouting. What's going on? Are you in some sort of trouble?'

'Not me,' replied Diane. 'It's my sister who appears to have landed herself in some sort of mess, and I wanted to warn her that the police are looking for her.'

Diane went on to explain about her car and the visits she had received from the police, and even as she told the tale it sounded more and more bizarre.

'I went to work, I came home, I went to bed, and they seem to think that when I was sleeping my car was taken and driven to St Fagans. You don't need to be the sharpest knife in the drawer to know they're trying to link my car with this kid that's been snatched but it's too bloody ridiculous for words.

'I came around earlier to warn my sister to get her act together but Dan told me he hasn't seen her for a couple of weeks, but I know that's not right.'

Before Diane even had the chance to explain about the perfume Mark interrupted. 'It's not right, I know that for sure. It's a big fat lie. I saw the two of them together yesterday

141

morning.'

Mark saw that he had captured Diane's interest and took the opportunity of sitting next to her on the sofa and finished off his coffee before continuing. 'Yes, it was definitely yesterday morning, about ten thirty because I didn't come home straight from work and Dan's car was parked outside his front door when I did get back.

'I heard another car pull up and I didn't take much notice but I know it only stopped for a couple of minutes as I heard it drive off again. Normally I'm out of it by nine o'clock if I've done a night shift, but I was late going to bed and just couldn't get off to sleep. I was eating toast and walking around when I saw Dan walking past my window. He is not in the habit of walking anywhere and I watched him going up to his front door.

'He didn't even go inside because your sister must have also been looking out for him and she opened the door before he got there. I thought they must be going away because she had a holdall and a small case and went to put them in the boot but he shouted something at her and then took the bags from her and flung them onto the back seat.'

'They seemed in an almighty rush to get away somewhere – maybe they had a plane or a train to catch?'

Diane interrupted. 'Well he hasn't gone anywhere with Susan, has he? I spoke to him earlier and he looked like death warmed up and then when I decided to come back and have a go at him I saw him drive off – and he was on his own.'

'Well, all I know is that I saw your sister and Dan Painter together yesterday morning, so he's lying if he told you he hasn't seen her for weeks. But why would he do that?' Mark offered Diane another cup of coffee but she refused.

'I need to get to the bottom of this,' she said. 'I could quite clearly smell my sister's perfume when I bent down to shout through the letterbox. That pair are up to something and normally I'd just let them get on with it but if my car has been involved in something they've schemed up then I'm going to make it my business to find out what it is.'

Suddenly Diane looked more worried than annoyed and she shook her head. 'Apart from that, she is my sister and even if most of the time she's a total pain in the arse I wouldn't want anything bad to happen to her. I keep getting this nagging feeling that she's next door and just isn't answering me. There was something when I listened through the letterbox. Not that I could really hear anything – it was more just a feeling that someone was in there.'

Mark hesitated and then came out with a suggestion. 'The layout of next door is a mirror image of this, so looking through the letterbox you can see most of the living space. There's no way you can see into the bathroom but you can see through the bedroom window from the back of the building if you lean over the wall between my place and Dan's.'

It occurred to Mark that this knowledge could sound a bit kinky so he quickly explained. 'It was Dan Painter's daughter who was originally allocated next door, and I think her name is still on the rent book, but she moved in with her boyfriend and Dan took the opportunity of getting a place to himself. Anyway, when the daughter lived there her kids were always sticking their heads over the wall and looking into my bedroom, so I know it can be done.'

'If she's in there she'll probably have drawn the curtains,' suggested Diane. 'Still, it's worth a try, and at least we know that he isn't at home.'

Mark's day was turning out to be very exciting by his standards, and he opened the back door that led to a small enclosed garden. It didn't run the whole width of the house, as one-third was made into the path leading to the steps to the upstairs properties. Next door was a mirror image and there was a wall about four feet high dividing the two gardens.

Diane was five feet six inches tall and she was starting to feel a bit stupid. 'I can't bloody well climb up there!' she said. 'Anyway, what if someone sees me?'

'Don't worry about that,' Mark replied. 'Most of the time people around here just mind their own business, and if you want I can climb onto the wall and take a look.'

'No, I really want to see for myself – that's the only way I'll be satisfied.'

'I can give you a leg-up,' suggested Mark.

Even though Diane was beginning to like her new friend, the idea of him fondling her bum was not yet on her agenda and she suggested he fetch one of his kitchen chairs for her to stand on.

With the help of the chair she easily managed to get herself into a position on the wall where she could see into Dan Painter's bedroom, but there was no sign of life. 'All I can see is a small bundle on the bed covered in a blue blanket, but even if my sister tried to hide she would never get herself curled up that small.'

Curiosity had got the better of him and Mark climbed onto the wall and jumped down into his neighbour's garden. Throwing caution to the wind he pressed his face against the window and was able to see every corner of the room, confirming what Diane had thought. 'Your sister definitely isn't in there, but what you said was a bundle on the bed isn't just a pile of clothes – it's a kid.'

'A kid! Are you sure? Knock the window. Go on Mark, bang on the window. What's a kid doing in Dan Painter's bedroom?'

To begin with Mark tapped gently on the window. He had younger brothers and sisters and he knew how easy it was to scare kids. Unable to contain herself Diane had now managed to scramble down the wall and stood next to Mark. The child's face wasn't visible to them, but a small white freckled arm was lying still on top of the blue blanket.

Diane banged the window much harder and called out. 'Hello there, are you alright? Are you there on your own? Don't be frightened, we only want to help.'

She squashed her face hard against the glass looking for some sort of response from the child but there was nothing. No sign of movement, and now she stared really hard to see if there were any signs of life.

Although she was very tired Diane had never been more wide awake in her life and the level of adrenaline that was charging through her was more effective than a dozen shots of espresso. She stared in disbelief at Mark. 'I think the kid's dead – I really think the kid's dead. What the hell is going on here? If Susan's mixed up with this I'll kill her myself. What the bloody hell do we do now?'

Mark pressed his own face next to Diane and followed her line of vision to the small limb that lay lifeless and he agreed. He didn't feel pumped up by nature's 'fight or flight' mechanism – he just felt sick. A few minutes ago he had been thinking how exciting today was but that feeling had now turned to one of absolute terror. Climbing over the wall had been easy but now his knees seemed to have turned to jelly and getting back was more difficult.

It wasn't until he was back in his own garden that he realised that Diane was still next door and without a chair to help her get up the wall. He stood on the chair himself and leaned back over so that she could grab hold of his arms and he could lift her up. In a mixture of panic and fear, she climbed over the top but they both lost their balance and ended up falling off the chair and crashing into Mark's rubbish bin.

They both swore and Diane quickly got to her feet, but Mark had twisted his ankle badly and was in considerable pain when he attempted to walk on it, so Diane helped him hobble back to the kitchen.

'We need to phone for an ambulance for that kid,' said Mark looking around for his mobile phone.

'I think he's past needing an ambulance,' Diane said. 'What we should do is ring the police, but what in the name of hell do we tell them? We climbed over your neighbour's wall looking for my sister and instead found a dead child? They already think Susan is in some way involved with that kid that's gone missing from St Fagans.' As soon as she spoke the words Diane froze and from his expression it was obvious that Mark had read her mind.

'Jesus Christ. Oh bloody Jesus Christ, it's him isn't it? It's the boy that went missing yesterday,' said Mark as he punched 999 into his phone.

When asked what service he required Mark just blurted out

that he had found the kid that the police were looking for and was instantly transferred to Martin's team in Goleudy. Even whilst he was still on the phone giving the address he could hear voices in the background ordering immediate police and medical response. He reluctantly gave his own name and contact details. 'I live in the house next door,' he told the officer. 'You won't need an ambulance though, the kid's had it – he's dead.'

It was the news that the team had been dreading and Martin and Matt rushed to the car park and within minutes they were following the patrol car driven by Tom Coleman, one of the unit's designated drivers, with flashing blue lights and sirens wailing at top volume. Sergeant Evans and two of his officers were in the leading car and a further three officers in the car behind.

The traffic was heavy but the trained skills of PC Coleman ensured that ordinary motorists were soon made aware of his need to overtake and without exception they moved to accommodate the police convoy.

Having made the phone call and waiting for the consequences Mark and Diane stood on the doorstep and waited. Diane's thoughts were not so much on wondering about the boy but pondering on her sister's involvement in this drama. Surely to God she hadn't got herself mixed up with kidnapping and ransom. The ransom part would fit because sadly she reflected that there was little Susan wouldn't do to get her hands on ready cash. She loved money and all her life had been attracted to any low life that could provide her with the means to live without having to work for it.

The kidnapping was a different story. Diane knew that her sister and kids didn't mix well and Susan had been on the pill since she was fifteen. Kids in her view were a pain in the arse and there was no way she was going to have such a millstone around her neck. She didn't have a maternal bone in her body, and if she had been involved in the kidnapping then there was little wonder that the boy had ended up dead.

But where was she? It was obvious that she and Dan Painter

must have been involved, but where were they now? Diane had heard on the news that there was a ransom involved and although this information had been leaked to the press, it hadn't been denied. Had Dan and her sister picked up the ransom and got away with it? Had they killed the boy and left his body on the bed? The thought made her feel physically sick and she leant against Mark who, in spite of the circumstances, didn't miss the opportunity of holding her close.

The screaming siren of an emergency response unit heralded the first vehicle to arrive and even before it had come to a stop the paramedic had opened one of the doors and was jumping out.

'Where's the lad?' he shouted.

Mark stepped forward and pointed to Dan's door. 'He's in there but we don't have a key – we just saw him through the back window. He's on the bed.'

The ambulance crew were in a quandary and the three members of the team considered their options. They had no authority to go breaking down doors, but if there was a little boy in there with even the faintest chance of benefitting from their expertise then they had to do something.

If they had been praying for divine intervention their prayers were answered and the police sirens could be heard just seconds ahead of their arrival. Sgt Evans didn't need to be appraised of the situation, as years of experience told him that the medical team needed help to get through that door, and he signalled to two of his officers who within seconds had splintered the lock.

The officers went in first to ensure the safety of the paramedics and they were the first to call out the good news.

'The boy's alive! He's just about alive but he's very sick.' As Philip, the senior paramedic spoke his colleagues were working on their patient and in no time at all the boy was receiving oxygen and intravenous fluids.

'He's unconscious and needs expert paediatric attention, and I don't know if he'll survive the journey to the hospital,' Philip explained to Martin. 'We'll get him there as quickly as we can. What's his name?'

Martin looked at the deathly white body of the seven-year-old child as the paramedics stretchered him past.

'He's Jason Barnes,' answered Martin. 'I'll get on to his mother straight away – she's desperate to know where he is. I just hope she can reach him before he gives up on us. God only knows what trauma this poor kid has endured.'

Even before the ambulance siren had faded Matt had been on the phone to DC Cook-Watts and given her the news. She was with Tina and they would now be on their way to the hospital. All everyone could do was pray that she would see her son whilst he was still alive.

A familiar white van pulled up and Alex and the SOC team were briefed. 'It's brilliant that the boy is alive,' he said. 'The news from the ransom team is that the kidnapper has been picked up. It was done according to your instructions as soon as they got your call that the boy had been found. There was always the possibility that the boy wouldn't be Jason but from the description given by the 999 caller it was worth the risk.'

Matt was taking another call and confirmed to Martin that the man picked up and in possession of the ransom money was indeed Dan Painter. Martin knew from Tina's confession that Dan was Jason's father and there were so many questions he wanted to ask him. How long had he known about his son? How could he just leave the boy like that, possibly not even knowing if he was dead or alive? Martin was impatient to interview this evil bastard and spoke to Alex.

'There's nothing I can do here so it's all yours and it would be good to know who has been in and out of this place recently. To begin with, the car he used has been traced to a Diane Evans and having interviewed her I am convinced that she wasn't involved. It's her sister Susan that I would like to speak to as I'm positive that Painter didn't do this on his own. I'm going to have a quick word with the neighbour who made the emergency call and then I'm going to see what Painter has to say for himself.'

A few minutes later Martin and Matt were surprised by one of the people who was waiting for them next door. When they had left Diane Evans earlier she had expressed an overwhelming desire to get some sleep and now Martin was beginning to doubt what he had just said to Alex. It couldn't just be a coincidence that she was now sitting in the house next to where the boy had been found – she had to be involved in some way.

Before he had time to ask what the hell she was doing there Diane got a whole load of stuff off her chest.

'Hello again, Chief Inspector,' she began. 'I expect you're wondering what I'm doing here and so it's best that I tell you everything.' She went on to explain how she had initially just set out to warn her sister that the police needed her to explain about the car.

'I knew as soon as you told me that the car had been seen at St Fagans that Susan must have taken it. Honest to God, I still can't believe that she had anything to do with snatching the boy – she must have just got my keys for Dan Painter to use. Perhaps I shouldn't have come to warn her but she is my sister and you'd do the same for your sister, wouldn't you?'

Martin said nothing and Diane rambled on with the rest of her account of events up to the point where Mark had dialled 999.

Everything she said was too unbelievable not to be true and Matt even had to hide a grin as he imagined Diane Evans and Mark Davies falling into a heap as they returned from their over-the-wall escapade. Mark had his foot up on a chair and his ankle was very swollen and all he did was nod from time to time as Diane related the details of their activities.

When she had finished Martin asked if she had any idea where her sister was now. 'With him, I expect, but what I told you this morning is the truth, I haven't seen her lately.'

Mark interrupted. 'I have, I saw her yesterday morning. She was next door waiting for Dan who had been somewhere on foot – not like him at all, he drives everywhere. Anyway, I saw them both get into Dan's car and drive off and I got the feeling they were off on holiday, but according to Diane he was there earlier today without her.'

Patiently Martin got all the details of the comings and goings next door and pieced them together in his own mind. He had some ideas about what could have happened but he had no ideas regarding where Susan could be now.

Diane asked a question. 'Do you think my sister and Dan Painter did the kidnapping, and have they had the ransom money?'

Martin could see no reason for not telling Diane the latest. 'Dan Painter did collect the ransom money but it was just before we got your call that a boy matching Jason's description had been found. Consequently we picked Painter up and he's been arrested.'

'What about my sister?' Diane asked. 'Was Susan with him, and has she been arrested too?'

'No, your sister has not been arrested and as far as I am aware she has not been identified on any of the surveillance cameras that we put in place around the area where the ransom money was left.' Martin looked enquiringly at Matt who confirmed his understanding.

'So maybe my sister isn't involved after all,' Diane said hopefully.

'It's unlikely that she had no involvement. At the very least it looks as if she gave your car keys to Dan Painter to avoid him using his own for the actual act of snatching Jason. That definitely muddied the waters from our point of view, and although it was easy to trace the car to you we had no way of making a connection between your sister and Painter. Now if you had told us earlier that they were an item we could have found the boy a couple of hours ago.'

Diane avoided looking at Martin when he spoke as his words only echoed her own thoughts. She had already worked out what he was saying and felt guilty that her actions may have resulted in a delay in getting the boy to hospital. But at the time she hadn't felt able to just drop her sister in it with the police, and anyway she wasn't absolutely certain that Susan was still with Dan.

She shuffled uncomfortably in her chair and looked near to

tears and it was Mark who came to her rescue.

'Look, mate, there's no need to give her a hard time – she was only looking out for her sister and I would have done the same. Even if the police had come here earlier they would have just knocked the door and gone away again when they got no reply. It was Diane who thought there was something wrong next door and persuaded me to get over the wall. She deserves some credit for that.'

Mark got a feeble smile of gratitude from Diane and Martin nodded. 'That's as maybe, but are there any other things regarding your sister that you could share now. I'm thinking of possible friends she may be with or places she is likely to visit – anything at all? Mark has already told us that Dan Painter and your sister were together yesterday and I will be interviewing him shortly so perhaps I'll get something from him.'

Diane shook her head. 'If there was anything, believe me I would tell you, but my sister is her own person and most of the time I have no idea where she is or who she's with. I don't even like her particularly, but at the end of the day she is my sister and family-wise she's all I have. If she has had anything to do with the kidnapping of that little boy she deserves to be locked up. I just hope she raises her ugly head soon and tells us what the hell has been going on.'

Martin could see that Diane was fighting back tears and remembered from the interview earlier that she probably hadn't slept for about twenty-four hours. 'I would suggest you try to get some sleep, especially if you have to work tonight, but I also suggest that Mark gets that ankle looked at and if it helps one of our cars will take you to the hospital.'

Martin didn't wait for a reply but nodded to one of the uniformed officers as he left. There was nothing more to do here and he and Matt had an appointment with a certain Mr Dan Painter. At the moment the man faced a charge of kidnapping but if the boy died there may be a very different set of charges to answer.

Chapter Twelve

With the exception of a couple of ten-minute breaks Martin and Matt had spent three hours interviewing Dan Painter, who had not held back on anything regarding the kidnapping. He had confirmed that he was likely to be Jason's father although it was not something he had known about until recently and it had never been confirmed. For the avoidance of doubt he had shown the detectives the photograph he had taken to carrying in his wallet. It was the one of him as a small boy, and apart from the very different backgrounds it was just like looking at the most recent photograph of Jason.

The likeness was uncanny but that was where the father-son connection started and finished. There was certainly no paternal love in evidence and Martin was sure that at this moment in time Dan deeply regretted his few minutes of pleasure with Jason's mother. On the other hand he was equally sure that if things had gone according to plan Dan Painter would have been raising a glass to that coupling from some distant beach in southern Mexico.

Painter had been apprehended within minutes of picking up the ransom money and then formally arrested and taken into custody. Examination of the surrounding CCTV footage soon tracked him back to his car and then that too was impounded. Alex Griffiths and his team had since crawled all over the vehicle and there was plenty of evidence to show that at some point Jason had been transported in the boot.

The blue blanket that Jason had been found partially wrapped in on Dan Painter's bed bore traces of having been in the boot, but more convincingly there were a few strands of that ginger hair that barely needed forensic investigation – they were obviously from the head of a certain seven-year-old boy.

During one of the breaks from questioning Matt had received an update from Helen Cook-Watts and the news was much better than they had dared hope for. 'It was a bit like a miracle,' she told Matt.

'When we got to the Paediatric Intensive Care Unit the doctors were standing around shaking their heads and the prognosis for Jason seemed dire. He was already on a ventilator because even the effort of breathing was too much for his small, crumpled body and two separate infusions seemed to be pumping fluids in at the rate of knots.

'Tina went straight over to her son and has not let go of his hand for one second. It's, by a factor of ten, the longest I have ever seen her go without lighting up a cigarette but she seems to be working some sort of magic on Jason. According to the senior registrar the boy's condition improved from the moment his mother touched him and he's getting stronger by the minute. I must admit I queried the science of such a possibility, but the doctors put me firmly in my place and I was told that there is more to medicine than what is contained within medical textbooks.

'Anyway, Tina's love and the doctor's skills appear to be bringing Jason back to us, although the next twenty-four hours will still be critical. I'll keep you posted.'

Matt relayed the positive news to Martin and the two men returned for the final session with Dan Painter and his duly appointed legal aid solicitor. To his credit, albeit for the first time since his arrest, Painter enquired about Jason, but Martin did not feel inclined to salve any part of the kidnapper's conscience and didn't respond to the question.

Martin was ready to believe the account given by Painter regarding the planning and execution of the kidnapping. No matter how many times he was asked to go over the preliminary stuff there was never any deviation. Painter emphasised how much he wished he had never told Susan Evans about being Jason's father, and the interview tapes recorded how Susan had begged him to snatch the boy and demand some money.

According to Painter's version of events she got him to believe that it was no more than he deserved because Tina Barnes should never have kept him in the dark about his son. Over and over Painter insisted that there was never any intention to harm the boy and he would have followed through on his promise to tell Tina where to find her son as soon as they were on the plane.

'The boy getting sick was nothing to do with me,' he protested. 'I remember my own kids spiking a temperature and looking very poorly and then the next day they were up to all sorts of mischief. It's what kids do, and it's the same with Jason, isn't it?'

If Painter was fishing for information about the boy his luck was out and all he got was a tongue-lashing from Matt. 'How would you know if it's the same with Jason? You left him for dead and how you left him is how we found him, so that's something else you have to answer for.'

Although Dan was able to stick to what had actually happened prior to the kidnapping, his recollection of events following the act was a different kettle of fish and changed with each telling. At first it was that he and Susan had fallen out and she had left him to sort the boy out on his own. Dan said that they had taken Jason straight to his house and that's when he and Susan had quarrelled.

'Do you expect us to believe that she would walk out on you when the most difficult phase of the operation was complete and you had two tickets for Cancun tucked under your dashboard? You and Susan Evans were seen driving from your home yesterday, just after Jason was snatched, and she wasn't with you when you returned this morning. Was Jason in the boot of your car when you both drove off, or had you already left him where we found him?

'According to an eye-witness you and she were the best of friends when you left here, so when did this so called quarrel happen? When and where did you and Susan Evans part company and where is she now?'

The sudden barrage of questions from Martin completely unnerved Dan Painter and he fell back on the familiar 'no comment' position, suggested by his solicitor and so often used by criminals when the going got tough.

Undeterred, Martin persisted and reiterated how important it was for them to interview Susan Evans.

'We know you were both in this together and we need to hear her version of events so that the Crown Prosecution Services can decide on appropriate charges. When exactly did you last see her, and did she give you any idea where she was going?'

All Dan Painter did was close his eyes to shut out the sight of this determined detective, but it was enough to wake Susan in his mind and she spat bits of decaying teeth and gum so realistically in his direction that he physically ducked.

His sudden movement, followed by an unexpected bout of sobbing gave his solicitor the opportunity to bring the session to an end. It was agreed that no further interviews would be conducted until the next morning, and Painter was escorted to the cells followed by his solicitor but not before he had demanded an update on the condition of Jason Barnes.

'My client has every right to know what the position is with the boy. The fact that he is sick is regrettable but Mr Painter can hardly be blamed for that – it would have happened in any event.'

'Bloody hell,' said Matt. 'What are you people like? 'It's true that the boy's sickness may have nothing to do with the kidnapping, but leaving him without the medical attention he needed was in my view tantamount to killing him.'

The solicitor looked shocked. 'So the kid is dead then?' he asked sharply.

'That's not what my sergeant said,' Martin answered. 'He was simply giving what I have to say is a shared opinion on Painter's actions. The situation with Jason is that he is at the University Hospital of Wales on a ventilator and fighting for his life, and that's all I can tell you.'

A few minutes later Martin and Matt stood in Interview

Room One and considered their position. 'For some reason when the news came through about Jason's disappearance I had a bad feeling, and my initial thinking was that it was the work of a paedophile and I couldn't even bring myself to think of the possible outcome. I certainly didn't think that he had been kidnapped and held to ransom. I suppose that was based on the fact that the call came through about a pupil from Holly Road School, and I wouldn't expect any of the parents there to have bank balances to support the requirements of a ransom demand.'

Matt took a mouthful of the coffee they had picked up after leaving the interview and then nodded. 'Yes, that's what I thought too. It just goes to show that we don't know who we rub shoulders with in the local shops. Would you ever guess if you saw Jason and his mother in the supermarket that she is a multi-millionaire? Apart from her excessive nicotine habit I quite like the woman, but if she was having trouble coming to terms with her fortune before all this God only knows how she'll cope now. The media will be hounding her for a good few days at least and again when the case gets to court, and there will almost certainly be people out there more than happy to help her during her hour of need but with at least one eye on her money.'

Matt continued. 'The really sad thing is that I believe if Painter had told her that he suspected Jason was his son she would have been OK, with it and they may even have sorted some sort of relationship. There's a sizable age gap between them and at the moment Painter looks like a broken old man but he's fundamentally a decent-looking bloke. And can you believe that photograph of him as a kid – it's just like looking at Jason. What's the plan now, guv?'

'Well, to my complete amazement, I can see no reason not to make good our arrangements to celebrate Shelley's birthday. Jason is in good hands, Dan Painter is safely locked up, and the world and his wife are looking for Susan Evans. With any luck we'll be interviewing her tomorrow and the rest of the day will be taken up with a press conference, getting some more out of

Painter, and sorting out the reports. Providing the news stays positive regarding Jason then things will be done and dusted a lot sooner than I would have expected, so I'm off home and I'll see you later.'

Two hours later on a still and relatively mild October evening Martin and Shelley were sitting in the back of a taxi as it headed down the M4.

'Where are we going?' asked Shelley.

'That's for me to know and you to find out,' teased Martin. 'I've not been here before, but Alex and Charlie rave about the place and you know what those two are like when it comes to discovering places that are a bit out of the way and serve really good food. According to Charlie the surroundings are sensational and second only to the menu – and when it comes to judging the quality of food I would always back Charlie's judgement.'

Martin looked at Shelley, and would have liked to ask the taxi driver to pull off the road so that he could show her how much he loved her and to hell with some out-of-date bylaw that precluded public demonstrations of intimacy. The wicked look in those amazing deep blue eyes told Martin that her thoughts and his matched completely and they giggled like a couple of schoolgirls, but their bubble was burst by the driver seeking precise directions.

Martin consulted his phone and gave out the instructions provided by Alex and within minutes they were turning into the driveway of Llanerch Vineyard.

It had been a pleasant day. Not exactly an Indian summer but certainly warmer than could be expected in Wales at this time of the year. However it was October and almost eight o'clock and so the light was fading fast and the buildings were lit up and looked welcoming.

Shelley pressed her nose against the window of the taxi and shouted with delight. 'Martin, you're a genius! This is where Angela Gray has her cookery school, isn't it?'

'I'm happy to be regarded as a genius, but as far as cookery schools are concerned you've lost me. If Charlie has set me up to do my own cooking I'll swing for her.'

'No, relax, I don't think you'll be asked to sauté anything but coming here has reminded me that I must look into the courses that are on offer. I've got one of Angela's cookery books – it's about the amazing variety of cheeses that we produce in Wales nowadays.'

Martin grinned at her obvious enthusiasm. 'I think it's Charlie who should really be held up as the genius, and now I know something else to get you for your birthday. Get the details of the courses while we're here and book yourself on one – it's the best idea for a birthday present as I won't even have to wrap this one!'

Shelley poked him in the ribs and he retaliated by pulling her hair and inevitably their fun led to a passionate kiss.

'Put her down,' suggested a smooth deep voice from the entrance to the restaurant. 'Happy birthday, Shelley – come on, we've got some champagne on ice.'

Reluctantly Shelley broke away from Martin and went forward to receive an exaggerated French-style kiss on alternate cheeks from Alex and then bent down to embrace Charlie.

Even before the first taxi had left the grounds a second one was heard crunching on the gravel and they all turned to watch Matt and Sarah jump out and join them.

More birthday greetings and kisses came with the last two arrivals and Sarah handed over a beautifully packaged present.

'Oh, thank you, but it's too beautiful to open,' said Shelley but even as she said it she was tugging at the silver and purple ribbon.

'We didn't get you a gift as such,' explained Charlie 'but the evening is on us, so let's get inside and start enjoying it.'

They were shown to a table reserved for them and as she sat down Shelley finished opening the present. 'I've never had such a fantastically coordinated set of presents,' she laughed. 'First Alex and Charlie bring us here and then Martin promises to buy me a cookery course of my choice and then you very cleverly give me one of Angela Gray's recipe books. I've already got one of her books but that's exclusively about Welsh cheese.'

She addressed her last remarks at Sarah who shared a knowing look with Matt. 'I knew you had one book because I saw it when we had a coffee at your dad's house. When Charlie suggested we were coming here I asked your father if you had any of the other books and he had a rummage around to make sure we weren't duplicating anything.'

Matt laughed and joined in. 'Sarah and I met because she has a nose for finding out things, and I said at the time she would make a good detective but so long as she sticks to investigating cookery books that's fine with me.'

Alex signalled to the waiter who ceremoniously popped the cork of the champagne and everyone raised their glasses to once again wish Shelley a happy birthday.

The atmosphere was brilliant, and no one looking at the six people enjoying an evening together would have guessed that just that morning the three men were involved in looking for a seven-year-old boy who could have been taken by a paedophile with horrendous consequences, or brutally murdered by some homicidal maniac.

All three of them knew that their jobs brought them in direct contact with the darkest side of human nature and recognised the importance of evenings like this. Time out with friends and colleagues – and an unwritten rule that there was never a mention of work – were critical to maintaining a balanced view of the world.

Martin knew that if he and Shelley were not together, then there was every chance that he would, now, be at the cottage and constantly in touch with the hospital regarding the status of the little boy. He would be badgering his team for constant updates on the search for Susan Evans and planning the next day's work schedule.

It wasn't that he had fallen out of love with his job, but he had fallen hopelessly in love with tonight's birthday girl and just the sight of her doing nothing more than studying the menu put thoughts of anything else out of his mind until tomorrow.

The menu caused quite a commotion because, to quote Charlie, 'What I would really like is to have a tiny helping of everything and slowly work my way through the lot. It's just not fair to offer such fantastic dishes and expect people to just choose one.'

There was no disagreement but Alex tweaked his wife's nose and reminded her that the concept of eating for two was not something for her to put to that much of a test. Charlie nodded and drained the last of her smaller than usual glass of champagne. She was coming to the end of the first trimester of her pregnancy and outwardly there were no signs, but she shared some of her thoughts. 'Well at least I'm over the few weeks I had, when I was falling asleep at the drop of a hat. If we had come out for a meal then you then, would have been waking me up for each course.'

They laughed and talked and laughed and talked and the evening flew by. Shelley came up with a compromise regarding Charlie's inability to decide on what to eat and they did the same for the starters, the main course, and the dessert. Each of them selected a different dish and there was a fair amount of tasting and sharing and oodles of enjoyment as new flavours were experienced.

The few mouthfuls of champagne were the only alcohol that Charlie allowed herself to indulge in and after that it was water for her, but as several bottles of wine were finished by the others, it was Charlie who became more bubbly. She was feeding off the effects it was having on her friends and kept them amused with stories of her Irish family that at times seemed almost unbelievable.

'You can't possibly have *two* uncles that are able to mimic Winston Churchill,' laughed Sarah, after Charlie's description of how such impersonations aided by fat cigars had been used on the streets of Dublin.

'Oh yes she can,' grinned Shelley. 'We went to their wedding and I have never laughed so much in all my life – some of the characters are really larger than life and we all had a whale of a time. Do you remember, Martin? We danced almost all night and the entertainment was still going on at breakfast time.'

Martin did remember, and much as he had enjoyed the Irish hospitality, it had been pleasantly overshadowed by the time he had spent with Shelley. He would always have fond memories of the small fishing harbour they had wandered to in the early morning – it was the time and the place where he had realised that he had found his soulmate.

Coffee and liqueurs followed a perfect meal and this was the only time when moments of discord were struck, but they were nothing more serious than differences of opinion regarding the best parts of the meal.

Charlie opted for the Welsh lamb which she had eventually selected for her main course. It had arrived with the tiniest of new potatoes and a redcurrant jelly. She licked her lips again at the memory of it and guessed at what Alex would choose as his favourite. She was spot on, as the man in her life had the sweetest tooth and she had watched him drool over a chocolate and raspberry pudding that looked as good as it tasted. It was, however, the one dish that wasn't shared, as no one had been brave enough to suggest the idea to Alex.

Martin said that his seafood starter was amongst the best food he had ever tasted, and Shelley, who had helped him scoop up some of the prawns and crab meat, agreed.

Matt wouldn't be moved from his choice of fillet steak and Sarah suggested that the best course was the cheese course. They all changed their minds at least once and relived the tastes and textures that had led to very little being left on anyone's plate.

'Thanks for suggesting this place,' said Martin, 'and I can't let you pick up the bill for everyone – what say we share it?'

'Shut up for once,' replied Alex. 'It's our treat for Shelley's birthday, and if you feel guilty we will think of somewhere twice as expensive to go for Charlie's birthday next month and let you pick up the tab.'

It came as a shock to everyone when the waiter walked over with the news that the taxi for Mr Matt Pryor and party had arrived.

'That can't be right, I ordered ours back here for eleven –

it's nowhere near that, is it?' Matt looked at Sarah, who replied that it was actually ten past, and so they reluctantly they said their goodbyes. Whilst Alex was sorting the bill Charlie made her way to the loo and Shelley and Martin took a stroll through a door at the back of the restaurant and walked into a partially lit outside eating area.

There were a few tables and they looked out onto the actual vineyards. 'I bet this is spectacular on a balmy summer afternoon, and a bit like being in the South of France.'

'I agree about the setting,' replied Martin 'and I marvel at your optimism. How many balmy summer afternoons have we had in recent years? But here's a promise. The next time one of our summer days manages to creep up to anything vaguely resembling balmy I will drop everything and bring you here.'

'Murder, rape, or a crime epidemic permitting, I will hold you to that,' laughed Shelley and then it was their turn to climb into a taxi and hope that the driver had other things to occupy his mind than the besotted couple in the back.

Chapter Thirteen

It was business as usual in the morning but Martin whistled as he showered and couldn't resist taking several peeps at Shelley as she slept soundly in the bed that he had just vacated. She had told him that she had an evening session with some new recruits to the police force and so didn't need to get to work until lunchtime. It had taken a lot of resolve for him to get up and leave her there and he couldn't remember a time when setting off for work was really not what he wanted to be doing.

Overnight the weather had taken a turn for the worse and Martin grimaced as he closed his front door and walked down the path to where he had parked his Alfa Romeo in front of Shelley's Mini. He looked out towards the coast and saw banks of dark grey clouds that usually signalled heavy rain, and the sky looked as if it was set for a very wet day.

Matt looked a bit the worse for wear when they met in the staff dining room some thirty minutes later. 'Great night last night but unfortunately Sarah and I thought it was a good idea to have a couple of nightcaps when we went home. My head is regretting it this morning and just in case I got a taxi in to work and Sarah will pick me up when I want to get home – which is now actually but I guess there's not much chance of that.'

'Not a hope in hell.'

Another voice interrupted and Iris placed two cups of coffee and a mountain of toast in front of the two detectives. 'If you don't mind me saying, you two look as if you've seen better days – work is it?'

Matt already had a mouthful of toast so it was left to Martin to explain that they had been celebrating Shelley's birthday last night and had possibly over-indulged.

Iris let out a laugh that made Matt cringe. 'Oh that's alright then – I thought you may have been out all night chasing some nasty criminals. You should do more of getting out and enjoying yourselves; it's what you need to keep you sane, some of the stuff you have to deal with. Is there anything else I can get you, like bacon and eggs or maybe a sausage sandwich?'

The men decided to take a rain check on the offer and Iris went back to her job of ensuring that all the staff who worked in Goleudy were provided with the best she could muster in terms of home-from-home cooking.

'What's the order of play for today?' asked Matt, piling some strawberry jam onto the last piece of toast. 'I feel half human after that.'

'I spoke to Helen just before I came in search of coffee. She's already at the hospital, where the news on Jason is very positive. He's physically out of the woods, and it will just be a matter of time before he makes a full recovery, but they are worried about his mental state. Apparently he keeps asking where the lady is, and his mother has no idea who he's talking about. My own immediate thought was that he is talking about Susan Evans, because I really believe that she's involved with this and more than Dan Painter is willing to admit. Helen will stay with Jason and Tina and keep us posted if the boy is able to remember anything about what happened to him. She seems to think that he will remember quite a bit but for the moment "the lady" is the only thing he will talk about. I suggested going there to speak to him, but Helen says the medical staff want him kept as quiet as possible so basically whether we like it or not we will have to be patient.'

'There's a press conference arranged for eleven and much of what we wanted that for has been sorted, but it will be a good PR exercise and give us a chance to thank the public for their efforts in looking for Jason yesterday. The other thing will be to use the opportunity for us to ask for any sightings of Susan Evans. See if you can get a recent picture of her from her sister and then meet me in the interview room. Let's see if we can get some more out of Dan Painter.'

The two men parted company and Martin walked up the stairs to his office. He passed Sergeant Evans, who brought him up to date on the search for Susan Evans.

'The last person to have seen her as far as we can work out is Mark Davies, the neighbour of Dan Painter – we both met him yesterday when we found the boy.'

'That's apart from Dan Painter himself,' replied Martin. 'When Mark Davies saw her she was getting into Painter's car and then they drove off. The next person to see Painter was Diane, Susan Evans' sister, but she definitely wasn't with him then because apparently he told Diane that he hadn't seen her for a while – that was obviously a lie. Something went on between those two and we need to speak to Susan Evans urgently to find out what – but she seems to have disappeared into thin air.'

Martin was getting an uncomfortable feeling about the safety of Jason's 'lady' and it became more tangible when the sergeant shook his head and muttered. 'Something just doesn't feel right, does it?'

That did it for Martin and a few minutes later he walked into one of the interview rooms, determined to find out what had happened to Susan Evans. Sergeant Evans' famous nose had now convinced him that there were more pieces of this puzzle to put together before the total picture could be revealed.

Matt went through all the preliminaries as he and Martin faced Painter and his solicitor in the usual format of a formal interview under caution. It was difficult to read this man accused of kidnapping as his face was deadpan and there was none of the lack of self-control that had resulted in the previous interview being terminated. His demeanour was not arrogant but neither was it contrite and he had obviously been coached by his solicitor regarding the way in which he answered questions. In fact as soon as Matt had spoken the statutory opening words it was the solicitor who set the ground rules.

'My client wishes to read a statement we have prepared and to answer only those questions that are relevant to the account he has provided.' The solicitor was a well-spoken man and most definitely from the other side of the Severn Bridge. If the tape had been capturing thoughts as well as words it would have recorded Matt suggesting the solicitor was a 'bloody pompous English twit'.

It was not the way Martin would have chosen to go but he had learned from experience that going along with criminals and their legal advisors sometimes lulled them into a false sense of security. He nodded and was pleasantly surprised by the brevity of the statement on offer.

Painter explained how, until recently, he was unaware that Jason was his son and that even when he had found out there was nothing that he wanted to do about it. He had made the mistake of telling his girlfriend Susan Evans about Jason and she had convinced him that as he had missed out on being part of his son's life he was entitled to some of the money that at some point would be his son's inheritance.

He described in detail how he had easily persuaded Jason to hide in the cricket bag and how he had used Susan's sister's car. Quite suddenly the statement came to an end and his final sentence was 'I confess to kidnapping Jason and asking his mother for one million pounds for his safe return, and it was never my intention to harm the boy in any way'.

'Well, thanks for that,' said Martin not even bothering to disguise his sarcasm. 'It ticks a few boxes for us, but to be honest the discovery of white flannels and a cricket bag at your home with some obvious traces of Jason having been inside it didn't make it too difficult for us to figure it out. Perhaps that's why they call us detectives.'

'The kid must have been terrified when some strange bloke bundled him into a bag and zipped it up,' suggested Matt, and got the reaction he was looking for.

'He knew who I was – well at least he knew me as Megan's granddad, and I didn't shove him into the bag in the way you're saying it. I just suggested we could play a trick on his mother and he was happy to hide inside. I told you, I never hurt him, not at any time. It's not my fault the boy is sick and it won't be my fault if anything happens to him.'

Painter pulled himself up straight in his chair and looked straight ahead. He desperately wanted to ask if the boy had survived the night but dreaded the answer and for the moment no one on the other side of the table was going to put him out of his misery.

'Where did you go when you left St Fagans?' asked Martin.

'I took Jason to my house.'

'Was Susan Evans waiting for you there?'

'Yes.'

Dan Painter was about to add something to his one word answer but his solicitor stopped him.

'You only need answer the question as we agreed.'

'In reality he needn't say anything, as you and I both know, but it will benefit him later if we are able to say that he cooperated fully with the investigation,' returned Martin.

The immaculately dressed solicitor sneered. 'Believe that and you will believe anything.' To his client he added, 'Just stick to what we agreed.'

For no other reason than to annoy the solicitor Martin called a ten-minute break suggesting that there were things he needed to check.

Outside the interview room Matt questioned his boss. 'Why the interruption?'

'Don't know really, maybe the over-indulgence of last night is catching up on me, but whatever it is that pair is seriously getting on my nerves. Anyway, let's have a coffee and let them stew for ten minutes.'

The plans for coffee were put on hold as they heard a shout and both turned to face John Evans who was hurrying towards them.

'There's a message from DC Cook-Watts and I think it'll mean a trip to the hospital for you.' He noticed the concerned look on Martin's face and hurriedly explained the position.

'The boy is fine and according to Helen they are having difficulty keeping him in bed as he's certainly bounced back to health – but that's kids for you. His mother is not sure if he's making up stories, if he is confused as a result of being so unwell, or if he is actually relating something that happened. It all needs unravelling and Helen needs some help.'

Martin nodded and was pleased to have something to do other than go back into the interview room. 'Tell our friends in there that the interview will resume when we return from an urgent call to speak to Jason Barnes at the hospital. That will make them aware that Jason is still in the land of the living and one would expect that to be a relief, but I suspect the fact that we are going to talk to the boy may give Dan Painter something else to worry about.'

To avoid the hassle of parking at the hospital a squad car dropped them off and they made their way to one of the children's wards. It seemed like nothing short of a miracle that a child who yesterday was fighting for his life was today sitting cross-legged on a bed in a side room of the busy ward.

Obviously re-hydration and intravenous antibiotics had saved the day but the real saviours had probably been Diane Evans and Mark Davies. If Diane hadn't been hell-bent on looking for her sister the boy would still be on that bed and could have been found too late for even the miracles of modern-day medicine to be of any help.

Helen was deep in conversation with Jason and Tina was pacing around but smiled when she saw Martin and Matt.

'As they say in the song, "what a difference a day makes", and for me the difference is sitting there on the bed. Thank you so much for everything you've done. Helen has told me what happened to Jason and then as soon as he got better Jase gave us exactly the same story.'

Jason had noticed the two men who had entered his room and not surprisingly he was eyeing them with a high level of suspicion. His mother noticed her son's concern and introduced the detectives as very good people and someone Jason could trust.

Martin did a 'seriously grown-up' handshake with the little boy and told him that everyone thought he was one of the bravest kids on the planet. This pleased Jason and he and

170

Martin were soon chatting away like old friends.

'My mum thinks I'm making up some stories and I'm not, mister, but some things I can't quite remember.'

'I'm not surprised,' said Martin quietly. 'You've had an amazing adventure, most of it not very nice, but if you start at the very beginning and tell me all about it, just as it happened then we may be able to help with some of the things that are still worrying you.'

'It's the lady – do you know what happened to the lady?'

Martin admitted that for the moment he didn't but then eased Jason back to St Fagans and went step by step over the events that were now known from every angle.

'It was fun getting into the big bag and I only did it to play a trick on my mum but I soon wanted to get out and it was really dark after I heard a bang, like I was shut in a dark cave.'

Tina sat at the side of the bed and took her son's hand. 'We have explained to Jason that the bang was probably the sound of a car boot being closed.'

'It was so hot and dark and I felt sick and I shouted that it was OK and I would even eat Mum's sandwiches – I just wanted to get out.' Tears welled up in his eyes and his mother squeezed his hand. 'I was bloody scared, mister.' Unlike before Tina didn't reprimand her son for swearing and there was no one in the room who didn't think he had every reason to do so.

'The worst part was the bumping around but then I started feeling sleepy and I just couldn't keep my eyes open but I was scared to close them in case I wouldn't ever wake up and never see my mother again.'

It was Tina's turn to fill up with tears. Hers spilled down a face that held a mixture of love for her son and hatred for the man who had put him through such torment.

Knowing that the session was going to take time Martin waited a few minutes before asking Jason what he remembered next.

'The lady was there when I woke up and so was Mr Painter. I didn't know that was his name 'cos I just knew he was Megan's granddad but Mum says his name's Mr Painter. We

171

were in the caravan.'

Martin and Matt exchanged glances and Tina caught the look of surprise on their faces. 'This is where I think Jason has got hold of the wrong end of the stick and things have got a bit muddled in his mind.'

Quite unexpectedly Jason got angry and shouted at his mother. 'Stop saying that, stop saying I got it wrong about the caravan. It was just like the one we stayed in when we went on holiday with your friend Carol. I know you say I was only little and I can't remember it but I can – I can.'

Tina shook her head and it was Martin who re-engaged with Jason.

'Tell me what it was like.'

'Dirty.'

'And the one you stayed in with Carol, was that dirty?'

'No, course it wasn't.'

'So this wasn't the same caravan?'

'No.'

'Apart from being dirty how else was it different?'

Jason thought for a moment. 'It was quiet and you couldn't hear the sea. In Carol's caravan we used to fall asleep listening to the waves, didn't we Mum?'

He looked at his mother who confirmed what was being said and expressed surprise that Jason remembered things so clearly.

'OK,' said Martin. 'I totally believe that Mr Painter took you to a caravan but I have a bit of a problem because he says he took you to his house.'

Jason shrugged and Martin attempted to find out more about the caravan.

'So it was dirty and quiet and not by the seaside, but did you sometimes hear cars or trains or even aeroplanes?'

'No.'

'Perhaps it was in the country,' suggested Matt. 'Did you hear any animal sounds like cows or sheep or horses – anything at all that will help us know where you were taken?'

'No.'

'But you are absolutely certain it was a caravan?'

172

'He said he believed me,' mumbled Jason looking from Matt to Martin.

'Yes, I do,' confirmed the DCI. 'What happened when you got to the caravan?'

'I don't remember going there, I just remember waking up on one of those seats that you can make into a bed. I was too hot and didn't want to be wrapped in a blanket but my arms wouldn't work properly and I couldn't get it off me.

'I didn't like it there and I didn't feel very well and I don't really want to remember about it.'

Jason's bottom lip began to quiver and his mother sat on the bed next to him and persuaded him with a cuddle.

'Look, Jase, you've been very brave and we're all very proud of you, but if you just try and tell us what happened these policemen will be able to sort things out so that the people who have done wrong will be punished. Will you try?'

Slowly Jason told Martin as much as he could remember. 'The lady wasn't very nice, you know, and she said lots of very naughty words and she shouted all the time. She called Mr Painter Dan and I think her name was Susan but I didn't speak to her. She kept getting angry at me because I wanted my mum and then she got really angry when I kicked the table over and spilt her drink.

'I didn't mean to do it – the table only had one leg and that was all wonky. She wasn't only mad at me, she didn't like Mr Painter either and they had a fight.'

'Do you mean they were quarrelling or did they actually hurt one another?' quizzed Martin.

'This is one of the bits I don't want to remember,' answered Jason. 'They were really fighting and afterwards she was lying on the floor and she looked like someone very ugly.' Jason closed his eyes as if he didn't want to see the things he was remembering, but unfortunately there was a very real need to find out more.

'We've nearly finished,' coaxed Martin. 'If you could just explain what you mean when you say she looked like someone very ugly.'

Jason thought hard. 'She didn't move. She didn't shout like before. Her eyes poked out and her lips looked like she'd been eating blackberries or she'd been stung by a wasp or something.'

'This is my last question, Jason, and then I'll leave you in peace. Did you see what happened to Susan after that?'

Jason shook his head. 'I don't know if I saw the lady after that. I don't remember. Could be I went back to sleep.

'You have been brilliant, young man,' said Martin as he said his goodbyes. 'You deserve a medal and I'm sure your mother is very proud of you.'

'You bet!' was the response from Tina, and as she sat on the bed next to Jason she looked as if she would never let him out of her sight again.

The three officers congregated in the corridor outside Jason's room and Helen filled the senior officers in on what had happened prior to her asking for them to attend.

'It was every time Jason spoke about the lady, as he called her, that he got really agitated and I knew there was something going on in his little head. His mother has been tremendous and determined to help him get things off his chest but we seemed to be reaching a point beyond which he couldn't, or maybe it was more that he wouldn't, remember.'

'Bloody hell, I'm not surprised. He's just a kid and it sounds to me as if he witnessed Susan Evans being murdered. I don't think he realises that yet but it makes sense. Why else would she have disappeared?' Matt let rip on what he thought of Dan Painter and hoped that Jason would never have to find out that the man was his father.

They agreed that Helen should stay at the hospital and if appropriate get more information from Jason.

'I don't get the caravan bit, but I do believe the boy when he says that's where he was taken. If Dan Painter did kill Susan Evans it wouldn't have been something he planned to do. He had the tickets for them both to jet off to Mexico so it sounds as if they had a violent quarrel and something went very wrong.'

Martin continued to think out loud. 'My guess is that the

caravan was the original destination and would probably have been the place where we were directed to find the boy – always supposing that Painter did intend to keep that part of the bargain.

'If he and Susan Evans fought and she ended up dead then I can see that he would have to change his plans and maybe that's when he took Jason back to his house, where we actually found him.

'Come on, Matt, let's get back to that interview we left. I'm looking forward to it now and can't wait to see Painter's reaction when we mention caravans and murder.'

Chapter Fourteen

It was almost eleven o'clock when a squad car picked up DCI Phelps and DS Pryor in the grounds of the University Hospital of Wales. The press conference concerning the kidnapping was arranged for the hour and they were going to be late. Ideally Martin would have liked to postpone his date with the media until after he had re-interviewed Dan Painter, but there was no chance of that.

Matt radioed ahead to say there would be a slight delay to the agreed start and grinned to himself as he imagined how well that news would be received by the waiting press. He thought longingly of the cup of coffee that he and his boss had almost had before getting the call to go to the hospital. The bottles of water that were always provided on the front table in the conference room didn't seem as appealing but they would have to do for now.

As expected there was a general air of impatience as Martin took the centre seat and immediately spoke into the microphone.

'I'm sorry to have kept you waiting but we have just returned from the University Hospital and I am delighted to be able to tell you that Jason Barnes is making a very good recovery.'

There were the expected spontaneous interruptions.

'Did the bastard hurt the boy?'

'Was he assaulted?'

'Is it true that the kidnapper is a friend of the family?'

'Where was he found?'

Martin tapped hard on the side of the microphone, 'If you

give me a chance I will put you in the picture and then you can ask your questions.

'First of all I want to say a very big thank you on behalf of the police and especially from Jason's mother, Tina Barnes. The teachers and parents from Holly Road School were brilliant, as were the staff of St Fagans. Their security cameras made it possible for us to quickly identify the car that was used in this wicked crime and a series of events led us to finding Jason at the home of Mr Daniel Painter.

'He is currently under arrest. We also want to contact a Ms Susan Evans, who may be able to help us with our enquiries. So far we have been unable to locate Ms Evans and we have some information that gives us reason to be concerned about her safety.'

There was nothing more that Martin could say for a minute or two as questions and comments were shouted from all corners of the room. He had learned from experience to ignore this type of outburst, and true to form the room settled down spontaneously and he continued.

'There is really nothing more I can tell you at this moment in time but you have my word that as soon as we find Susan Evans we will share that information with you. Now, as promised at the beginning I am happy to take a few relevant questions.'

Although the gathering at a press conference always resembled a mass of people wrapped up in pieces of technology there was in fact some sort of unwritten order and it didn't surprise Martin when a woman with a fashionable sleek bob, dressed in a dark green suit and cream high-neck sweater, was allowed to take centre stage.

Laura Cummings was the woman behind a face that most of the audience had seen on local television. She and Martin had crossed swords a few times in the past but she was generally polite and always well briefed.

'A good outcome for the boy and his mother, DCI Phelps, and we are all grateful for that. You left out a number of facts regarding the relationship between Tina Barnes and Dan Painter – or maybe you are unaware of it?'

'I have spoken to Mike Barnes, Tina's father, and he told us that before Tina left home she and Painter had a lot of time for one another. What he actually said was that his daughter "had the hots" for his friend Dan and did little to hide it.'

Martin swore under his breath and regretted the direction that Ms Cummings was taking her colleagues. He had visions of newspaper headlines screaming that Jason had been kidnapped by his estranged father, and that wasn't the way for a little boy to find out who his dad was.

Suddenly Martin felt very claustrophobic and did what he had to do to bring the press conference to an end. He wouldn't endear himself to Laura Cummings but that wasn't his biggest concern.

'I said I would answer relevant questions, not go on fishing trips based on information from a man who has been out of contact with his daughter for many years and has never even met his grandson. You will be informed of any new information but for now that's it as I have work to do.'

One cup of coffee led to another and was joined by a couple of ham rolls before Martin and Matt had summoned up the strength for what they suspected would be a lengthy interview with Painter.

They walked into the interview room and Matt fiddled with the tape recorder whilst Martin half-listened to a series of complaints from the posh solicitor. In his view his client had not been given sufficient information regarding the charges he faced and it was unacceptable that they had been kept waiting with no explanation about what was happening.

'I have urgent business which means I must leave here by one o'clock at the latest, and so we will have to be finished by then.' He checked his watch as he spoke and without waiting for a response took the seat next to his client.

'We will be finished when I say we're finished, but if you can get your client to cooperate and answer my questions you may get your wish on the timescale. That's down to you. DS Pryor, will you do the introductions for the tape please?'

Martin sat down and deliberately stared hard at Dan Painter.

The man looked as if he was struggling with a recurring nightmare and Martin's first question brought it into sharp focus.

'Where is Susan Evans?'

There was no response and so the question was repeated.

'Where is Susan Evans?'

Painter stared into space, space that mercifully for him was not occupied by a vision of Susan Evans.

Martin shrugged his shoulders and looked towards the solicitor. 'Well, I've got all day if necessary but I was under the impression that you need to be somewhere else.'

'My client has no idea where Susan Evans is.'

'Well, would he like to tell me that?' suggested Martin.

Painter picked up on the conversation and said that it was true.

'Just for clarification,' continued Martin. 'You say you have no idea where Susan Evans is?'

'Yes.'

'I don't believe you – I think you know exactly where she is.'

'Where are you going with this?' asked the solicitor. 'Mr Painter has already told you he doesn't know the whereabouts of Susan Evans.'

'Yes, and as I have already said, I think he does, so are we going to go round in ever-decreasing circles or is he going to tell me what happened in the caravan? I'm anxious to know if your client left her there dead or alive.'

Martin's words were not lost on the solicitor, who had clearly not been as well briefed as he'd imagined. The words were not lost on Dan Painter either, who felt physically sick, which brought back memories of his vomiting over the dead but still-warm body of Susan Evans. He felt a burning sensation as acid bile entered the back of his throat and he swallowed hard to keep it down.

Surely this detective hadn't found the caravan? Surely if they had found Susan's body he would now be under arrest for murder? He could feel the eyes of everyone including his solicitor staring at him and willing him to speak, but his voice had forsaken him and all he could do was keep swallowing.

'I would like some time alone with my client. This line of questioning is not something we had anticipated and I need to be sure he understands his legal position and his rights.' The solicitor stood up and Martin spoke into the tape. 'Interview suspended at 12.10.'

'We will re-convene in ten minutes, that should give you more than enough time to advise your client to make a clean breast of things. In spite of your lack of trust you must tell him that it will be in his best interests. Be assured we will find Susan Evans and we have very grave concerns regarding her safety.

'With Mr Painter's cooperation it could take us a few hours to find her, but if it takes weeks or even months then so be it. Most judges will look favourably at an accused who has saved the police force that level of unnecessary work. You should advise your client to think carefully about that.'

After what was considerably less than the agreed ten minutes Matt re-started the tape and the interview recommenced.

'My client wishes to withdraw his original statement and to give a full and honest account of the kidnapping. He still maintains that Susan Evans pushed him into it and that were it not for her he would never have contemplated taking the boy.

'The caravan that you mentioned is the place where they had always intended to take Jason and his mother would have been given directions to find him there. I cannot express sufficiently that Mr Painter never intended the boy to come to any harm and it was when he believed the boy was at risk that the accident happened.'

Before the solicitor could continue DCI Phelps set out the rules. 'I would like Mr Painter to tell me everything from start to finish and in his own words.'

Nearly two hours later Matt systematically recorded the time the interview was terminated and sat back in his chair.

Everyone looked a bit shell-shocked and if anything it was Dan Painter who was now the most relaxed. Matt considered the expression 'confession is good for the soul' and concluded that there was some merit in it.

He and Martin had a busy time ahead of them and Matt excused himself to make calls to the SOC team and Professor Moore.

'I wasn't expecting that,' grumbled Matt as for the second time that day he and Martin were being driven in one of the squad cars. 'Well so much for my desire to have an easy day. I thought we would just be sweeping up all the details of the kidnapping, not adding murder to the list. Mind you, when this case came in I had visions of finding the body of a child, but thank God that didn't happen. Painter has certainly painted himself into one hell of a messed-up picture. Do you believe his final version of events?'

Martin was looking through the window of the marked police car as it left the main traffic routes and headed down a little-used coastal road. 'Yes I do. It's tragic really because I don't think he is intrinsically an evil man. I think he was flattered by the attention of a much younger woman and one who would apparently do almost anything for money. I certainly believe he wouldn't have harmed the boy, and as we know from the hospital Jason was made ill by a particularly nasty virus, and that wasn't something Painter could have predicted.

'So leaving aside the kidnapping you think this body we are about to find is basically the result of a domestic that got out of hand?' Matt shook his head. 'What a bloody mess. There definitely won't be any young women to console him where he's going.'

The car bumped over some rough ground and the driver swerved to avoid some large stones. 'I'm not sure this road is taking us anywhere,' he complained and brought the car to a standstill. The three men got out and scanned the area and the detectives agreed with the driver.

Matt stared at the ground ahead. 'It looks as if it comes to a full stop just up there and there's no sign of any caravan. If this is a wild goose chase ...'

Martin was looking back at the ground they had covered and thought there was a chance they had missed a turning to the left of the makeshift road they were on.

'I can't see anything,' responded the driver, 'but jump back in and I'll reverse back to where you think it is.'

'Bingo,' shouted Matt as simultaneously all three men spotted a small a dirt track. 'Painter forgot to tell us we had to turn off the original road, but it's clear to another vehicle's been here very recently.'

'Double bingo – I spy a caravan.'

The rain that had been coming on and off throughout the day suddenly returned with a vengeance. It lashed against the windows of the car as the driver pulled up alongside the caravan. No one really wanted to get out and fortunately there was no real hurry.

'I suggest you give Alex a ring,' Martin told Matt. 'Get him to pick up Professor Moore and bring him here in the SOC van. I don't think my budget will run to paying the bill for repairing the suspension on his Lexus if he drives it up here.'

Matt grinned and phoned the head of SOC. 'They're all on their way,' he relayed to Martin after ending the call. 'Alex and his team are ahead of the Prof so they'll wait at the start of the side road and give him a lift from there. Brains seems to think the Prof's biggest decision for today will be whether to leave his beloved car unattended on the road side or risk the suspension, but he'll offer the choice.'

Martin smiled at Matt's use of Alex Griffiths' nickname. He could remember a time when everyone knew Alex as 'Brains', but now only a handful of close friends occasionally slipped back to using it.

Staying dry was not going to be an option and Martin was the first to brave the elements. He walked up a slope at the side of the caravan and looked out towards the coast. Painter had told them as much as he knew about the house that had been planned and even on a wet late afternoon in October it was easy to see the attraction of the site.

PC West, the officer who had driven the car, offered to go

back to the main track and ensure that the SOC van didn't miss the right-hand turn. Martin and Matt walked past the caravan and looked at a seemingly innocent pile of building rubble – one they knew covered a dark and guilty secret.

'It's exactly as he described. I guess Susan Evans' body is in there somewhere. Come on, boys, let's get to the bottom of this – in more ways than one.' Martin had barely finished his sentence when the familiar SOC van pulled in, followed by another squad car.

Alex jumped out and nodded in the direction of the other car. 'Sgt Evans seemed to think a few extra pairs of hands wouldn't go amiss and I didn't argue. From what Matt has told me we could be digging for a body.'

Before he answered Martin went around to the passenger side of the white van and spoke to the professor. 'There's no point in you getting soaked to the skin at this stage so I suggest you stay where you are until the body has been found.'

Prof. Moore looked over the top of his half-rimmed glasses, and, as was his way, looked very directly at Martin. 'What you really mean, Chief Inspector, is that you don't want an old fogey like me getting in the way, but I will take your words kindly and stay where I am until I'm needed.'

Matt had overheard the exchange and raised an eyebrow towards his boss. 'Hold on, you nearly got a thank you there, the old git is definitely mellowing.'

Alex was quick off the mark and in no time a canopy had been erected over the pile of rubble and his team, helped by the welcomed uniformed officers, were carefully removing pieces of wood, bricks, and general rubbish from the area. Everything was photographed and documented and it wasn't long before one of the officers jumped back startled.

Although he was expecting it, he was still taken aback by the sight of a hand that by now was a mottled grey colour but still displayed the chipped scarlet nail polish. 'Over here, sir,' he called to Alex.

'Stand back, everyone,' Alex called out. 'You can leave that end and careful remove things from around this area.'

Martin and Matt were partially sheltered from rain picked up by a wind blowing from the coast, and held on to one another as they leaned forward to get a better view of the proceedings.

'You can come around the other side now,' shouted Alex. 'Just be careful where you tread, there appear to be a lot of stones and bricks but there are some big holes that you could fall into – and it's very slippery.'

In order to reach the space that Alex had indicated would provide a better view, both men had to leave the shelter of the canopy and walk through longish grass that was soaking wet.

'This is fun, my feet are wet through,' complained Matt, 'and he's right about it being slippery.'

They picked their way carefully over pieces of wood and rubble and then there was an almighty cracking sound and Matt seemed to have shrunk to four feet tall. The bottom two feet or so of him had dropped through one of the holes that Alex had warned them about.

'Bloody hell!' shouted Martin. Are you alright? For God's sake don't move – I don't know how safe things are.'

Everyone had heard the sound of something giving way under Matt's weight and stopped what they were doing in favour of a more urgent rescue. Several pairs of strong arms soon got Matt, who brushed off any suggestion that he was hurt, declaring that it was only his pride that was damaged, back on a firmer footing and Alex declared the ground around the subsidence a no-go area.

Alex brought Martin up to date with the recovery of Susan Evans' body. 'I know that you and the Prof both like to see the body as it was found but this case is a bit different to most. You know who killed the woman and you also know how the body was hidden, so there's no real purpose in either of you risking life and limb to clamber over that lot.

'If you agree we'll erect a small tent at the side of the caravan and get the body moved there. We have masses of pictures to show everything as it was found.'

'That suits me perfectly,' replied Martin. 'What about the caravan, can we have a quick look inside?'

'Sure thing, we've finished with it.'

Whilst the body was being moved Martin had a quick look around the inside of the caravan and saw the one-legged table that Jason had worried about kicking over. Everything fitted with Jason's description and there was little to keep Martin's interest. He was more concerned by the fact that Matt had hobbled up the step of the caravan and noticed that his sergeant was rubbing his left leg. There had been a time when the two of them had been at the mercy of a particularly evil killer and Matt had sustained a life-threatening injury. A knife had pierced an artery in that same left leg and Matt had been lucky to survive.

'Are you sure your leg is OK?' he asked Matt.

'Fine, guv, no need for you to worry this time, and don't forget I've now got my own personal nurse to look after me.'

'Yes and I'll be getting Sarah to ensure you get checked out when we get back.'

Matt raised his eyes to heaven but if anything now seemed to have more difficulty with walking than he was willing to admit.

The professor was already under the most recently erected canopy and studying the body of Susan Evans when they ventured back out into what was now torrential rain. 'If you don't already know, Chief Inspector, I can confirm that this woman was strangled and unless I find something else on post mortem then that will be the cause of death.'

'That fits in with what I've been told,' Martin said. 'When do you think you'll have the results of the PM?'

'Not today for certain as I already have an unexplained death waiting for me and there are people who have been waiting for answers since yesterday. Best I can do for you is an early start in the morning so if you want to see the full show it will be knife to skin at 8 a.m. How does that suit you?'

'Perfectly, thank you,' Martin replied but Prof was already back examining the throat and neck of the victim and simply assumed his suggestion would be acceptable.

Martin turned to Alex. 'Unless you want me for anything I'm going to head back and make it my business to ensure that Matt gets checked out.'

Alex looked across to where Matt was walking gingerly towards the patrol car and nodded in agreement. 'The last thing he needs is to open up old wounds; it's not worth taking any risks.'

'We've got the usual to do here and then we'll be moving the body back to Goleudy and sealing off the area. For the moment the likelihood of people trespassing onto the crime scene is as remote as the site itself but it never fails to amaze me how word gets out.'

'Well you know my views on that,' added Martin. 'I'd love to know who leaks information to the press, they deserve to lose their pensions, and it would give me great pleasure to boot them out of the force.'

'See you later, but if you could do one thing for me I'd be grateful. I'll need to inform Diane Evans that we have most likely found her sister, and if she's up to it I'll get her to make a formal identification. Will you ensure the body goes to one of the viewing rooms first, and make her look as best you can?'

'Of course I will,' said Alex. We should have her back at Goleudy by five o'clock so any time after five thirty will be fine.'

Their driver set off and Martin gave instructions for Matt to be dropped off at the A&E Department of the University Hospital and silenced his sergeant's protests. 'Get on the phone to Sarah and I'm sure she'll come and hold your hand. You've probably just twisted your ankle but that hole you fell into contained all sorts of rubbish and I won't take no for an answer.'

They were not to know that at that moment one of the SOC officers was clearing up next to the hole that Matt had crashed into and he called his boss over. 'Take a look through there, Alex. Ignore the beer cans and takeaway cartons. What do you think that is?'

Chapter Fifteen

For the second time in one day Martin found himself in Gower Road, Ely, and this time it was DC Helen Cook-Watts who accompanied him. Word had obviously got around that Diane Evans had been in some way involved with the finding of Jason Barnes because the road was ten times more busy than usual and neighbours and journalist were on the lookout for any titbits of information.

At least the rain had stopped and Martin had been able to dry out whilst waiting for Helen to come from the hospital. She had brilliant news regarding Jason and told Martin there was every chance the boy would be allowed to go home tomorrow. Some other news she had was more disturbing but Martin couldn't see a way of avoiding its publication.

En route to Ely Helen had talked non-stop about the case. 'I've been amazed by Tina Barnes in all of this, and I think she's been more than a little surprised by her own strength. She hasn't smoked a cigarette since we got the call to say Jason was found and being taken to the hospital.

'Claire Masters, one of the teachers from Jason's school, has been a huge support to Tina and she's the one who warned her to prepare for the news I told you about earlier. I suppose schools are a bit like police stations in that they're hotbeds of gossip, and at the moment the talk has moved on from the kidnapping to the shock that Dan Painter is Jason's biological father. If I were Tina I'd be asking for an inquiry into how this information got into the public domain. Tina told us but she is absolutely certain she hasn't revealed her secret to another living soul. Have we got a leak, guv?'

189

'I don't think our ship is as watertight as we'd like it to be, but on this occasion I think we could look towards Tina's father. He's definitely been talking to the press about his daughter's one-time infatuation with his friend Dan Painter. It'll be interesting to see if the headlines announce that Jason was kidnapped by his father or if they ask "Could the kidnapper be the boy's real father?" That will tell us if they actually know or are just putting two and two together.'

Helen nodded. 'Yes, but whatever angle they take it'll be headline news, and there's no way Tina is going to be able to stop her son finding out about his dad. I wouldn't like to be the one to tell him.'

Martin pulled the car up outside the path to Diane Evans' house and they were immediately surrounded by reporters, some of whom had been at the press conference earlier.

'You promised to keep us up to date so what's the line on the kid's father?'

'What are you doing back here? Did Diane Evans just find the boy or did she put him there in the first place?'

'Have you found Susan Evans? Do you think she and her sister were both involved?'

Martin could see Diane's face in the window and he wondered how she would react to the news about her sister. There had been no traces of sibling affection when she had spoken about Susan earlier but actions speak louder than words and Diane had gone to warn her sister that the police were looking for her.

DC Cook-Watts walked up the path and Martin turned to face the questions. 'There is a press statement in relation to Susan Evans being prepared at this moment in time, but before it's released I need to speak to her sister. That's what I'm doing back here and that's all I have to say for now.'

It was obviously not enough and a barrage of questions ensued but Helen had already been let into the house and Martin followed her. The sitting room was exactly as it had been earlier that day but Diane had company. Mark Davies introduced himself to Helen and acknowledged Martin. He was making the most of suddenly being catapulted into Diane's life and stood manfully beside her.

'I didn't come straight back here after finding the boy and then we had to give statements to the police. With everything that had gone on I didn't think I had a bloody cat in hell's chance of getting any sleep but I collapsed in a heap on Mark's comfy sofa and woke up about an hour ago.'

Diane went on to say that she had walked back and then had a shower and Mark had done the same at his place. 'He arrived just ten minutes before you but then I don't think you've bloody well come to hear about our domestic arrangements – it's about Susan, isn't it?'

Martin nodded. 'It's very bad news I'm afraid – do you want to sit down?'

Diane shook her head fiercely and no one was surprised when her bloodies turned to effings. 'She's fucking well dead, isn't she? She's *fucking well dead*!'

There was no denial and Martin expressed his most sincere regrets for her loss. Bad news, grief, and loss affects different people in different ways and during his years in the force Martin had seen countless reactions, but this was a new one on him.

For the next ten minutes only Diane spoke – or rather shouted. She lambasted her sister's behaviour, from the time she was a young girl up to her most recent relationship with Dan Painter. It was incredible that for a woman who professed not to give a damn about her younger sister, Diane seemed to able to recall most of Susan's flings. One was simply referred to as 'that bastard Len who took her to Brighton' but many of the others had much more lengthy and colourful expletives attached to their names.

For as much as she laid heavily into the men who had been in her sister's life, she also didn't hold back with similar descriptions of Susan herself, and if only half of what she said was true then Susan Evans had been a pretty nasty piece of work. The phrase 'do not speak ill of the dead' had never been so totally disregarded, and Helen Cook-Watts was getting a first-hand lesson in the unpredictability of breaking bad news.

Her lesson didn't end there, the next part being even more bizarre as suddenly Diane stopped shouting, sat down, and burst into tears and spoke in a whisper, almost to herself. 'She may have been an out-and-out cow, but she was my sister and I loved her.'

'Phew, follow that,' said Helen under her breath and although she couldn't have heard the comment Diane did her best for an encore by brushing away her tears with the back of her hand and staring intently at Martin.

'Well you wouldn't be here if Susan had died of natural causes so what was it – an accident, suicide, or murder?'

'We have reason to believe that there was a row between your sister and Mr Painter and ended with him choking her to death. We can't be absolutely sure until after the post mortem but that is what he has told us and superficially your sister's injuries match that probability.'

'To be honest I have a certain sympathy with the bloke and there have been times when I could have been in his position. She really could try the patience of a fucking saint. What happens now?'

The matter-of-fact question took Martin by surprise but he outlined the arrangements for a formal identification if she felt able to do that.

'Let's get it over and done with, and if it's OK I'd like Mark to come with me?'

The four of them drove off in Martin's car but not before the press had challenged every step they took towards it.

How Martin wished he could have the freedom to say to the press what Diane readily told them and so graphically. She left them in no doubt that they should mind their own business and they would need to be contortionists to perform some of the obscene actions she suggested. They looked suitably shocked and there was an uncanny silence as Martin drove off and he and DC Cook-Watts exchanged something of a smirk.

They entered Goleudy by the back stairs. Sgt Evans must

have been told of their arrival as he pulled Martin to one side almost immediately.

'Matt just called and he's fine. He's twisted the muscles in his calf and is badly bruised, but in his words he'll live to tell the tale and will see you in the morning. Now, Alex got the body of Susan Evans brought here but he didn't accompany her himself because of the new discovery at the building site. He asked me to speak to you as soon as you got back and to ask you to give him a ring straight away.

'He wouldn't ring you directly because he said he knew what you were doing and it didn't seem right to disturb you. If you like I'll stand by while Helen conducts the official identification and arrange a squad car to take these people back home.

Martin was relieved to hear about Matt, but for the moment was more anxious to know what was up with Alex.

Sgt Evans wouldn't be pushed on handing over any information and just gave a knowing smile.

'I think the big man wants to tell you himself, so I'll make your excuses here and you make the call.'

'Alex. What's the mystery?'

Martin could feel his friend and colleague grinning on the other end of the phone.

'You were barely out of sight when one of my lot spotted something in the place where Matt almost disappeared. Looking at that area now I would say he had a lucky escape because it drops down about eight feet onto a concrete base. It looks like part of the foundations for the house that was supposed to be built here. If he had gone through he would have had a nasty surprise waiting for him, as we have discovered a second body.'

'You what?'

'Yes, it's a body alright, and like the first one it's the body of a young woman – but according to the Prof this one's been there for years. It's unlikely that she crawled into that hole and died but it's possible, just like Matt, that she fell and was not as lucky as he was. We can't rule out foul play but you know what the Prof is like: he won't commit himself until after he's had a proper chance to examine the body.

'To him the body of Susan Evans represents bread and butter work for a pathologist, but the second body got him quite excited. He was on the phone to some of his cronies who specialise in putting a date on these types of corpses, and by the sound of things there was no lack of offers of help.

'I think we've done everything you would have wanted and I can brief you and your team fully in the morning before the post-mortems. The body is already on the way to Goleudy with the Prof in charge so if you want a sneak preview they should be with you at any moment.'

'No, I think I'll leave that level of excitement until the morning,' replied Martin. 'I know some of my team have been trying to chase up the owners of the building site but they weren't having much luck. All we wanted to do initially was inform them about the recent activity in their caravan but this new discovery throws a very different light on things. It may have nothing to do with them but I certainly want to know why work on the site came to an end and who the last people were that had reason to be there. Thanks, Alex. I knew things were too good to be true. I had a kidnapping that was sorted and an unlawful death where the killer had confessed. All I had left to do was sort out the paper work – but you had different ideas!'

'Don't thank me, mate, thank that sergeant of yours. If he hadn't ploughed through that debris the body would still be down there. Now all you need to do is find out who she is and how she got there – easy peasy. See you in the morning.'

Martin suddenly felt hungry and remembered that Shelley had an evening training session and so nine o'clock would be the earliest she'd get home. It wasn't that long since she had effectively moved into the cottage and he couldn't make up his mind which part of their day he liked best. Waking up in the mornings was like continuing to dream and parts of her warm body were always draped over his. At first he had taken time to slowly remove her arm or her leg so that he wouldn't wake her but now he knew that nothing would wake Shelley until she was ready to open her eyes.

They had made a conscious decision not to fall into the trap of routine and they ate, made love, and slept when they felt like it and not according to the clock. It was all part of the excitement of discovering each other and they knew that eventually life, work, and possibly kids would make spontaneity more difficult but for now it was brilliant.

He made his way to the staff dining room and although Iris had knocked off for the day she had left the usual selection of sandwiches and freshly made meals that could be heated up in one of the microwaves.

Martin chose a beef cobbler and wasn't disappointed. The gravy was rich and the meat tasty and tender, and topped with scones and cheese it went down a treat.

'Looks like you enjoyed that, guv,' suggested Helen as she watched her boss mop up the sauce with the last piece of a bread roll. 'I'm just having a coffee as hopefully I'm getting treated to dinner tonight. Do you want a coffee?'

'No thanks but sit down and tell me what happened with the identification, and I'll tell you about something that is going to keep us busy for the next few days at least.'

'I'm intrigued but as far as the Susan Evans case is concerned it was straight forward. Diane Evans identified Susan and there was no shouting, no swearing, no tears, just nothing but a simple acknowledgement that the body was that of her sister Susan.' Helen looked at her DCI and asked if he had ceased to be amazed by people's behaviour and Martin laughed.

'I don't think I ever will be and perhaps we never should be. We human beings are a pretty mixed-up bunch. You won't come across the likes of Diane Evans and her sister very often but there will be other relationships just as complex.'

Helen nodded and asked Martin about his news. Not having been at the scene when Susan Evans' body was discovered Helen asked a lot of questions about the logistics of the site.

'We'll all be treated to images of how the first and the second bodies were found when Alex briefs us in the morning. As I understand, it the Prof and some of his university colleagues are hoping to re-enact one of the episodes from

Waking the Dead, and I for one am looking forward to their findings.'

Chapter Sixteen

Matt was bearing weight on his left leg with no signs of the pain from the day before, and even the stairs up to the fourth floor were no problem. In response to Martin's enquiry, he put his rapid recovery down to the expert massages of his personal Florence Nightingale and confessed to encouraging the hands of his masseur to stray.

'Far too much information,' laughed Martin.

'I can't believe I nearly landed on a corpse, but Alex was telling me about it when we arrived together earlier. Have you got any ideas about the woman?'

Martin shook his head. 'I'll have a better idea where to start looking when we know how long she's been there. We have had some joy from the council's planning department, who have tracked down the plans for the development on that site and have the owner listed as a Manuel Romanes. There was apparently one hell of a rush to get the plans through the various committees something like five years ago and then the whole project came to a sudden halt.

'Carol Price from the planning department is trying find out more about this Manuel Romanes. Apparently they sent out letters to his home address at the time, asking about progress on the building. There are copies of everything and she seems to think that Mr Romanes would have received the first couple of letters but then there was one returned to sender, indicating that he no longer lived there.

'There's a note in the file describing how one of their inspectors visited the site at the time and followed his visit up with a letter advising Mr Romanes of the need to make the site secure if, as it had appeared, work had been suspended. Apparently such an instruction should have been followed up with a compliance visit, but Ms Price told me it had been overlooked and the file hasn't been opened since the inspector's letter was added.'

Reaching the top of the stairs the usual odour, one of disinfectant mingled with death, caught the noses of both detectives simultaneously.

'This would have really churned up my stomach if it was yesterday and I was still recovering from the great night we had with Charlie and Alex.' Matt patted his stomach. 'Thankfully today my breakfast is nicely settled and I've no hangover to contend with.'

Mrs Williams, the professor's right-hand woman, was not her usual calm self and it wasn't difficult to understand why.
Not one but two of the PM rooms were set up for business and she had three distinguished professors to cope with instead of just the usual one she knew so well.

She seemed pleased to see some familiar figures and smiled broadly as Martin and Matt approached the changing room and indicated where she had put out two sets of scrubs for both of them.

'The professor is even more keen than usual to ensure there is no cross-contamination between the two PM rooms, so it will mean a second change of clothing if you intend witnessing both examinations.'

'Which room first?' asked Matt.

'Well, as you can see, the main focus of interest for our visiting professors is that poor woman in there – or at least what's left of her. The only comments I've heard so far are that she was probably a fit and healthy young woman until someone broke her neck. I heard my Prof telling them how she was found in quite a deep hole and I don't know how they know she didn't simply fall into it and break her own neck.'

Martin was surprised by Mrs Williams' comments. In fact he was surprised to hear her say anything as usually she just got on with her job very quietly and efficiently. This morning she had plenty to say.

'As you can see Prof. Moore is in PM Room One, and the body on that slab is Susan Evans. He seems certain that he'll complete a full examination on her within the hour but has warned me that the other one will take us well past lunch time. Excuse me, I'm wanted in there.'

She had seen the Prof beckon her and disappeared through the adjoining door, leaving Martin and Matt to follow behind.

Susan Evans' body was partially covered with a white mortuary sheet but the cause of her death was clearly visible. The bruising around her neck was livid and the skin had already started to break down, partly due to the initial damage but mainly because her death had immediately cut off the vital oxygen supply needed to facilitate tissue repair.

Dafydd Moore looked over his half-rimmed glasses at Martin. 'I will be very surprised if I'm able to tell you anything you don't already know about this woman or about the cause of her death. The contusions you can see around her neck are commensurate with the confession you've already obtained from her killer. You're welcome to stay and watch the full PM, but I'm sure you have better things to do and I'll let you know if anything unexpected turns up.

'The other corpse is a different kettle of fish, and has got two of my colleagues more excited than I've seen them for some time.' He stopped as he noticed Matt smirking beneath his mask. 'Excitement gets more sparse as you get older so you grab it where you can – and each to his own.

'They don't expect to find anything special about the woman and have already figured she's not some ancient relic, but they don't get many bodies that have been dead for years to work on. They know the theory of decomposition and the factors that delay or speed up the process and this is a rare opportunity to test theory against reality.'

Matt grinned more broadly. 'Whatever floats your boat! And they know exactly how she died?'

'We think that's something the two women have in

common,' replied the professor. 'With Susan Evans it's easy to witness the damage done but with our unknown corpse there's no tissue left to examine and so we will be looking at other factors. Our initial thoughts are that they both died because something or someone prevented air and de facto oxygen from getting to their lungs. You know how that happened with Susan Evans but it's going to take some effort and possibly a bit of science to unravel the mystery of the lady that interests my colleagues.'

Martin looked at Matt who had, as always, looked away to avoid watching the Prof make a mid-line incision and begin the systematic process of the PM on Susan Evans.

Smells and sights he could cope with but that surreal moment when the Prof's scalpel cut through dead flesh was one he liked to miss.

The two men changed and went into the second room where the set up was very different and where two absorbed professors didn't even notice their arrival.

'Sorry to interrupt your deliberations, I'm Detective Chief Inspector Martin Phelps and this is my colleague Detective Sergeant Matt Pryor. Professor Moore has suggested you may be able to give us a bit more information on this body.'

'It's hardly a body, guv,' remarked Matt. 'I didn't expect this – it really is a skeleton. How can you tell that it's a woman?

One of the visiting professors was a Moore look-alike, but the other was much younger: more of an Alex Griffiths double, but even taller and very imposing. He introduced himself as Patrick Harries and his colleague more formally as Fedar Yeltsov, visiting Professor of Forensic Medicine from Lithuania.

Professor Harries answered Matt's question. 'It's actually relatively easy, Sergeant, although people have been known to get it wrong. The overall size and general robustness of the skeleton is different between men and women, although that differential gap may be closing as stereotypical roles change.

'Traditionally we've seen more bone development at muscle attachment sites in the male skeleton, but with modern woman taking up labouring jobs and men choosing to be house-husbands there will, in my opinion, eventually be evolutionary changes to consider.

'Our best indicator is the pelvis, as even when a woman has never borne children her pelvis was designed for the purpose and there are several significant differences in this area. Take a look at the sciatic notch here. It's much broader than one would expect to see if this was a male skeleton, and the angle where the two pubic bones meet in the front is much wider.'

Matt looked at the pelvis and nodded. 'What about when she died? What are the scientific factors that help with that?'

Professor Harries smiled. 'Well, I just said that scientists have been known to get the sex of a skeleton wrong, and when it comes to dating the period of death they have occasionally proven to be wildly out. There are dozens of variables to consider. Was the body left indoors and protected, or out in the elements of a warm or a cold climate? A cold, dry environment will protect the body for longer than a hot and damp one, and contrary to most people's beliefs a body will decompose slower in water than in open air.'

Martin joined the conversation. 'In this woman's case we have more tangible evidence on how long she's been dead, because we know the last time work was done at the site where she was found. It was originally thought that financial or relationship difficulties had caused that building work to come to a full stop but it looks like there's a more sinister reason.'

'If we didn't have that information, how would you go about determining the period of death?' Matt and Martin were both enthralled with hearing about the scientific methodology and Prof. Harries readily obliged.

'We would take account of where she was found and factor in some beliefs that have become forensically acceptable. For example, we could assume that within a few days the body would be infested with insects and they would eat their way through the flesh. Inevitably there would be flies and maggots and it could take anything up to a couple of months for the body to dry out and cease to be of interest to the original predators.

'There may have been a few rodents helping with the flesh-eating but when things get down to just ligaments and tendons it becomes the domain of the minibeasts and in particular the beetles, who can chew their way through anything. All of that could take up to a year depending upon the level of activity and when there is nothing left except bone, teeth, and hair, there are types of bacteria and some moths that will consume the hair.'

Matt grimaced. 'It sure puts a whole new angle on recycling doesn't it?'

'Yes and with individual skeletons we can never be sure how nature secretly and randomly selected the methodology of decomposition, but there is a vast body of knowledge to which we can refer. It will be your detective work that will find out who she is and how and when she ended up in that place and then what we have described will add to that body of knowledge.'

Whilst the three men had been talking Professor Yeltsov had not uttered a word but had taken dozens of measurements and made copious notes. He seemed blissfully unaware that there were living people around him and all his attention was on the skeleton that he had decided to call 'Вера', which was 'Vera' written in Cyrillic.

'You won't find a skeleton in any of the universities world-wide that has not been given a name,' smiled Patrick Harries. 'We are privileged to have Fedar Yeltsov taking an interest, he is a world-renowned forensic anthropologist and I couldn't see why he shouldn't name this one.'

Martin shook his head. He liked the taller version of Alex and asked him a few more questions. 'Are you able to tell us any more about the woman? Her age, for example, and any clues to the cause of death?'

'Happy to oblige on both counts, but with the understanding that we will need to finish our work before my initial thoughts are confirmed. I would put her as around five feet eight inches, perhaps a bit taller, and her age as no more than thirty.'

'I could guess at the height myself, but how can you tell her age?' asked Matt.

'As we age the process of ossification occurs and bones throughout the body fuse at reasonably standard times and in a known pattern. If you look at this part of her hip you can see that the bones are fused but if you look here at these bones in her skull you'll see there isn't total fusion.'

Patrick Harries was enjoying himself and in this respect he was more like Prof. Moore than was originally evident – they both liked an audience. 'It's impossible to say if she was fat or thin as layers of fat do not leave distinctive marks on the bone.

'Her teeth are perfect and it's not often you see a complete absence of cavities. The fact that she has all thirty-two, including her four wisdom teeth fits in with the age profile. She had quite a wide jaw and I suspect that she could have been a candidate for toothpaste advertising.'

'On a more serious note, you asked about the cause of death and our first thoughts are that she was asphyxiated. How that happened is for you to discover but if you look at that small U-shaped hyoid bone in the centre of what would have been her throat you will see that it is damaged. There is also slight separation of some of the cervical vertebrae and that could be significant.

'Although we believe she was a young woman when she died she had during life received more than the average share of trauma. Her left tibia and fibula and her right femur have all been broken but all have been simple fractures with none of the injuries requiring surgical intervention. Her collarbone has healed on more than one occasion and she's had several cracked ribs.'

'Quite a story from a heap of bones,' commented Matt as he and Martin changed and made their way back to Incident Room One where Alex was already set up and waiting for them.

The whole team had assembled, and initially it would have been to close two crimes, but there was an extra buzz of excitement as everyone became aware of possibly a third. Martin only had to listen to a few comments to know that there was some confusion and quickly brought everyone up to date.

'We couldn't have asked for a better result from the kidnapping of Jason Barnes. He has been discharged from hospital and is safely at home with his mother. The man who actually snatched him is locked up downstairs and as you will have all seen from this morning's newspaper revelations it is being suggested that Dan Painter is Jason's biological father. It is not something Tina Barnes wanted her son to know but DC Cook-Watts spoke to her earlier and Miss Barnes is not going to deny it. She realises her son may be taunted with the fact when he returns to school and is doing her best to put a positive slant on things before that happens.'

'He's a great little kid,' Helen added. 'Tina has done a cracking job raising him on her own and now she's got to tell him that his friend's grandfather is his dad and that his dad is the man who kidnapped him. If you add to that the fact that he may have actually witnessed his newly discovered dad strangle a woman, then God only knows how a kid of his age will cope with all that.

We haven't questioned Jason in any detail about what happened in the caravan because we have an actual confession from Dan Painter, but it's something that will have to be done. The boy's recollection of events may support Painter's statement that describes an almighty great fight between him and Susan Evans that got out of hand. It could make the difference between murder and manslaughter.'

'Given that the two of them were planning on flying off to Mexico I can believe that it was a domestic that went badly wrong,' Matt opined. 'From what Diane Evans has told us about her sister my guess is that she was always destined for a sticky end. I get the feeling from talking to Painter that he would have held his hands up to choking Susan straight away, but of course he was in one hell of a mess with a sick, kidnapped child on his hands.'

Martin nodded. 'That's how I see it, but unfortunately for Painter what he did after killing Susan Evans will not bode well for him in court. Hiding the body the way he did shows his intent to try and get away with it, and not seeking medical help for the boy will be the final nail in his coffin. However it's an ill wind that blows nobody any good, and if Painter hadn't buried Susan Evans, Matt wouldn't have found Vera.'

Chapter Seventeen

Manuel Romanes basked in the warm sunshine of a glorious October afternoon on the Costa del Sol. He watched his five-year-old son diving off the side of the pool and swimming almost the whole length under water, and then his eyes scanned the shaded area of the garden and stopped beneath a crimson hedge of bougainvillea. Rachel was sitting beneath a multi-coloured parasol, just about managing to balance cross-legged on the edge of one of the sun-loungers.

'You look decidedly uncomfortable,' called out Manuel. 'Why don't you go indoors and rest for a while?'

'I'm summoning up the courage to jump in the pool with Anton, but as soon as I get in, he'll get out. I think he's afraid that I'll give birth in the pool and the water will turn into a blood bath. He has a vivid imagination backed up by a poor understanding of the facts.'

Manuel laughed but as he watched Rachel stand up and walk towards the pool he could understand the concerns of his young son. She looked like a balloon ready to pop, and he could imagine that any normal little boy would want to be out of the way when that happened.

As expected Rachel waded into the shallow end and at the same moment Anton heaved himself out of the deep end. Manuel and Rachel exchanged knowing looks but it was Anton who spoke.

'My friends are coming over soon and we're going to play football if I can find my ball. Have you seen it?' he asked his father.

'Yes, it's under the hedge over there,' replied Manuel,

pointing to a spot near the garage. 'Both our cars are inside so why don't you use the outside parking area as your football pitch, and that way we won't have any more broken windows.'

Anton made a face at his father and responded in Spanish. It pleased Manuel that his son always spoke in English in Rachel's company, and he was over the moon that at just five years of age his offspring was fluent in two of the world's most widely spoken languages.

Rachel was not Anton's mother, but she had come to love the boy as if he was her own and she hoped he would take to his new half-brother or sister as well as he had done to her. The baby was due any day and the delivery couldn't come soon enough for Rachel, who had struggled with being pregnant at the height of the temperatures churned out by a Spanish summer.

She had sometimes longed for the cool, often downright cold, and wet summer days of her home: the seaside resort of Porthcawl in South Wales, but on the whole she wouldn't swap Nerja for Porthcawl's Coney Beach. Everything anyone could possibly want was at her fingertips and as a partner she couldn't ask for better than Manuel.

They had met through Manuel's wife Catherine, who used the riding stables where Rachel worked. The two women had a mutual love of horses but little else in common, with very different personalities and backgrounds.

Catherine Romanes came from a privileged horse-racing family whose home was not far from Ascot racecourse. She had ridden horses practically since before she could walk and had met Manuel when his family had come to the UK to purchase two horses for breeding.

The handsome Spaniard had fallen hook, line, and sinker for a woman who looked like the epitome of an English rose but who underneath was as hard as nails and used to getting everything she wanted. Their wedding was one of the social events of the year but was the beginning of a serious rift between the two families.

The rift was over religion, as in the eyes of her new in-laws their son's wedding in a quintessential English Anglican church did not see him married in the sight of God. A compromise was reached and the couple went through a ceremony that blessed their union in the Baroque-style Roman Catholic Cathedral in Malaga.

If he was honest Manuel would have to admit that he had felt equally out of place in both settings, as like the majority of Spanish men of his generation religion did not figure high on his agenda. Since becoming an adult he had only attended weddings and funeral services, and avoided family discussions on faith. The spectre of religion did not raise its head again until after their son was born.

The start of their married life had been difficult for the couple, as due to some bad investment decisions Catherine's father's business had folded dramatically and the family had lost everything, including their spectacular Berkshire home. Her parents, Peter and Margaret Washington, were helped by Margaret's sister Elsie, who since the death of her husband had lived alone on a small farm in South Wales.

At the time Catherine and Manuel were living in Nerja with José and Claudia Romanes, and on hearing the news José offered to help.

It was less than a two-and-a-half-hour flight from Málaga to the Cardiff International Airport and within days the two families were sitting around a huge farm-kitchen table at Elsie Hopkins' home, deciding strategy.

Peter Washington was a proud man and was adamant that he would not accept financial help for himself from this recently formed 'Spanish alliance'. He was already struggling with having to be the non-contributory guest of his wife's sister and this foreign aid was out of the question.

In spite of their differences the families stayed together at the farm for almost two weeks and during that time Manuel fell in love with the surrounding countryside and the coastline that looked out over the Bristol Channel.

Catherine had always been close to her father and she could see how the crash of his business had affected his health. She colluded with Manuel and his father and they came up with a plan that would put the Washington's in a good position and at the same time save face for her father.

She described the perfect place that she and Manuel had found for a home. There was a notice to say that the land was for sale and it was ideally positioned in the cradle of two hills and with a view across the Channel. It had always been understood that José Romanes would put up the funding for the couple's marital home, but he had supposed that home would be in Spain as traditionally in his family couples lived near their husband's parents.

Before he returned to Spain Señor Romanes had made an offer for the land and instructed architects to draw up the plans for a spectacular single-storey building with a two-storey annex. Catherine told her delighted mother that she could design the annex exactly as she wanted it and live there in return for a generous amount of baby-sitting. It all sounded idyllic and Peter was relieved for the first time in months to have something to take his mind off his business failure.

Unfortunately, the purchase of the land was fraught with a number of legal difficulties. It was almost a year before a spade was sunk into the ground. Manuel had to spend most of his time in Spain as he was still playing a vital role in the family business. There were plans to open a UK branch of the Spanish stud farm in the Vale of Glamorgan, but the negotiations were dragging on and Catherine started to feel neglected. She sometimes went to Spain with Manuel but hated the tight family set-up, where she felt constantly under the microscope and surrounded by Romanes women while her husband worked long hours.

She took more and more to staying at the farm, where she was footloose and fancy free. Manuel had bought her a horse that was kept at the stables where Rachel worked as a riding instructor. It didn't take Catherine long to get in with some of the exceptionally affluent users of the stables, and horse riding turned to other forms of socialising, and then to all-night weekend parties.

Rachel had met Manuel when he purchased the horse, and it had been the only time in her life when a complete stranger had made her stomach flip. She thought Catherine was a complete idiot to risk losing such a man for the likes of the morons she had attached herself to. Suddenly Catherine stopped coming to the stables and the owner was given instructions not to allow her to ride during her pregnancy. Rachel had several thoughts when she heard the news, and the first was to hope that the baby would be Manuel's child and not the result of one of Catherine's several flings, liaisons that were openly boasted about by some of the men who used the stables and rode more than just the horses.

She also wondered how they would stop Catherine riding if she turned up, because the woman was certainly not one for doing anything other than exactly what she wanted. In reality, it wasn't something that needed to be considered, because it was almost a year before Catherine showed up at the stables again.

She had endured a nightmare of a pregnancy – it was like a textbook of everything that could possibly go wrong. Even before she knew she was pregnant Catherine had been blighted by morning sickness, and in her case it had been the all-day variety. She constantly felt sick and was actually retching and vomiting dozens of times throughout the day. It was discovered that she was suffering from hyperemesis gravidarum and was admitted to hospital several times for rehydration and assessment.

Catherine hated what the baby was doing to her and heaped some of her anger onto Manuel. It seemed that instead of bringing them closer together the boy that they had seen on the scan was driving a wedge between them. At about twenty-four weeks gestation the sickness disappeared, and as if attempting to make up for months of not enjoying food Catherine ate her way through mountains of cakes and chocolate.

She piled on the pounds and gave herself a new reason to be angry with her unborn son. It could have been on the cards anyway but excessive weight gain and minimal movement didn't help with her blood-pressure levels, and she screamed abuse at her baby when her ankles disappeared and in their place formed a mound of pitting oedema.

With all the signs of pre-eclampsia escalating a decision was reached to perform a caesarean section at thirty-six weeks and Anton weighed in at just under six pounds.

Manuel had assumed that his wife would breast-feed their baby but Catherine had other ideas and she was more than happy to let anyone who wanted to bottle-feed her son and change his nappies.

All she wanted was a return of the figure she had once had and for her, not some scrawny newcomer, to be once again the centre of attention.

Because the pregnancy had been difficult and Catherine was showing no signs of bonding with her child the family were advised to be on the lookout for signs of post-natal depression. Manuel did everything he could to raise his wife's spirits and chased the architects, planners, and builders for progress on the building of their new home.

He had come to realise that Catherine was very much a material girl and buying things to turn the house into her dream home would surely lift her spirits. When Anton was just six weeks old he brought her the news that all the legal stuff had been sorted and that the builders had actually moved a caravan onto the site and were prepared to crack on with the development.

Like the majority of the population neither Manuel nor Catherine's parents properly understood the complexity of post-natal depression and they just went along with Catherine's mood swings. There were sunshine days when she was up before the birds and by lunch had purchased various items for their new home, and there were black days when she stayed in bed and cried. There was only one constant common denominator and that was Anton, but whether it was a good or a bad day for Catherine there was no place in it for the child.

It seemed that progress with the house was doomed, as one set of builders went into liquidation and a new company had to be engaged. Manuel struggled to find anything to keep his wife sane. He stayed in the UK as much as he possibly could and was both mother and father to his son whilst he was there and in his absence Catherine's parents took on that responsibility.

Suddenly, when Anton was six months old, Catherine returned to horse riding and to the party-loving set she had once been part of. Her parents, whilst not approving of her staying out late and sometimes not coming home at all, were so pleased to have their daughter back that they kept quiet about her activities. However, as her behaviour got more outrageous, they felt compelled to challenge her.

She had told them that she was not prepared to hang around and look after 'Manuel's Spanish brat' whilst he swanned around Andalucía with some of his old conquests, and that she was thinking of leaving her husband for someone who appreciated her. That night Manuel had telephoned and asked to speak to his wife but her mother, who had answered the phone, had no idea where her daughter was and suggested there were things they needed to talk about. In return Manuel told her that his family were concerned about Catherine's lack of love and concern towards their grandson and had some suggestions of their own to make.

It was agreed that Manuel and his parents would fly over the next day. Margaret Washington tried ringing her daughter's mobile to tell her about the arrangements. The phone kept diverting to voicemail and Margaret didn't feel happy about just leaving a message. She wrote a note and walked to her daughter's room with the intention of leaving it on the bedside table. When she entered the room she got the strangest feeling that something was wrong, but superficially everything looked to be in order.

Maybe it was the order that was causing her concern! Catherine wasn't the tidiest of women, but today everything looked neat: only one drawer was partially open, and that was because the buckle of one of Catherine's belts was preventing it from closing. Margaret left the note and wondered where her daughter had gone this time and when she would be back.

She had never been an easy child but she was still

Margaret's baby, and it was obvious to her that her daughter's mind was in turmoil. It would have been easy to blame post-natal depression or the absence of her husband, but Margaret knew that it was deeper than that. When Catherine was just twelve years old she had deliberately thrown herself from her horse because she had come second in a local gymkhana. She reflected that she and her husband should have sought professional help for their daughter then, but instead they had thrown money at the problem, giving Catherine every material thing she wanted.

It was her pregnancy that had exposed the extent of her unstable mind and as Margaret closed the door of her daughter's room, she wondered where it would all end.

Chapter Eighteen

Martin cleaned off the previous notes on the whiteboard and drew three new columns before putting a bold heading, 'VERA'.

'Apart from the paperwork and the judicial process we have concluded the investigation of the kidnapping of Jason Barnes and the killing of Susan Evans. We have a signed confession and more than enough forensic evidence to prove that almost everything happened in line with what Dan Painter has told us.

'The only thing that is open for discussion is the lead-up to her death, as according to Painter it was she who started the physical fight between them and he hadn't realised his own strength when he tried to shut her up. At some point Jason may be able to tell us what he saw, but the boy has been through a lot and we can wait until he is fully recovered before attempting to question him.

'I had expected to be here this morning just winding up and confirming the results of the post-mortem on Susan Evans, but instead we have opened a new investigation and I'm going to ask Alex to give us a pictorial account of the new case.'

Alex sat at his laptop and with an air of theatrical intrigue controlled the images that emerged on the largest whiteboard in the room. He explained that the beautiful location was to have been the setting for a luxurious home, but work hadn't got much further than the digging of the foundations, with the positioning of a caravan for the use of the builders.

Martin interrupted. 'As most of you will know, this caravan is where Jason Barnes was taken and where Susan Evans was killed.

'We know from the confession that the woman was killed in the caravan and there is evidence of Dan Painter's vomit – just as he described.

'In the next ten minutes you will see a video of how the body was found and carefully removed from beneath all the bricks and debris that you can see. Given the remoteness of the place and the fact that the site had been abandoned, Susan Evans' body would probably have stayed there indefinitely if we hadn't been told where to find it.'

Martin nodded. 'Yes, thank God Painter couldn't live with his nightmares.'

'I didn't record DS Pryor's sudden and spectacular disappearance, but he must have trodden on some rotten wood and loose stones because part of the ground gave way beneath him.' Alex waited and was not disappointed to hear comments about Matt's weight and the size of a hole needed to swallow him up.

Matt retaliated. 'Not funny, guys, I could have broken my neck!'

Because everyone knew no serious damage had been done they felt able to continue with a bit of banter, but then it was back to business as Alex flashed up an image that looked directly into the hole that Matt had vacated.

Now it was Matt's turn to comment. 'How come we didn't see that when I was pulled out?'

Martin replied. 'We were all concentrating on getting you out safely and didn't really want to disturb the area again.'

'Apart from that, the skeleton that we can all see clearly now was not as visible at the time. It was only when Ken was making some final checks that he removed some pieces of wood and could see this exact image.' Alex continued. 'This is proof of what we were saying a few minutes ago, about the feasibility of Susan Evans' body not being easily found. We can see that this second body had been in that hole for some years – hopefully DCI Phelps will be able to tell us more about that.'

Martin, with some input from Matt, spent the next fifteen minutes relating the fascinating time they had spent with Prof.

Moore's colleagues. When they had finished Martin's first column, 'Actual Facts', was surprisingly full considering all they had to base the facts on was a skeleton.

'The professors are keen to remind us that some of the facts are still not fully substantiated, but in any event they give us quite a lot to work on.' He moved to the second column and began scribbling the facts that needed to be considered and handing out chunks of work.

'I agree with Prof. Moore's suggestion that the dumping of what would have then been a complete body is likely to have coincided with the cessation of building on the site. We urgently need to speak to Manuel Romanes about why the work was stopped. The planning department seem to think it was a mixture of frustration due to non-compliance with planning regulations and possibly some sort of family dispute, but they aren't really sure.

'The address that the council planners gave Matt for Mr Romanes is a farmhouse, but we've checked the electoral register and according to that there has never been anyone with the surname Romanes living there – but nevertheless it is the address to which the council sent his letters. Helen, you, and I will take a trip there after this session.

'Matt, you can get some of the team working on the missing persons files. You know what you're looking for?'

Matt nodded. 'A woman, approximately thirty years of age, who may have been reported missing about five years ago. Of course we have no idea if she was from this area and so we may have to look into UK-wide records. She would have been around five feet eight inches tall, with a perfect smile, and could have been into sport as she had during her lifetime suffered a number of broken bones.

'Our visiting professors particularly noticed that her collarbone had been broken a few times, and isn't that something that happens quite a lot to people who ride horses?'

'Yes,' Helen said. 'It happens in contact sports as well, and according to the facts on the board she also broke her leg and her arm at some time so it could have been skiing or even a traffic accident.'

'It could have been one of a million things, but just knowing about these details will help with the identification.' Martin rubbed the side of his face and called the meeting to a close. 'One other thing you need to do, Matt, and that is talk to the people upstairs and put out a press release regarding the discovery of this second woman. Some of the reporters go back a long time and they may even be of some help on the missing persons front.'

Martin walked out and Helen joined him and asked if he needed directions to the farmhouse, but he shook his head. 'I recognised the address as soon as Matt said it, and if I'm not very much mistaken a couple called Elsie and James Hopkins live there – or at least they did.'

During the journey to the farm Martin told Helen how his aunt had taken him to the farm a few times when he was in school. 'Elsie Hopkins used to sell farm produce at the open-air market in Cowbridge, and my aunt loved her yoghurt and goat's cheese. I remember kicking my heels for what seemed like hours whilst they chatted on a Saturday morning, but my patience was rewarded when we were invited to the farm.

'I remember it being a great place and Mr Hopkins being exactly what I expected a farmer to look like.' Martin laughed. 'I've learned since that there is no such thing as a typical farmer, or a typical anything else if it comes to that, but I really enjoyed our visits there.'

'Why did they stop?' enquired Helen.

'I don't think there was actually any reason other than my aunt probably got work and that often meant spending all my free time on film sets or such like.'

'Sounds more exciting than visiting a farm. I'm surprised you still remember where it is as it must be years since you were last there.'

'Oh, at least a hundred years!' mocked Martin as he turned the car into a narrow country road and followed the sign that told them they were heading for Celtic Valley Farm. A few minutes of bumping over some rough ground and he brought the car to a stop and got out to open a wide metal gate.

'Exactly as I remember it,' said Martin as he got back in and drove the car to a hard-standing near the farmhouse and parked it next to two other cars and a small van.

Their arrival had set the dogs barking, but there were no dogs to be seen and so cautiously they made their way to the front door. Before Helen had the chance to knock the door was opened, and although it was something like twenty years since Martin had last seen her he was practically certain that he was looking at Elsie Hopkins.

She was thinner than he recalled, but the years had treated her face well and even two complete strangers at her door received the cheery 'hello' he remembered from the past.

He had been a boy of around ten years of age when they had last met and he would not have expected her to recognise him and in any event he was obliged to make the formal introductions and show her proof of identity. That was when she surprised him.

'DCI Martin Phelps?' she asked. 'Oh, sorry, it's not that I'm suggesting anything different, it's just that many years ago I was friendly with a woman whose nephew was called Martin Phelps and she brought him here a few of times – what a coincidence.'

Martin smiled warmly at the woman and shook her hand. 'No coincidence. I did come here as a child with my Auntie Pat, and I was telling my colleague on the way here what fond memories I have of those visits and how kind you and your husband were to me.'

Elsie smiled back, though a little sadly. 'My husband died of testicular cancer ten years ago just last Friday, and as you will see the farm is not what it used to be. Come on in, heaven knows why we're standing on the doorstep. It's a real pleasure to see you again, but what about Pat – what's she up to these days?'

Helen felt like a gooseberry, as for the next ten minutes her boss and Mrs Hopkins caught up on the last twenty years or so. It wasn't often that Martin had the chance to talk to someone, other than his next-door neighbour, who had known his aunt. Somehow between the words a pot of tea was made and some home-made scones were produced.

'Matt will be cursing me for getting this visit,' said Helen as she bit into the most delicious scone she had ever tasted.

Before he tasted anything Martin felt compelled to explain their visit to Elsie. Initially he just said that they were hoping to speak to a Mr Manuel Romanes, who had at one time given the farm as his address.

'Has this got anything to do with Catherine?' asked Elsie.

'Who is Catherine?'

'Manuel's wife,' Elsie said.

'So you do know Mr Romanes? Is he here?' Martin could see that their host was getting anxious and slowed down on the questions. 'Look, Mrs Hopkins, perhaps you could just put us in the picture, there is nothing for you to worry about but we really do need to speak to Manuel Romanes.'

'Please call me Elsie,' was the reply. 'It's a long story, and with your permission I'll get my sister Margaret to join us. Catherine is her daughter and as far as I know Catherine is still legally married to Manuel.'

Elsie got up and crossed the kitchen, opening a thick wooden door at the back.

'Margaret, will you come here? There are some police officers who want to talk to us about Manuel.' There was no response from the other side of the door and Elsie continued walking away and calling out.

'What do you make of that?' Helen asked Martin.

Martin shrugged. 'Let's just wait and see what they have to say. At the moment I can't make anything of it, but one thing I do know is that these scones are even better than the ones I remember as a kid.'

Elsie returned with her sister, whom she introduced as Mrs Margaret Washington, and Martin immediately decided that unlike her sister she would be expecting the use of her full title. 'Mrs Washington, it's good of you to see us, and as I understand it the man we want to speak to is your son-in-law.'

'Yes, Manuel is our son-in-law but he doesn't live here, he lives in Spain.'

'And you daughter Catherine, does she live in Spain too?'

Mrs Washington had sat on one of the wooden chairs opposite Martin and he watched as her lips tightened and he wondered if there had been some kind of family dispute.

'It's possible that my daughter lives in Spain, Chief Inspector, but if she does it isn't with Manuel – he has got custody of our grandson and is currently shacked up with someone who is about to produce another offspring for him. He has obviously forgotten my Catherine ever existed.'

Suddenly and violently Elsie banged her fists on the table, causing everyone to jump. 'That's enough, Margaret. I mean it – that's enough. I am sick of you bad-mouthing Manuel when in reality the man couldn't have done any more to support you and your ungrateful family.

'When Peter was in danger of being declared bankrupt it was Manuel's father who put up the funds to stop that happening.

'Catherine was never faithful to her husband and everyone in the farming community knew what she was up to with that crowd from the stables. He trusted her and she made a fool of him, and don't pretend you didn't know any of this.'

It was as if Elsie had been bottling up her disgust for years, and now that the cork had popped there was no stopping her outpouring of feelings.

'It was hardly Manuel's fault that Catherine had a tough pregnancy, and if the man could have borne the child for her he would have done. She had no time for the baby and although I sympathise with anyone who suffers post-natal depression most of Catherine's symptoms were self-inflicted.'

Margaret Washington looked at her sister in total disbelief. Not only had Elsie decided to tell her exactly what she thought about Catherine, but she had decided to do it in front of two strangers. Martin had lost count of the number of times that a visit from the police had unleashed years of pent-up tension within families and he had learned to let the exchanges run. When people were letting go of their feelings they were off their guard and said things they may otherwise have thought twice about.

'She was sick, really sick.' Catherine's mother spoke in her daughter's defence.

'I didn't see anything different to what we had all seen before when Catherine couldn't get her own way. She stayed in bed most of the day – well, I can't remember a time when she *didn't*, unless there was something she wanted to get up for. Her so-called sickness didn't stop her partying and staying out all night, though, did it?

'Did you think I couldn't see what was going on in my own house? You covered for her with Manuel when he phoned and she did the dying swan act whenever he was here so the poor man had no idea what his wife was up to.

'It came as no surprise to any of us when she left her child and didn't come back, but Manuel and his family were devastated.'

At this point Martin started to interrupt, but Elsie was suddenly embarrassed by her outburst and got in first.

'I'm sorry you had to hear all that, family business should stay within the family and I don't know what came over me. Maybe it was just that I remember your aunt as a woman who spoke her mind and somehow thinking of her gave me the courage to speak out.'

Helen picked up on what she guessed Martin had been about to ask. 'You say that Catherine left her child and didn't come back? What happened?'

It was Mrs Washington's turn to express her feelings and she turned on Helen, who had asked the questions.

'I thought you came here to speak to Manuel, not ask a load of pointless questions about my daughter. Catherine will have had good reasons for leaving and I have tried for years to get her father to help me figure out what those reasons could have been. Unfortunately he chose to wrap his sorrow at the loss of his daughter around the neck of a whisky bottle, and now his liver is past recovery. What a bloody mess.'

Elsie stood up, walked around the table, and drew up a chair next to her sister.

'I'm sorry for my outburst, but maybe it has cleared the air and now we can talk about things that we should never have left unsaid.' She looked towards Martin and addressed him formally.

'Perhaps we should ask you to explain things more fully, Chief Inspector Phelps, starting with why you want to speak to Manuel?'

Martin explained that he was trying to contact the owner of a piece of land that had been earmarked for development a few years ago. 'The Council's planning department have this farm as the address for all correspondence with Mr Romanes when the plans were submitted and we need to speak to him regarding why the work was halted.'

Mrs Washington shook her head. 'Are you seriously telling us that a detective of your ranking has been sent here to find out why some building work hadn't been completed? I don't think so but in any event you don't need Manuel for that. I can tell you exactly why Nuestro Abrigo was abandoned.'

Seeing the slightly quizzical look on Martin's face she explained that the Spanish name that meant 'Our Shelter' had been chosen for the home that Catherine and Manuel were planning to build on the site.

'We were going to live there too, you know. The plans included a beautiful two-storey annex for me and Peter and although I know all Catherine really wanted us for was full-time child care I would have been happy there.'

Martin was afraid that they were going to be treated to a long trip down memory lane as she started to describe the colour scheme she had chosen for her kitchen and he rather curtly moved the conversation forward.

'I am more interested to learn about why the plans didn't go ahead and I'm assuming they stopped when your daughter left her husband.'

'She didn't just leave her husband – she left me and Peter too, and Peter almost had a nervous breakdown.'

'Do you know where she went?' asked Helen.

'If I knew that I wouldn't be standing by watching my husband slowly die from the results of wallowing in whisky. Cirrhosis of the liver is not a pretty disease, young lady, it's not pretty for the sufferer and it's downright ugly for anyone close to the victim.

'There was no consoling Peter when Catherine left and as time went on and we heard nothing from her for weeks and then months he became more and more withdrawn and that was when the drinking started.'

Elsie could see that her sister was struggling and so she took over and told the officers that Manuel had stayed at the farm for weeks after Catherine had left. 'He of course wanted to ensure that his son was OK, and to be fair to him he also made strenuous efforts to find Catherine. I think their marriage was already on the rocks but he wanted to hear from Catherine, face to face, that she was not coming back.'

Having regained her composure Mrs Washington weighed in with no small degree of sarcasm.

'Looking for Catherine, was he? More likely chatting up someone he hopes will be the second Mrs Romanes. He practically lived at the riding stables and even took Anton to see his "new mother"!'

Although she probably felt like banging the table again Elsie refrained and tried to reason with her sister.

'I don't know why you continue to blame Manuel for Catherine leaving home. She knew what she was doing and didn't have a second thought for any of us – not even her young son. Manuel spent time at the stables but only because Catherine's circle of friends were always there. As you know, he discovered that one of the men had also stopped going there at the same time as your daughter disappeared and there was a lot of gossip about their relationship.

'The man was someone called Simon Davidson and Manuel tried to contact him but his family intervened. Apparently Simon's mother was quite frank with Manuel and said she knew about her son's affair and told Manuel that her son had ended it. She confirmed that Simon was living at home and that

Catherine was most definitely not with him and was not going to be.'

She turned to Martin. 'Nevertheless, the rumours that Catherine had taken off with him continued and as time went by it seemed the most likely thing.'

'How long ago was that?' questioned Martin.

'Four years, five months, three weeks, and two days ago,' said Mrs Washington, seemingly without even having to think about it. 'That's when my daughter left this house and we haven't seen or heard from her from that day to this.'

Chapter Nineteen

You could have heard a pin drop as the two sisters noted the effect that Margaret Washington's words had had on the detective chief inspector and his constable. Martin didn't believe in coincidences and the words had been the final link in the chain he had already forged concerning the skeleton 'Vera' – or as he now believed her to be, Mrs Catherine Romanes.

He wanted to know more about the circumstances surrounding Catherine's disappearance and knew that he had to hold out on telling the women what had been discovered at the building site. It was likely that once they knew the two would fall to pieces and he would have to wait for his answers.

He spoke quietly and asked Mrs Washington if she would tell him exactly what she remembered about the last time she had seen her daughter. 'Had you and she quarrelled? Did she drive away in her car? Who else saw her go? Tell me anything that you can remember, please.'

Margaret Washington had a gut feeling that the man sitting opposite her was about to give her the most terrible news regarding her daughter. She also sensed that he would not be rushed into anything and so she explained that Catherine walked out on a Friday evening.

'There had been a big argument that afternoon and she as good as told us that she was planning to leave Manuel and didn't much care happened to Anton. Her father was angrier than I have ever seen him and he told her that her husband and son would be better off without her.

'She laughed in his face and told him that the only reason he wanted her to stay with Manuel was so that he and I would have the benefit of the Romanes' money. It was a dreadful row and afterwards I heard Catherine banging about in her room and thought she could be packing up her things to make the get-away she was planning.

'Then it all went quiet and it was sometime later that I thought I heard her car drive off, but it must have been a taxi because her car is actually still here.

'Later that evening we got a call from Manuel and Peter made me tell him that things were bad and that Catherine had possibly left for good.'

'Were you the last to see her before she left?' asked Martin.

'No, I don't think I was, because I thought I heard raised voices later but when I asked her father about it he said he had heard nothing and that it was probably loud music.'

She turned to her sister Elsie. 'You wouldn't have spoken to Catherine that night because you didn't get back from your craft fair until very late. Do you remember?'

'Of course I remember, we've been over and over that night a million times.'

Something had been bugging Helen from the beginning and she looked for an answer. 'Why didn't you inform the police of Catherine's disappearance? Maybe not immediately, if you believed she had taken off with somebody – but when you didn't hear from her for such a long time why didn't you simply report her missing?'

'She wasn't a child and she had as good as told us she was leaving her husband for someone else. We had already endured the scandal of Peter's business disaster and we couldn't face any more public humiliation.'

'Are you sure when Manuel phoned you on that Friday night that he was phoning from Spain?' questioned Martin.

'I can answer that,' said Elsie. 'It was me who picked Manuel and his parents up from the Cardiff International Airport the following day and they stayed here just as they had done whenever they came over to visit.'

'Now will you please tell us what this is all about?' Margaret asked.

Martin leant forward. 'You will probably have heard the news regarding the little boy that was kidnapped on a school trip.' Both women nodded, wondering what that had to do with anything, and Martin continued. 'I'm not sure how up to date you are but the boy was taken by a man and there was a woman involved. While they were holding the child captive they quarrelled violently and the woman was killed. After his arrest the man told us what had happened and directed us to where he had left the woman's body.'

Elsie had cottoned on and explained things to her sister who still looked puzzled. 'I knew there was something familiar about that place – I said so when we were watching the news – but I only went there a couple of times to be shown the view looking down to the coast.'

'That's why these officers want to speak to Manuel, it's got nothing to do with Catherine. It's because he owns the land on which this woman's body was found and presumably the caravan we saw on the television is the one he had placed on site for the builders to use. Oh, that is a relief.'

She turned to Martin. 'I had come to the conclusion you were here to tell us that you had found Catherine's body and were looking for Manuel in connection with her death.'

Martin looked at the two women who in spite of all they had said were obviously relieved to think that Catherine wasn't the subject of this official visit. Their mood had gone from one of extreme anxiety to cautious optimism and for Martin that was going to make the next few minutes even more difficult.

'I'm afraid ownership of the land is not the only reason we want to speak to Mr Romanes, and if Mr Washington is around it would be helpful if he could join us.'

Margaret Washington verbally jumped on Martin as if he alone was responsible for her husband's predicament. 'When I said that my husband had taken to drinking after our daughter left I didn't mean he liked the occasional tipple. In the space of a few years he totally pickled what had previously been a very healthy liver. I won't go into the details of his personality change, or his itchy, jaundiced skin, but I think the latest development will give you some idea.

'Three days ago he started vomiting blood and collapsed in the bathroom, and we had to call an ambulance. He is now in hospital and the vomiting is apparently as a result of something called oesophageal varices – or to put it more bluntly his liver has virtually stopped doing what it should do and he is dying.'

'The doctors talked about an end-stage condition and palliative care but what they really meant was "send for the undertaker" – so no, Chief Inspector, he is not *around*, as you put it.'

Martin was more than used to being the punch bag when people were faced with desperate situations and simply said how sorry he was to hear about Mr Washington.

'As I said there was another reason we want to speak to Mr Romanes, and I'm afraid that there is no way I can make this easy for you. During the retrieval of the body we had been told about we discovered the remains of another body.

'The second body is also a woman and she would have been around thirty years of age at the time of her death, approximately five years ago. She would have been about five feet eight inches tall and the only other thing I can tell you is that she had perfect teeth.'

Martin stopped and waited for a reaction, but neither Catherine's mother nor her aunt said a word, and so he continued.

'From what you have told me about Catherine's disappearance and from what we know about when the building work stopped we believe that we have found Catherine. Obviously we will be making further tests to establish that fact but in my opinion those results will only serve to confirm our belief.'

Elsie put her arms around her sister, the only sign that either woman had heard what Martin had said. Not feeling comfortable with the silence, DC Cook-Watts collected the cups and plates and put the kettle on. She had on such occasions suggested something stronger than tea but in light of what had been said about Mr Washington she decided against it and made a strong brew instead.

Martin also felt the need to give the women some privacy and wandered to the far side of the kitchen. He hadn't noticed them before but there were wooden framed photographs on the wall nearest the back door. He recognised Elsie and her sister and guessed the eldest of two men shown must be Peter Washington. There was a photograph of a swarthy, good-looking man holding a baby, but the one that most caught his eye was a beautiful young woman showing prefect teeth in what had been described by one of the professors as a toothpaste advert smile. If the picture was correct, 'Vera' almost certainly was Catherine Romanes.

There had not been the wailing and gnashing of teeth that Martin had been expecting from Margaret Washington and as he returned to his seat he watched her drinking the tea that Helen had given her and wondered if she had even understood what he had said. Outwardly she looked totally composed and there was only the faintest hint of a tremble in her voice as she spoke.

'I've been expecting one of two things for the past five years. One, that my daughter would breeze back through that door as if barely a day had passed since she left and expecting everyone to forget her behaviour and lack of communication. My second expectation has been the one you just delivered on and I've rehearsed that possibility so often. Now that it's happened it's almost a relief.'

Elsie squeezed her sister's hands and nodded in agreement. 'I think we've known for at least the past couple of years that something must have happened to my niece, but none of us wanted to speak the words. Do you know what happened to her?'

Margaret looked up to see for herself what Martin's response to her sister's question would be. He shook his head and confirmed that until he had spoken to the sisters he was not aware of the identity of the woman that had been found. Even now it was on the balance of probabilities and explained that

231

there were tests that would give positive proof.

Margaret's hand went to the gold locket she always wore and her hands trembled as she unclasped it. 'I have always kept a couple of Catherine's baby curls in this locket and if it's DNA comparison you're looking for then I suppose they would help. Failing that I could simply identify the body – that's what you get people to do, isn't it?'

As he was looking for sensitive words to explain why physical identification would not be possible he was spared the problem as Elsie answered her sister's question.

Margaret's hand went to the gold locket she always wore and her hands trembled as she unclasped it. 'I have always kept a couple of Catherine's baby curls in this locket and if it's DNA comparison you're looking for then I suppose they would help. Failing that I could simply identify the body – that's what you get people to do, isn't it?'

Martin was spared the unpleasant task of explaining why physical identification would not be possible as Elsie answered her sister's question.

'I can see why that wouldn't be possible, Margaret, and so will you if you think about it. You know that when we bury one of our animals on the farm, only the bones are left after a few years, and I suspect that is the case with Catherine. We have our memories of her, and some of them are precious, so let's just think about the happy little girl who used to come here for her summer holidays.'

The awakening of those tender thoughts did more to bring on the tears than the stark reality of anything Martin had said and Margaret began to sob. Quietly at first but then with a torrent of tears she poured out years of heartache.

Elsie moved away from her sister and suggested they all give her some space.

'We were going anyway,' said Martin. 'Will you be alright?'

'Yes, we'll be OK, but to go back to the question I asked earlier: do you know what happened to Catherine?'

'At the moment I have no idea, I'm afraid, but we will be working hard to find out and I will definitely need to speak to

Mr Romanes and Mr Washington.'

Elsie walked over to the telephone and looked at a list of numbers that was kept on the table. 'I can give you Manuel's number or if you prefer I can ring him and tell him you want to speak to him.'

'No, don't do that,' said Martin. 'I want to be the one to tell him.'

Elsie looked Martin straight in the eye. 'You mean you want to assess his reaction and try to decide if he had anything to do with Catherine's death. You haven't said if she died of natural causes but I don't see that being a possibility. My guess is that someone murdered my niece and for some macabre reason left her body in the place that was going to be her home.

'Whoever is on your list of suspects, you can rule out Manuel, and not just because he was in Spain the night she disappeared but because he's a genuinely nice person. What about the man Catherine is rumoured to have left with? Simon. You'll need to speak to him.'

Martin watched Elsie as she spoke and was once again taken back to his childhood. No wonder his aunt and this woman had hit it off so well, they were well-matched in their direct speaking and clear observations.

He nodded and asked about the possibility of speaking to Peter Washington.

'I'll ring the hospital and see what the position is with Peter. Margaret didn't exaggerate his condition and it sadly looks as if my sister is going to finally lose her daughter and say goodbye to her husband within days of one another.'

'Really?' questioned Martin. 'His death is imminent?

Elsie nodded as she let the detectives out and waited at the door until they had driven off.

On the way back to Goleudy Martin asked Helen to call Matt and arrange for the team to be ready for an immediate briefing session. 'Tell him to forget about the missing persons trawl and see if he can get our trio of professors to give us some options regarding cause of death. For me everything points to murder, although I suppose there is the outside chance it could have

233

been an accident. I just can't think why she would have gone to the building site, though.

'On second thoughts keep the team on the missing persons files but get them to switch to looking for any men reported missing in the same timescale we were considering for Catherine. Speak to the people who run the riding stables that she frequented. If there was any particular gossip around the time of her disappearance somebody will remember.

'Before we all meet I want to speak to Manuel Romanes, so I'll go straight to my office and hopefully he'll be available on the number Elsie gave us.'

On the way to his office Martin picked up a large mug of very strong coffee and a ham and cheese sandwich and then settled down to make the phone call to Spain. There was no problem getting hold of Manuel, but it was more than twenty minutes later when Martin ended the call.

Everything he had heard was in accord with what he'd learned when visiting the farm and Manuel had agreed to get the first available flight to Cardiff.

'I was just coning to find you, guv,' said Matt as Martin entered Interview Room One. 'Helen said you wanted the team rounded up immediately but anyway we've spent the last quarter of an hour listening to her account of your visit to that address I gave you.'

'Great,' replied Martin and he walked across to the whiteboard he had started to write on earlier and added some facts to the first of his three columns. 'I'm sure Helen also told you that she has given Professor Moore some of Catherine Romanes' hair which could well prove a positive DNA match with the skeleton. We now know the date and approximate time of Catherine's disappearance and although it was five years ago we will go through the same process as if it were yesterday.'

He turned to Helen. 'Did you get anything from upstairs regarding a possible cause of death?'

'Yes, the professor told me that when you and Matt spoke to his colleagues you were shown a damaged bone in the neck of the skeleton. They are putting the damage to that bone down to

234

something or someone that caused intense pressure. He said that if we had found Susan Evans' remains five years after her death she would have given us a similar picture.

'I asked him if that meant that Catherine Romanes had been strangled and he said it was the most likely conclusion. However he warned us not to forget that suicide by hanging could produce comparable injuries, though this would depend upon what material had been used for the purpose. He lost me a bit when he went into details of the different injuries caused by rigid things like leather belts versus softer things like bed sheets.'

There was a general discussion as officers remembered suicides they had attended and the bizarre pieces of equipment that had been used to carry out the act.

'I don't buy the idea of suicide,' said Matt. 'There was nothing in the area she was found that she could have thrown a rope over, and if she killed herself somewhere else how did she end up there? From what we learned at the farm her mother was the last of her family to see her alive, although she thought she had heard Catherine arguing with her father sometime before she left. We haven't been able to speak to Peter Washington yet and time is running out on the possibility of us speaking to him at all.'

'Did you manage to speak to anyone at the riding stables?' he asked Helen.

'Yes, and you were right about there being someone who would remember the gossip. The owner, Laura Green, didn't have a good word to say about Catherine, but she did give me what she called a "comprehensive list" of all the people she hung out with at the stables. She has even promised to email me with their addresses and telephone numbers – and unlike most people nowadays, who delight in hiding behind the rules of confidentiality, she positively relished the thought of each one of them getting a call from the police.

'There were several men who chased after Catherine but only one, Simon Davidson, that she paid any attention to and – here's the good bit – no one saw him after Catherine disappeared, and apparently there's no shortage of money in his family. He sounds like her sort of man, doesn't he?

'When Catherine's husband went to the stables to ask if anyone had seen his wife it apparently gave everyone a great deal of pleasure to tell him about his wife's antics. They are such a snobby lot – the only decent thing about that place is the horses. I couldn't stop Laura Green talking, and she told me that her most recent reason to dislike Catherine is that Manuel has taken the school's best riding instructor, Rachel, to live with him in Spain.'

Martin explained to everyone that during his phone call to Manuel Romanes he had been told that Rachel was living with him and his son and that she was expecting a baby any day. 'Obviously under the circumstances Mr Romanes didn't want to leave her, but I could hear her persuading him to get the first flight and get things sorted. According to Elsie Hopkins she picked Manuel and his family up from the airport the day after Catherine disappeared, but we can't take it for granted that he had flown in with his parents. He could have already been in the country, strangled his wife, dumped her body at a site he knew well, and met his family off the plane before Elsie even got to the airport. Matt, we need to check the planes from Malaga to Cardiff that day and see if his name actually is on the passenger list and that his ticket was used. Based on my phone conversation with him I agree with Elsie Hopkins, who rates him as a decent bloke, but as we all know that doesn't mean he didn't kill his wife. There is plenty of evidence to show that she publically made a fool of him; maybe he paid her a surprise visit and caught her up to no good.'

'That would be a crime of passion,' interrupted Helen. 'Maybe he killed both of them! Perhaps Simon Davidson had raided his family business with a view to running off with Catherine and Manuel caught up with them. Perhaps we should be looking for another skeleton – what do you think?'

Martin let the general buzz of speculative conversation that followed Helen's words continue for a few minutes before answering her question.

'What I think is that we can't rule anything out and the sooner we get to work on some of the information we have got the better. I may have made a mistake in disclosing as much as I did to Mr Romanes. On the other hand I could hardly have got him arrested by the Spanish Guardia as we have nothing to support such an action. I hope my gut feeling about him is right and that Simon Davidson is alive and can be found to answer questions about what really happened that night. Everyone knows what has to be done so it's a question of checking and double checking and reconvening here at nine o'clock tomorrow morning.

Chapter Twenty

'This is it,' said Matt as Martin drew up to the security gates of a property known as Vale Cottage. 'Is it some form of inverted snobbery to call your home a cottage when in reality it's a bloody mansion?'

He got out of the car and looked for a way of opening the security gates and jumped out of his skin as a voice boomed out and seemed to come out of one of the pillars. 'Yes, can I help you?'

The voice was not unfriendly and actually came from a circle of holes in a steel plate attached to Matt's talking pillar. He could see a set of buttons that enabled him to respond.

'I am Detective Sergeant Pryor, the driver is Detective Chief Inspector Phelps, and we have been given this address in connection with our enquiries into the whereabouts of Simon Davidson.'

The voice didn't reply but some mechanical device began to operate and the gates opened inwards. Matt jumped back in the car and Martin drove into the grounds of the cottage.

The drive took them past an oval-shaped ornamental pond surrounded by several mature trees and some shrubs.

'Now this is what I call taste,' remarked Matt. 'Consider this in comparison with the properties surrounding Tina Barnes' home and they come a very poor second.'

Martin nodded. 'Yes, but this is also in a different price bracket, and I'm guessing that this set up would be something like three times the asking price of any of those. What doesn't square with me at the moment is that one of the rumours from the riding school suggests that Davidson wiped out the family business accounts before running off with Catherine – but if that was the case they couldn't have continued living here on a shoestring.'

Surprisingly there were no other cars parked near the front door, but there were several stone-built outhouses and Martin guessed that one or more of them were used to garage the cars.

As they got out of the car they were met by a tall, slim woman dressed in a burgundy waxed jacket, denim jeans, and knee-high boots. Martin tried to guess her age but gave up; she was one of those women who aged well and could have been anywhere between forty and sixty. She hadn't come from inside the house but from one of the buildings that in years gone by had probably housed the livestock. The place had clearly been a working farm at some time.

Matt showed his official identification, but she brushed it aside and suggested they all go inside as she had just finished bedding down the horses and needed a drink. She didn't seem surprised to see two detectives on her doorstep and they followed her through a large but higgledy-piggledy lounge into a very modern farmhouse-style kitchen.

'If you've come to talk about Simon then we could be in for a long session, so what's it to be – tea, coffee, or something stronger? I'm Fiona Davidson and Simon is my son.'

Martin wondered if he was in danger of being beguiled by older women, as this was the second one recently that he had liked. She was self-assured but didn't come over as arrogant, and soon handed over two mugs of strong coffee and poured herself a substantial gin and tonic before asking Martin the obvious question. 'Why are you looking for Simon?'

'Before I go into that can you tell me when you last saw your son?'

'Yes, of course I can. He and Melanie had lunch with us last Sunday. I haven't seen him today but I spoke to him on my mobile just before you buzzed from the gates. If I hadn't done I might have assumed that you were here to tell me he had been involved in an accident or something but as it was I knew he was well.'

Martin and Matt exchanged a look and remembered that they had earlier considered a very different possibility.

'We want to go back a few years when, as we understand it, your son was involved with a woman called Catherine Romanes.' Martin watched as the first signs of emotion showed on Fiona's face – and that emotion was anger.

'I was hoping to never hear that woman's name mentioned again, and if you have come to tell Simon that one of his old flames has met with a terrible accident then don't expect me to shed any tears. She nearly ruined my family, Chief Inspector, and if she is wanted by the police for anything it won't come as a surprise to any of us – but what has it got to do with Simon?'

'In what way did she nearly ruin your family?' asked Martin without answering her question.

Fiona poured herself another gin and looked through the kitchen window onto acres of rolling countryside.

'I was born here and my ancestors have farmed this land for generations. My husband's business is property investment and when we married we transformed this farmhouse and the buildings surrounding it from years of neglect into what we think is our perfect home. Although my family were potentially sitting on a goldmine in terms of all this land there never seemed to be enough money for even basic repairs.

'It wasn't until after my parents died that our solicitors discovered all sorts of bonds and insurance policies that they had stashed away over the years and I became a very wealthy woman in my own right.

'Simon is our only child and he went into business with his father but fell in with the wrong crowd. Oh, don't get me wrong, Chief Inspector, I don't blame anyone other than Simon himself for his behaviour, but when Catherine appeared on the scene he became impossible.

'We knew through the grapevine that she was a married woman, and most people seemed to think she was unstable and manipulative. He was besotted with her and apparently they hatched up a plan to run off and make a new life together, and it got as far as Simon transferring vast sums of money from the company accounts to his own.

'I will never forget that Friday afternoon when I got a phone call from my husband Brian and he told me about serious irregularities and how the finger was pointing at Simon. He sounded worried sick and neither of us was able to contact our son as he wasn't responding to our calls. Brian told me that it had to be Simon who had potentially bankrupted the company and we discussed what would happen when the truth was discovered.

'We decided to use my money to restore six accounts back to their original position and my husband managed to persuade his fellow directors that there had been some sort of glitch with bank transfers. I don't know what they actually thought but as nothing had been lost to the company they didn't really care and it wasn't investigated further.'

Martin wanted to ask a couple of questions but Fiona was at full throttle and so he let her continue.

'I don't know if Simon would have run away with Catherine Romanes if I hadn't intervened – I just don't know. I had barely finished agreeing certain transfers with my bank when I heard Simon's car pull up outside this house. Of course he didn't know that I knew what he'd done, so he just walked into the house and I heard him rummaging around in his room.

'I wanted to throttle him and to this day I don't know how I kept my cool, it was as if something was telling me that I was holding my son's future in my hands and I made us both a cup of coffee. I hadn't done that for a while because since Catherine had appeared on the scene he was hardly around. He looked reluctant to join me and I knew he had good reason to want to get away but it really caught him on the back foot when I told him that I hoped he would be very happy.

'Of course I didn't know then, at least not for sure, that he was planning a new life with that Romanes woman but it was a fair guess. He asked me what I meant and somehow I calmly told him what his father had discovered and also that he had no need to worry because we had sorted it so that his theft would not be discovered.

'During the next few minutes I saw my son go through every possible emotion and when he was sobbing with his head on this table I left him and went to be with the horses.'

'Did he leave with Catherine?' asked Martin.

'No, he stayed, and that night marked a turning point in our son's life. I know he didn't leave the house as he got very, very drunk and I covered him with a blanket when he passed out on the sofa. Brian was still in London and so I slept on one of the armchairs in case Simon was sick. You hear of it, don't you? People get drunk and then die when they choke on their own vomit and I was scared that could happen to Simon.

'As you can imagine, world war three broke out when Brian returned from London the next day, and it has taken years for my husband to trust Simon again. He told us that after I had spoken to him he had been overwhelmed to think that we would risk everything we had to cover for him. He had also considered my wish that he should be happy and finally realised that his happiness would be at the expense of a man losing his wife and a little boy growing up without his mother.

'With the courage of half a bottle of scotch he told us he had phoned Catherine and informed her it was all over. He was a bit sheepish when he explained that he made several attempts to speak to her directly but she wasn't picking up and he had resorted to leaving her a message. To the very best of my knowledge he has not seen her from that day to this. There, that was very good. I've never told anyone about that black Friday but it has been very therapeutic, so thank you for listening.'

Matt, who had been making a few notes, checked back on some of the points that had been said and asked a few questions. 'What time did your son arrive here on that Friday, and what was the first time he left the house after that?'

'It was a few minutes after five when I heard his car, and I know that for certain because I had just been speaking to someone from my bank and she told me that she would normally have left the branch by that time but had been waiting for my call. As to when he left, it wasn't until after the weekend.

'Now you know all our sordid family details, Chief Inspector, will you answer the question you so neatly sidestepped some time ago? Has something happened to Catherine Romanes, and if so what has it got to do with Simon?'

Martin accepted the offer of another coffee and this time Fiona had the same. At first she was confused when Martin referred to the kidnapping that had recently been in the news but then things became clear as he described how the arrest of the kidnapper had led to the discovery of more than just the one body they had been expecting. She sat forward in her chair when Martin revealed that the bodies had been found on the site where Catherine and her husband were planning to build a house, and she put her hands to her mouth as she realised what he was saying – that the second body was more than likely her son's ex-lover.

'How long had she been there?' Fiona asked.

'It looks as if she died soon after she left her home, and that was on the Friday night we have been talking about.' Martin spoke firmly. 'So you will see why it is so important that we have your son's movements for that weekend and that they can be positively verified.'

'That means that you believe Catherine Romanes was murdered and you came here believing that my son killed her.'

Martin interrupted. 'We came here hoping to speak to your son in connection with Catherine's disappearance, yes. Without knowing any of that you have been able to provide him with an alibi for what we believe to be the time of her death, but we will still need to speak to Simon and Brian.'

'Simon lives in Reading with his partner Melanie, but we see them frequently and will all be flying to St Lucia for their wedding in a couple of weeks. Then it's back here for a party the likes of which this old place hasn't seen for centuries – I'll send you an invitation if you like.'

As the security gates closed behind Martin's car Matt looked back. The daylight was fading and strategically placed solar lights were emitting a faint glow around the edge of the pond.

'Now that's what I would call a des-res, but I couldn't imagine living there with just one other person and I don't know many women who would fancy staying there alone, as she will be tonight.'

'You forget, Matt, she was born there and her family have always lived there, and so for her the place is simply home – it's what she's always known. Did you notice that in spite of the size of the place and the fact that she has money she isn't a slave to any interior decorator? Her lounge in particular welcomes you to curl up on one of those randomly placed armchairs. She is a woman with taste and I'll bet their son's wedding party will be spectacular.'

Matt nodded. 'No chance we can accept her invitation is there?'

'No chance!'

Matt's mind returned to business. 'If, as is likely, we are ruling Simon Davidson off our list of possible suspects, then where does that leave us? As you said earlier, it's possible that Manuel Romanes could have been in the country at the time Catherine went missing and he certainly had a motive.'

'I'm hungry and tired and any more thinking will have to wait until tomorrow.' Martin was about to suggest dropping Matt off at his home when a call from Sgt Evans sent them in another direction.

Matt had received the call and Martin quizzed him about it.

'What exactly did John say?'

'He said that Elsie Hopkins had called to say that she and her sister received a message from the hospital about an hour ago suggesting that Peter Washington's condition was deteriorating. Mrs Hopkins told John that she knew that you wanted to speak to her brother-in-law and under the circumstances you may want to do that now. Sounds as if she meant now or never. Apparently they were on their way to see him when she rang Goleudy to let you know, and so they're likely to be there already. Do you want to go straight there?'

'"Want" is not a word I'd have used myself, but I would like to speak to Mr Washington and I don't think it can wait until tomorrow.'

After driving to the hospital and parking the car the detectives were directed to a side ward on the Acute Medical Unit. Before they got to the ward they saw Elsie Hopkins sitting on a chair in the corridor, but there was no sign of her sister.

'Margaret is in the room with Peter,' she told them. 'I knew you'd come after I left a message with that very nice Sergeant Evans, but I'm afraid you're too late. Peter passed away about twenty minutes ago, and mercifully it was a peaceful ending, but I'm not sure if it was the fact that he was no longer in pain or the fact that he had told us some things that he's kept bottled up for years.

'When we got the message from the hospital we knew we were coming to say goodbye to Peter, and Margaret was in a dilemma regarding whether or not to tell her husband that there was the possibility that Catherine had been found. We decided to play it by ear and let it depend upon Peter's state of mind. In the event it was he who opened up the discussion about his daughter.'

'Look, Chief Inspector, what I have to tell you is going to take some time, and my priority just at this moment is my sister. Not only has she just watched her husband die but she has listened to a deathbed confession that will stay with her for the rest of her life.'

As she ended her sentence Elsie got up and opened the door of the cubicle to reveal her sister still holding the hand of her husband. Neither of the detectives had met Peter Washington in life and they were shocked by what they saw. He looked years older than his wife and his skin didn't just have the pallor of death, it was jaundiced and seemed to have some sort of subcutaneous lesions. It was hard to comprehend what dreadful secret had led a man to drinking himself into that state and Martin found himself wondering if Peter had confessed to killing his daughter.

'Is there anything we can do?' asked Martin. 'We can wait and give you a lift if that's of any help.'

Elsie shook her head. 'We've got another sister, and

although we aren't very close I did phone her when Peter died and she's coming to take us back to my place. If you could give me until tomorrow to sort out my thoughts I would be very grateful and then I'll tell you exactly what Peter told us.'

Martin nodded and Elsie closed the door.

'What do you make of that?' asked Matt. 'He obviously confessed to killing his daughter. It must have been during that argument that Mrs Washington thought she had heard. Well, it lets Manuel Romanes off the hook, and supports what Fiona Davidson told us about her son. Catherine's father would obviously have known about the building site. He ironically took his daughter's body to the new home she would never live in, and may have influenced his son-in-law to discontinue the work on the house – who knows?'

Martin was only half-listening to Matt as he was imagining what could have happened on that Friday night and came up with a sudden thought. 'I wonder what he did with her mobile?'

'What?'

'I wonder what Catherine's father did with her mobile phone?' Martin repeated.

'Why?'

'Well, it's just a box my brain feels the need to tick. Simon apparently left her a message breaking off their relationship and I would just like to know when in the timescale of events that happened.'

'But it doesn't make any difference now, guv. We know broadly what happened and it seems as if we will get chapter and verse when we speak to Elsie Hopkins tomorrow.'

Martin stopped on the stairs leading to the main entrance to the hospital and turned back.

'It's no good, you know what I'm like when something bugs me, and this is bugging me.'

'Where are we going?' asked Matt.

'Back to the ward, hopefully to get Elsie's cooperation.'

Half an hour later, and now with the need to have headlights fully on, Martin pulled up outside the farm he knew so well from his childhood for the second time that day. Elsie had given him a key and explained which room was still considered to be Catherine's.

It was apparently just as she had left it, even to the one drawer not being quite closed because of the belt buckle. 'Why do people do this? Turn a room into a sort of mausoleum. It's been dusted and vacuumed but nothing else has been touched and I feel a bit like a shrine raider.'

In spite of his words Matt was looking through drawers and cupboards until Martin told him to stop because the phone was sitting in full view on the dressing table.

'Come to think of it, I don't really know why we thought it would be hidden away and it's probably sitting more or less where she left it. Nothing else has been disturbed or taken and I guess her father had no reason to remove her mobile.' Martin picked up the phone.

'It's as flat as a pancake, and even if it wasn't we may not have been able to access it – but we both know someone who will have no trouble in making this thing talk.'

Chapter Twenty-one

Martin had refused Matt's suggestion of a drink and a pub meal and had instead dropped him off and headed for home. By ten thirty he and Shelley were sitting up in bed eating slices of pizza Margherita and drinking red wine. Not knowing what time to expect Martin home, Shelley had eaten earlier, and she watched him devour three large slices before he lay back on his pillow and put his half-finished glass of wine on the bedside table.

'I was starving and I think that's my favourite pizza. Nothing fancy, just a tomato topping with mozzarella cheese and fresh basil.'

Shelley grinned as she watched Martin adjust his pillow and close his eyes, and after the day he had had she was pleased to see him so relaxed.

'I agree about the simplicity of the Margherita but I like mine spiced up a bit so would go for a pepperoni every time. Don't you think?'

There was no reply from Martin and it didn't take a detective to discover why – he was fast asleep!

'I was expecting some red hot spiced-up lovemaking from you, Martin Phelps, but I guess there's always tomorrow.' Shelley spoke the words softly as she snuggled up beside Martin and joined his dreams.

Just before nine the following morning Martin was in Incident Room One and Charlie propelled herself towards him. 'It was no problem,' she said. 'It took me less than five minutes. It will take some time to re-charge but just keep it plugged in and you'll be able to listen to the last message – and from what you've told me it's the one you want it to be. There was an access password but it wasn't difficult to override it. Do you want me to put the message on speaker for you?'

Getting a nod of approval she pushed a button and a male voice was heard faltering over his words. 'I've tried ringing you and I've texted you asking you to call me but I've heard nothing … Look, I wanted to stop you going to our agreed meeting place because I won't be turning up.'

The voice was slurred and the man that Martin knew to be Simon Davidson was struggling to form his sentences. Martin remembered his mother saying that her son had needed a great deal of Dutch courage to make that call.

'My parents know about the money and they've put it right for me.' At that point his voice crumbled and the words were more difficult to hear but his message went along the lines the detectives had been told and ended with a grovelling apology.

'I would consider myself well and truly dumped if that message had been left for me,' said Charlie. 'Is there anything else you want from this phone?'

'Nothing for now, but you could just go through it and check things in case there is anything. We believe Catherine was killed by her father, and as he died last night he won't be standing trial. No rush, just have a look when you get a moment.' Martin turned to Matt and suggested that he ring Elsie Hopkins to see when would be a suitable time for them to visit.

'I'm meeting with Chief Superintendent Atkinson in a few minutes, but he says we shouldn't be more than half an hour so any time after ten will be fine for me.'

'Is it about the reorganisation?' asked Matt, and Martin noticed that Helen and a number of other officers were waiting for his reply.

'Probably, but I'm not expecting him to tell me exactly what the new structure looks like or who is being proposed for any new posts. I think we'll be discussing the process of appeal for any of us who find our jobs substantially changed. It's not long now before we'll all know exactly what's on offer but don't think I don't realise what a difficult time this is for everybody.'

No one said anything and Martin left for his meeting.

Matt had been told by Elsie Hopkins that they could visit at any time and so as soon as Martin returned from the top floor he and Matt set off. To his credit Matt didn't quiz his boss on the substance of his session with the Chief Superintendent, but he noticed that Martin was stern-faced and tight-lipped on the journey to the farm.

He tried to lighten the atmosphere. 'This shouldn't take too long, and there's always the chance we'll be offered some more of those delicious scones that Helen has been raving about. Do you think Mrs Hopkins would mind if I asked her for the recipe?'

'Given what they went through yesterday I think their minds will be on other things than scones, but if the going gets tough it might serve as an ice-breaker.'

Margaret was sitting in exactly the same place as she had been the previous day, and as before it was Elsie who let them in.

Martin spoke to Margaret. 'I didn't want to invade your privacy yesterday but I do want to offer my sincere condolences and to hope that what we have to go over now will not cause you too much distress.'

Margaret raised a faint smile and he saw for the first time how much alike the two sisters were. He recognised a familiar scene – one he had seen many times when a family had been dealt a tragedy. The two women had done their crying and were probably feeling wrung out but were desperately wanting to talk.

Elsie had arranged the coffee, but for the moment there were no signs of those famous scones, and they all sat around the table.

'My sister wants to be the one to tell you exactly what was said at the hospital, but she wants me to interrupt if I remember anything she misses out.' As she spoke Elsie moved her chair a bit closer to Margaret and waited for her sister to speak.

'We got a call from the hospital more or less saying that Peter was not going to be with us much longer and so we got there as quickly as we could. We were both in shock regarding the news you had given us and I wasn't sure how much, if any, I would tell Peter.

'As it happened I was spared that decision because as soon as we got to his bedside Peter started to talk about Catherine. At first I thought he was rambling and he did jump about a lot but eventually we got around to the night she left home.

'He told me that he heard her shouting at someone in her room and he thought that someone was me and so he went up to see what was going on. We had been quarrelling earlier and he thought she was having another go at me. Anyway when he got to her room there was no one else there and she was just shouting at her mobile phone.'

'He asked her who she was shouting at and she told him no one. What she actually said – and you must excuse me for repeating it – was "the fucking bastard didn't have the balls to tell me to my face, he left a fucking voice message." That's what Peter said she had told him.'

'Go on if you are able,' Martin said.

'Well, Peter had to stop for breath at that point, but then he told us that Catherine acted really strangely and that the best he could describe her actions was like someone putting their house in order. I didn't really understand what he meant, did you, Elsie?'

Elsie shook her head. 'Not really, but it did explain how we found her room so unusually tidy, and when Peter told us I had no idea what caused her to do it but I think I do now. I'll come to that later. Margaret, you just carry on telling the chief inspector what Peter said.

'I'm going to struggle with the next bit, and will you forgive me if I get muddled up or don't feel able to continue and ask Elsie to finish off?'

Matt told her not to worry and added what he thought would be a few words of support. 'I think you're being amazingly brave, and there aren't many people with the courage to speak as you are. Your husband obviously carried a terrible burden for years and it was probably a relief for him to finally admit to killing your daughter but now you are left with a double tragedy.'

'No! Oh, no! That's not what happened, although even I went through a period of time when I believed Peter had killed Catherine. That's not what happened, is it, Elsie? – that's not what Peter said.'

Elsie jumped in quickly. 'No, Matt, I realise how we may have inadvertently led you to that conclusion, but as my sister has just said it's not what happened.'

Martin could see the puzzled look on Matt's face and knew that they were both equally bemused by the turn this account of what they had believed to be a confession of murder was taking.

'Let me explain the next bit,' Elsie suggested and Margaret simply nodded.

'Peter told us that Catherine seemed to not even know he was there and was calmer than he had ever seen her, but the one thing she did say was "goodbye". He said there didn't seem any point in arguing with her and went downstairs expecting to hear her drive off to confront the object of her earlier anger.

'When after about half an hour he had not heard her car leaving he told us he had a feeling that she was calling out to him. We asked him what he meant and he said he could only relate it to when she had been a little girl and had a bad dream. She would call out in the night and it was always Peter who was able to comfort her.'

'He went back to her room, but she wasn't there or anywhere else in the house and something made him search the outhouses and the old barn – and that was where he found her.'

'She wasn't shouting at anyone, and wouldn't ever be again, because she was hanging from one of the low beams suspended by a series of her belts that she had buckled together. Peter said she had hooked one buckle onto a piece of metal on the beam and used a bale of hay to stand on. She didn't drop far, as he told us her feet were only inches off the ground and he was easily able to lift her out of the noose she had made and place her on the hay.'

'He felt the need to tell us every detail and I can only guess

253

at the effort it took as even relating it to you second-hand is distressful. The poor man must have lived and relived that scene and it's no wonder he felt the need to seek oblivion.'

Both Elsie and her sister looked drained and Martin told them how much he appreciated their cooperation and questioned if they were able to carry on. With a sudden new burst of determination Elsie got to her feet, made a fresh round of coffee, and finished the account of her brother-in-law's revelations.

'We asked him why he hadn't told us then what had happened and he simply said it was just too awful. We all knew that Catherine was planning to leave and so he went along with that scenario. He said he didn't even have to think about what to do with her body, and that the proposed site of Nuestro Abrigo came straight to his mind. He drove her there and, well, we can all fit together the pieces after that.

'That's everything that Peter told us and afterwards he did nothing but apologise and tell Margaret that he had done what he thought was best. He had hoped she would never have to find out but he also knew that without the truth she would never stop searching for her daughter. He didn't want to leave her with that hopeless legacy.'

Margaret had drunk her coffee and felt able to add to her sister's words. 'I know now why Peter got so distressed whenever we were out together and I thought I caught sight of Catherine. I never stopped looking for her and every time my phone rang or the door opened I expected it to be her. I don't know how I would have dealt with my daughter's suicide when it happened but I don't blame my husband for his actions. He thought he was protecting me and couldn't have known how heavy his secret would weigh on his conscience.'

The thought of her husband living with the constant image of their daughter hanging in the barn was suddenly too much for Margaret and she rushed from the room.

'Please, go after your sister,' Martin suggested to Elsie.

'No, she's going to be alright. We've done nothing but talk all night and we've even started making some plans. We are

254

both farmers' daughters and were brought up to know that life goes on and few things would be worse than what Margaret has endured over the last five years.

'I hope she will begin to see Manuel as the decent man I have always believed him to be, and that he will bring her grandson here for visits – Margaret would like that.'

Martin could see that Elsie was struggling to keep the lid on her own emotions and said that he and Matt would see themselves out.

'Don't be a stranger, Martin. Maybe one day you'll bring your children here to visit – your aunt would have liked that idea.'

· Her words reawakened the thoughts that Martin had been having lately and he smiled inwardly as he considered if it was possible for men to feel broody – surely that was an emotion exclusive to women. As they left the farmhouse he did feel that sometime he would go back there and wondered how Shelley would react if he told her he wanted to be a dad …

Martin's earlier discussion with Colin Atkinson had given him a great deal of food for thought, and if there were to be significant changes on the career front then why not go the whole hog? He wasn't getting any younger and he had even got to the point of contemplating marriage when Matt interrupted his thoughts.

He assumed that his boss had been mulling over what had been said and asked about the dreaded paperwork. 'It's been one hell of a week and I'm not sure where to start. We've had a kidnapping, a murder, and a suicide, and all are related but separate so it's going to take some sorting before things get passed to the CPS.'

Before Matt could say any more Martin interrupted and asked him to drive.

'I want to make a call to Spain, and if it's possible enable Manuel Romanes to stay in Andalucía and be present for the birth of his child. I don't think he will have left for the airport yet and there's no rush for us to speak to him now, but I do need to tell him what happened to Catherine.'

Martin zapped the remote of his car and then threw his keys to Matt.

'How do you think Romanes will take the news?' Matt asked. 'He must have had feelings for his wife, even if their marriage did end badly, and there's the little boy – I wonder what he'll tell him.'

'There's only one way to find out,' Martin responded, and after dialling a number he spent the next ten minutes talking to Manuel Romanes.

'My call couldn't have been better timed from their point of view, as apparently Rachel's been niggling all night and now looks to be in established labour. I heard her calling her thanks when Manuel told her he wouldn't be leaving. He was quiet and offered no comment when I told him about Catherine's suicide and I heard a sharp intake of breath when I explained his father-in-law's role in the disappearance of her body. Elsie Hopkins is right, he does seem like a decent bloke. He expressed his sympathy in relation to Peter and told me he would speak to Margaret immediately.'

'I still can't get my head around Peter Washington,' said Matt. 'Why the hell didn't he just raise the alarm when he found his daughter? He wasn't to blame for it – no one was to blame for it. She was obviously unstable and Simon Davidson's rejection was the last straw. They would somehow have come to terms with it – instead they have all, including Peter, endured five years of absolute hell.'

Martin made one more phone call, this time to Fiona Davidson. He didn't go into the level of detail he had with Manuel but he reassured her that her son would not be required to answer questions in relation to the discovery of Catherine's body and wished her well with the wedding arrangements. As he ended the call he thought about how another man who had once loved Catherine Romanes was now free of her and getting on with his life. In spite of the fact that, from what he had heard, he would have intensely disliked the woman, he was finding a speck of sympathy from somewhere deep down.

'Still no chance of us dropping in on that wedding

reception?' asked Matt when Martin had finished his call.

Martin didn't answer and was quiet for some time.

'I've been building up the courage to ask you, guv, but you were so serious after your visit with the chief superintendent that I'm still scared to broach the subject. I know you said you would let us all know our positions as soon as you could and I don't expect any special treatment but I'm going to ask anyway. Is there anything you can tell me?'

Somewhat mischievously, Martin grinned at his sergeant. 'I'm amazed you've managed to hold off the question so long but I guess we have had other things to think about. You know I can't share any details of the reorganisation until the agreed time but I will tell you that I am very happy with the proposals for all the members of my current team.

'As far as your future position is concerned, I believe you will be pleased if not delighted with what's on offer for you, but for the moment the most I can say is relax, you have nothing to worry about.'

'Really?' Matt replied. 'You're really pleased for all of us – so why the long face when you came back from your meeting with the chief super?'

The penny suddenly dropped with Matt.

'Oh God, you're not happy with what they are planning to offer you! That's it, isn't it? I'm so sorry, Martin, we've all been fretting so much about our own positions we haven't given much thought to yours. All of us have been assuming that with your reputation you'll be OK. Will you be OK?'

'I don't know, Matt – I really don't know.

Author Inspiration

The main event in *Money Can Kill* takes place at the National History Museum of Wales, commonly known as St Fagans.

St Fagans Castle, the sixteenth-century manor house, and the surrounding land was given to the people of Wales by the Earl of Plymouth and provides the setting for an amazing open-air museum. The gardens and lakes surrounding the castle are spectacular and freely available to the public.

There is no better way for Welsh schoolchildren to learn about the history of their country than to walk through St Fagans and see first-hand how their ancestors worked and played. There are over forty original buildings including a church, a tannery, a farmhouse, and various mills, with the old schoolhouse teaching how children in Wales more than a hundred years ago were punished if they were caught speaking their native language. A row of six cottages enable visitors to see the changes in everyday living between 1805 and 1985. All the buildings have been brought from various parts of Wales and re-erected on the site to give an experience of the Welsh lifestyle, architecture, and culture as it developed.

Throughout the year there are opportunities to see traditional crafts demonstrated and to join in some of the festivals of music and dance. In the fields around the farm visitors will see native breeds of livestock and an endless variety natural habitats for birds, insects and small animals. Whatever you are hoping to achieve from a day out there is something for everyone and visitors to St Fagans tend to return and find something new each time.

Jack-Knifed

Jack-Knifed is the first novel featuring DCI Martin Phelps and his team, based in the world-famous and vibrant Cardiff Bay.

Mark Wilson, a decent, well-liked gay man, lives alone in a beautiful house in Cardiff. One Saturday evening, his closest friends go to his house for an evening of drinks and catching-up.

Finding no answer, the concerned friends break in – to a horrific murder scene. For Mark Wilson has been brutally, sadistically murdered in his own home.

As DCI Phelps investigates, Mark's traumatic early life is revealed. Was his killer someone from his past? Was his sexuality a motive? What about his violent, homophobic father– a man who has already killed more than once …

Meanwhile, Mark's estranged sister Amy broods on the hatred she has for her brother, blaming him for turning their father into a killer. As she sinks further in to the depths of drug addiction, who's to say what her next move will be? As the body count rises, Phelps and his sergeant, Matt Pryor, soon realise they are on the trail of a serial killer …

The Coopers Field Murder

The first novel in this series, *Jack-Knifed*, saw the introduction of Detective Chief Inspector Martin Phelps, together with his sidekick, Detective Sergeant Matt Pryor, and their team, investigating a horrendous murder in Cardiff.

Now they are faced with a body found in Coopers Field, a Cardiff beauty spot – a naked body that has lain there so long it is almost unidentifiable. Pathology reports establish that the body is that of a woman – but who is she, and how did she die? Local nurse Sarah Thomas, a helpful passer-by when the body is found, soon finds that she has another unexpected death to deal with – at Parkland Nursing Home where she works. Colin James, one of her favourite residents at the home, dies suddenly – but the reactions of those closest to him are surprising. Was Colin's death due to natural causes – or is there something more sinister afoot at Parkland?

The Coopers Field Murder is the second in Wonny Lea's DCI Martin Phelps series, set in the thriving Welsh capital city of Cardiff.

Killing by Colours, the third in the DCI Martin Phelps series, takes Martin in search of a serial killer who appears to have somewhat of a personal interest in the DCI himself.

When the body of the killer's first victim is discovered at a popular Cardiff leisure attraction, key elements of the murder link her death to a macabre colour-themed poem recently sent to DCI Phelps. As the body count rises, the killer teases the team by giving possible clues to the whereabouts of victims and the venues of potential murders, in the form of more poems. Are the killings random acts by a deranged individual, or is there something that links the victims to one another – and even to the DCI himself?

Meanwhile, Martin's sidekick, DS Matt Pryor, is worried about the safety of his boss. Are his fears warranted? Is Martin Phelps on the colour-coded list of potential victims – or is he just the sounding board for the killer's bizarre poetry?

DCI Martin Phelps and the team are back in *Never Dead*, the fifth Cardiff Bay Investigation by Wonny Lea.

Newly promoted DI Matt Pryor looks forward to solving his first investigation as lead detective. He soon has the chance, as the sudden death of an elderly man on a local train turns out to be murder – and everyone is surprised by the cause of death. Matt soon has a double mystery to consider, courtesy of a photograph in the dead man's pockets, and his investigation leads him to a seemingly reputable charity organisation ...

Meanwhile, Matt's boss Martin Phelps attempts to solve the decade-old brutal murder of a young Somalian man. A possible lead at the time was strange pattern of smooth stones arranged nearby and Martin has finally discovered who was behind that – but is it crucial to the case?